About the author

C. R. Preston is an only child. As such, he does not like to share food, be wrong, or lose at Monopoly. At the tender age of four he learned how to write and immediately began practicing his Nobel Prize acceptance speech. Before becoming a successful writer, C.R. spent two years sleeve-polishing the multiple degrees he earned from University of Toronto. More recently, he married his partner of many years and is no longer living in sin—although their plants didn't quite make it. Due to his overwhelming rise to fame, the writer would like to maintain his whereabouts secret, in order to keep his stalkers at bay.

Acknowledgments:

I would like to thank the following people for their help and support during the writing of The Ostrich Farmer.

To my readers for their feedback and positive energy. Thank you for buying my books!

To my editor, Michelle Horn, for her diligent work.

To Mike Petroianu for yet another dazzling cover design.

To Philmore Almoida for reading my mind and then drawing it.

To Cristina Dirlea for Farah.

To Radu Caracaleanu and Andreea Iorga for promoting The Spanish Guru.

To Irina Costachescu and Alex Babut for Morocco and the opportunity to see the personality in some of the cars featured in this book.

To my beautiful friends—you know who you are.

And most of all, to Julian Avram, who makes everything possible... and is very cute.

THE OSTRICH FARMER

C.R. PRESTON

EMPIRE STATE PUBLISHING

Published by arrangement with Empire State Publishing.
ISBN-10: 0-9845457-3-5
ISBN-13: 978-0-9845457-3-5
http://www.empirestatebooks.com

To my family

CHAPTER 1

MARRAKECH ME IF YOU CAN

It is widely known that a man will not feel the measure of his own success until he is given a title. The title may mean something, or it may mean nothing at all. What matters is the confidence it brings to the bearer and the sense of importance that can be packed into any old bag and taken around the world like hot currency that will never drop in value.

For Leborio Borzelini, who had always known he was meant for greatness, inheriting land in the heart of Africa did just that. He was a landowner, the heir to an estate, and was on his way to claim it. Only a few days of travel stood between Leborio and his title. That and the means to travel from Marrakech, Morocco, to Bongoville, Gabon, where his inheritance awaited.

The air was hot and dry, deflecting in shimmering waves off the tiny, arid crevices in the dirt. Through the wavering heat haze, he could make out cauliflower clouds splashed against the milky blue sky, immutable and calm above the red city walls. There was not a hint of a draft blowing from either direction.

Sitting on the edge of the dry fountain, the young man stared silently into its bluish-green mosaic tiles. He had seen it working just the day before. In fact, the fountain was the reason he returned to this landmark—rather, the attractive amount of international coins along its bottom. One could easily fetch enough to cover a wholesome lunch complete with a cup of mint tea and a flavourful shisha pipe. The day before, he had almost managed to rake a few Euros off the bottom when a short and stubby genie of a man dressed in white robes appeared out of nowhere and chased him away, yelling something in Arabic.

Now that the fountain was dry, he could spot only copper-coloured coins at the bottom. Pennies, he thought, wrinkling his lupine nose with dissatisfaction. Someone else had beaten him to it. He'd have to skip lunch now.

He leaned back, lying flat against the wide ledge of the fountain and pushing the muddy heels of his shoes into the grooves between the tiles. He closed his eyes and turned his face to the sun, breathing in the heat. Not so bad, he sighed, relaxing his muscles and emptying his mind of all thought. Beads of sweat dripped along his glistening skin, gathering into a tiny pool at the base of his neck and vibrating with the rising tides of his breath. He uncrossed his magnificent arms, letting them hang down, his fingers almost touching the dirt. A stinging scent of perspiration rose into the air, and he quickly crossed them back over his chest, opening his eyes slightly to check for observers.

Suddenly, the fountain turned on, squirting brown jets of water at first to clear the pipes and making way for a clear stream that trickled steadily into the fountain. Bothered by this interruption, the young man stood up and cast a squinting glance into the bottom of the pool. There was something about the tiny bluish-green tiles staring back at him like a hundred pairs of scrutinizing eyes. He lowered his gaze. The next time he looked up, there was a moving cloud of dust cutting across the road ahead, getting larger and larger, and slowly shaping into a bus. That explained the water turning on, he thought, watching the tour bus pull into the parking lot behind the Ben Youseff Madrasa. Just as well. Watching tourists was preferable to having a stare-down with a fountain. He wiped his hands on the leg of his trousers and inspected his aristocratic fingers with a stern expression. He looked like he could use a good long shower. His once white pants were beige from dust and sand. There was dirt under his fingernails and sweat all around the gray Bedouin scarf he had tied around his head to protect it from the sun. The tank top he wore stuck to his chest like gauze, tapering into the ridges of a perfectly shaped six-pack. It made him look a little like a grubby G.I. Joe doll. He hadn't shaved in more than a week, and his bow-shaped mouth was peeking out from behind a thick, curly scruff.

The bus was yellow, with wide windows that looked freshly washed. An indefinite number of shiny star stickers looked to have been randomly picked off the spangled banner and thrown into incoming traffic, only to splatter against the windows of the bus like giant bugs. Some were peeling, others were drawn on, but all were unmistakably American. The doors opened with a pneumatic huff, and a small army of peroxide blonde teenage girls dressed in tiny jean shorts and suede boots rushed off into the heat. They spread out across the entrance square like a noisy whirlwind, yelling out names, acronyms, and soft-core profanity. A few found the view of the building intriguing and broke away from the others to take pictures.

"O-M-G! This is so sick!" he heard one of them say and unintentionally checked to see if a deadly epidemic had started in the square before remembering teen jargon relied heavily on oppositions between form and actual meaning. *Sick, phat, short*, and *bitchin'* were all compliments, whereas *cute, nice*, and *good* were polite synonyms for boring.

Reaching the end of the square almost at the same time, the young tourists stretched out their more able arms and fell back on the other. While pouting into an imaginary horizon line, the girls snapped a few shots with tiny phone-cameras. One of them held up a shiny handbag with a large buckle and walked up to the fountain. She inspected it briefly before sitting next to the man. With her, came a cloud of sweet-smelling perfume that reminded him of fudge. He covered his mouth just in time to suppress a sneeze.

"Bless you," she said mechanically.

He could see her from the corner of his eye, moving her small limbs with the deliberation of a ballerina. The girl flicked her Lady Godiva locks over a bare shoulder and put out her hand, holding up a camera, or a phone, or both.

"Do you need help?" he offered and reached out to take the camera. He held out his arm, flexing the rippling muscles ever so slightly right under her nose.

"Phew." She snubbed him, turning away from his arm and the smell that came with it. The girl placed the camera in his hand without looking at him and adjusted the pearly pink scarf she had folded over into a hair band. She clutched her purse in the picture, without notic-ing the crumpled piece of paper that fell out from one of its pockets.

"Ready?" asked the stranger, rushing to get the photo session over with. "Say cheese!"

"Oh, no, no! Thanks for holding it, but I prefer to take my own pictures," she said and grabbed the tiny camera from his hand. "No offense," she said, smiling. "I just know exactly what angle suits me best."

"But I thought…I mean, you looked like…"

"Yeah, I get that a lot," she went on. "Like Serena from *Gossip Girl*, right? Everyone thinks so. Oh my God, Siobhan!" She turned to another girl, dressed in equally tiny shorts, summer boots, and a blue hair band scarf. "This guy thinks I look like Serena. Can you believe it?"

"And who is *he*?" asked Siobhan, her small nose turned up in the air.

He raised one side of his monobrow at the two girls. "Actually, I was going to say you looked like you could use some help taking your own picture. I'm sorry. I don't know who Serena is."

Siobhan smirked and put an arm around her friend's bare shoulder.

"*Gossip Girl*? What is that?" the stranger dared to ask.

And just like that, the mild interest manifested by the two teens evaporated into the hot Moroccan air.

"Don't worry, Blake," he heard Siobhan say as they walked away from the fountain. "He's too old to know these things. Now, where were we? Let's take a pic together!" She stretched her arm, holding an iPhone at eye level. "Look! That's a fab pic of us. And the castle behind looks so cute. It's going on my Facebook profile."

It's not a castle, thought the stranger, staring at the Madrasa Ben Youssef with obvious admiration. It was one of the first Islamic colleges ever built, one of the largest in the Maghreb, a true representation of the magnificence of Saadian art. Cute would not be a word to describe it. Didn't they teach them that on *Gossip Girl*?

This was exactly the problem with the world. Young girls with androgynous names who spent more time taking pictures of themselves with their cheeks sucked in than enjoying the wonders of architecture. They wore boots in the summer and spoke like they thought, in abbreviated words.

He glanced in their direction with contempt and shook his head ever so slightly as he picked up the crumpled piece of paper that had fallen from Blake's jumbo shoulder bag. There was nothing wrong with being a little narcissistic, he thought, pushing his dark locks out from behind his ears until they framed his jaw perfectly. In fact, loving one-self was the duty of any person of worth. But to go as far as to decline a perfectly nice offer to snap a scenic shot in favour of stretching one's own arm at just the right angle, well, that was…distasteful, he decided, unfolding the paper in his hand and looking it over absent-mindedly. It was a map of the city with a circle around the name of a hotel—probably the hotel where these American girls resided. These neo-narcissists had done away with the mirror and instead stared back at the silly pictures they took of themselves. Snap and check, snap and check. There were countless images of outstretched arms online displaying oversized but well-positioned heads.

Sofitel Marrakech Palais Imperial

That was the name of the hotel that was circled. How this would serve his purpose remained to be seen.

Luckily for him, this world of shallow youths was behind him now. He sighed, shoving the crumpled paper into his duffle bag. He was headed for a simpler, more tasteful place, one where he would play a pivotal role as a civilising force. The girls were right. He was older—but not old. A man in his thirties had just the right amount of age to be considered refined. A refined person could only retire in a quaint but lavish setting. Being the proprietor of a large land endow-ment in a place where all one needed in order to be respected was a nice estate was all Leborio Borzelini needed. For now.

Ever since he was a little boy, Leborio knew he had been meant to live an extraordinary life. At first, he thought he would make a great explorer or an inventor of sorts. He poured odd-looking liquids into test tubes in hopes of discovering the elixir of life, collected pebbles looking for the philosopher's stone, and dreamed of marrying the daughter of the Costa Rican ambassador, who lived in the great big house next door, where he conducted his alchemy experiments, hidden in the attic. One day he found out there was no elixir of life, that only Harry Potter had access to the philosopher's stone, and that marriages could easily be broken by fathers who preferred younger women and by mothers who still carried a torch for an old flame. In the face of such perishable dreams, Leborio set out to find the ultimate absolute truth: his Destiny. Larger than life. Brighter than the sun. More constant than any human heart.

Until a few weeks ago, Leborio followed Destiny as a spiritual master, teaching yoga to the elderly—and very wealthy—housewives of the Lido Pool and Spa. His days as a self-proclaimed Spanish guru in an Eastern European country were now over. While he was traveling through Portugal to meet one of his Lido lady friends, he received a telegram informing him that he was the heir to his dead uncle's estate in Bongoville, Gabon. The catch was that he had to get there as soon as humanly possible to secure this inheritance before his cousin, Umberto, who had just as much right—if not more—to this land, could lay his own claim to the estate.

With prong-like fingers, he extracted a shred of paper from one of the pockets of his duffle bag, smoothing its folds with disgust. A single phrase neatly written in blue ink stared back at him: *So long, your feudal highness.*

He'd read it many times since he found it tucked in his bag but still couldn't make sense of it. The handwriting belonged to his cousin, Umberto Bore, who had presumably placed it there for him to find later.

For all the traits the two young men shared, physically and otherwise, they couldn't be more different when it came to their values. Leborio saw himself as a noble mind with a drive for success, while

Umberto was a humble soldier in God's Catholic army. They hardly wanted the same things in life—except for when the girl they both grew up with was around. Umberto must have thought he'd won, to bid him such a gloating farewell.

So, followed by his faithful—if not terribly clever—female companion, Snejana, the young man set on a quest to claim his inheritance. He had no idea what kind of world awaited for him at the heart of Africa, but whatever it was, he knew it would be as great as the land he now owned. He put the paper in his bag and shuffled to the raggedy palm tree where Snejana awaited.

"Tell me again," she started from under the precarious shade of the tree. "How did you come to inherit this land?"

"Why? Are you trying to find loopholes in my logic?" he said, staring down at the skinny girl whose head, even bundled in a creamy white hijab, bore an uncanny resemblance to an ostrich.

"No. But I'm very close to freaking out, and it helps me calm down."

Her eyes welled up as she gingerly stroked a small creature resting in her lap. The cat was hairless and pink, like a newborn piglet, with prominent ears and a heavy purr. It too did not want to move.

"Very well." He sat next to the girl, putting one of his magnificent arms around her bony shoulders. "Not so long ago, when part of Europe was under communist rule, some of the socialist republics made a bid for Africa. They were trying to convert the poorer, more troubled African nations to communism, you see. And, of course, in order to challenge the appealing glitter of capitalism, they bought land in these places. Lots of land. Land that the Americans couldn't touch now."

She closed her eyes and smiled, perhaps imagining luscious acres of pastures, where she, Leborio, their two children, and the hairless cat they picked up in their travels would run and play and have pastel-coloured picnics.

"And then what happened?"

"And then, when communism fell in Europe, all this land they had bought in Africa was given back to the people. Alas, it was given to the wrong people—the people of Eastern Europe, my uncle being one of them," he added. "But since he had the common sense to die before leaving a will, his estate was given to me. A far better turnout, if I may say so myself. I will make a fabulous master," concluded Leborio, raising his defiant chin with pride.

Just the thought of having a piece of land he could call his own made him sit taller, presiding over the reddish Moroccan dirt like an explorer over newly conquered territory.

"Master to whom?" pushed the girl.

"Why to those poor African people who live on it, I imagine."

"Do you think there are any? People, I mean. Some places don't have any people on them, you know."

"Like where?"

"I don't know." She shrugged. "The jungle, I suppose."

"Look around, dear. This is what Africa looks like: desert and sun. I mean, yeah, you get the occasional settlement in a gorilla-infested jungle, but trust me, my estate in Bongoville is not in one of those places."

"Where is it, then?"

The cat looked up at him. He cleared his throat and reached into the small duffle bag he'd strapped across his back with a greasy leather belt. He'd stolen the belt from the Asian boatman who helped them cross over from Portugal—not because the boatman had demanded Leborio's favourite silk shirt in exchange for a boat ride to Morocco, but because removing a man's belt while he dozed was incredibly difficult, and Leborio Borzelini enjoyed a good challenge.

He took out a Ziploc bag and dangled a few Euro coins at eye level with a desolate expression.

"We'll find out soon enough," he replied, pressing his chapped lips against each other. He could really use some fresh, cold water. "First, we're gonna need more money."

"Money," she sang, as if it were a limerick, "grows on trees, like lemons, overseas."

"Lemons?"

"My mother says that. She thinks people have these skewed ideas about what life is like in other countries. People dream of moving to better places, where life will somehow be easier than where they were before. They think they'll just arrive there and fortunes will await them."

"Fortunes sometimes do await them."

"Yes. Money grows on trees, like lemons, overseas." The girl sighed, resting her forehead on the diamonds of her knees. She closed her eyes and dreamed aloud. "My mother makes the best lemonade in the world. She stirs the honey with a silver spoon and pours it in a tall glass, garnished with a slice of fresh lemon. Sometimes she drops a few ice cubes in it, and I watch them float until they start to crack and melt. Such delicious lemonade! I gulp down the whole glass until the rim touches the tip of my nose. Then, I take the jug and fill up my glass again."

"You sound like you're thirsty, Big Bird." He kicked her gently with his foot, still searching through the bag. This time, he pulled out an almost empty plastic bottle that looked as if it had been run over by a train. He shook the opal-coloured liquid at the bottom, removed the cap, and sniffed it. It smelled like broiling plastic and toxic steam.

"Drink some water," he said, handing her the bottle magnanimously. "And don't fall asleep! It's dangerous to do that when you're not properly hydrated."

She refused to drink from it and tried to stand up, trying to stop her eyes from rolling back. He lifted her by the pits of her arms, mindful of the hairless cat. They stumbled down identical narrow, labyrinthine streets that kept the houses cool from the burning eye of the sun and followed the shade of pink-hued buildings into the heart of the city. Everywhere they looked, pushy vendors peddled souvenirs and treats to squeaky-clean tourists, and for the first time, he felt relieved to be filthy and tired. The folding streets took them away from the crowds and into the obscure stillness that only locals knew to find.

Sometime later, they stopped to catch their breath under the eaves of a freshly painted building with a flashy doorway. By the looks of it, it was a silver shop. He took out the plastic bottle and handed it to the girl, this time more forcefully.

"It's nice and hot." He pursed his lips. "Germs were boiled to death about twenty minutes back."

She obeyed and immediately recoiled in distaste, spitting it out on the asphalt. He watched her spit stain the ground for a mere moment and then disappear, hissing like a watermark under a hot iron. He scoped the horizon line, covering his eyes with his spare hand. Distant images wavered like ripples in the water.

"There." He pointed in a far distance, where a few lights glimmered like the promise of a Western oasis against the red mud buildings.

She pulled herself up, holding on to the crumbling wall with one hand and to the hairless cat with the other, squinting in the direction of the lights. Her long neck moved back as if held by strings, and her head turned to Leborio with the blank curiosity of a large bird staring at an unfamiliar creature. "What's there?" she asked.

"The airport, according to this," he said, waving Blake's tourist map in the air. "That's where we need to go to catch our flight to Gabon."

"But we don't have money."

"We're not going to be paying for it. Not if I can help it."

The girl puckered her lips in a disapproving gesture and for a moment stared at him blankly. Then, her big, gray eyes rolled back, and she started to fall. Agile as ever, Leborio caught her by the waist and threw her over his back, bending her over like a heavy carpet or a sack of potatoes. In the fall, Snejana had dropped the cat, and the creature was now looking up at Leborio with expectant eyes.

"Oh, stop it," he hissed and looked around to check if anyone had seen him. Then he stooped down and grabbed the cat by the skin of her hairless neck. The animal screeched and fought off the air around her dangling body.

"'Ot day, *n'est pas*?" He heard a voice behind him and turned to see a small figure leaning against the crimson wall of the silver shop, part of his face hidden under the wide brim of a brown hat. Leborio put the cat down, and the animal disappeared immediately between his trouser legs, peeking out suspiciously at the man in the brown hat. He might have been little, but he was still much larger than a cat.

"Aren't they all?" answered Leborio, adjusting the dead weight over his shoulder.

"*Non*," the man said in a nasal voice and shook his head slowly. "Not all days are zis 'ot. Only zis time of ze year."

Leborio watched him roll a cigarette and light it. From the way he covered his silver lighter with one hand, as if to prevent the wind from blowing it, Leborio knew he wasn't from around there. France, perhaps, judging by the accent. The man took a greedy drag out of the cigarette and held it in for a moment.

"Care for some good import brandy?" asked the smoker, taking out a silver flask from the inner pocket of his maroon jacket and holding it out with great pride. "Made it myself," he added, without specifying whether he meant the brandy or the silver container.

Looking at the flask, Leborio, who didn't care a whole lot for alcohol, shook his head.

"No, thanks." Then, his thick eyebrow rose ever so slightly. "Water would be nice though." He tapped Snejana's posterior, sticking out over his shoulder, as if it were the counter at a pub.

The other man grinned.

"Amal," he yelled through the small window behind him. He spoke a few words in Arabic. Moments later, a tall and lanky Moroccan man came out with an ice-cold bottle of mineral water. The stranger handed it to Leborio and watched him inhale half of it with one gulp.

"Thirsty?"

"You have no idea," he said, rolling the cold plastic bottle over his dirty forehead. "I've been standing outside the great mosque all day, trying to guess what the late Hassan II would have thought if he'd known it's being invaded by a bunch of American teens."

The man in the brown hat nodded and looked at Leborio through a carefully blown smoke circle. "Zese annoying little grass'oppers want to see ze world in fourteen days, and zen post pictures to show zeir friends where zey've been. We use to collect stamps, remember? Zese kids collect pictures of zemselves around ze globe. Like ze travelling gnome. Zey take 'undreds of pictures even if zey can't spell ze names of 'alf ze places zey visit." He pursed his lips in a gesture of disproval. "*Non*, I might be old-fashioned, but I sink ours was ze last decent generation," said the man, flicking the cigarette butt.

Leborio looked at the considerably older man with contempt and made a head gesture that was meant to suggest negation, but he collided with Snejana's dangling leg and ended up wiping his brow sweat on her shorts.

"Where're you from?" asked the Frenchman.

"Central Europe," said Leborio evasively.

"What a coincidence, so am I. But I suppose the center of a sing is wherever we are. In your case, ze center of Europe is more to ze East."

"That's a rather anthropocentric position, wouldn't you say." It wasn't really a question.

"No man likes to sink 'is talents are wasted in an inconsequential place. And so we stay or move like moths, to be closer to ze flame, closer to ze center of all sings. But you are welcome, my friend! Welcome to Morocco! You don't see too many people travelling wiz a pet," he noted after a while. As if she knew the Frenchman was referring to her, Regina looked up from between Leborio's ankles. "What brings ze three of you to Marrakech?"

"Just passing through," muttered Leborio.

"Most people are. You're very welcome. And what's your final destination?"

Leborio hesitated for a moment, unsure what the deal was with the incessant welcoming, and then, deciding it must have been a cultural thing, answered smugly, "Gabon. I own some land there, you see."

"Gabon? Never been, but I 'eard good sings about it. What are zey famous for?"

"Famous?"

"*Oui*. Morocco is famous for silver, falafel, and couscous; Sierra Leone is famous for diamonds and war; Angola is famous for gold. Zat sort of sing. What is Gabon famous for?"

"Diamonds," he said with the rising intonation of questions. He liked the sound of it. With a casual jerk, he shifted Snejana's weight over his shoulder the way a woman adjusts the strap to her handbag. "Gabon is famous for diamonds," he added, more confidently.

"Well, zen." The Frenchman put his arm around the young landowner, pretending not to notice the woman hanging off his back. "Fortune 'as smiled upon you, my friend. You must do me ze 'onour of visiting my business. I own zis silver shop," he said, inviting Leborio through the doorway. "Amongst other businesses, of course. I like to keep my options open when it comes to commerce. I am what you'd call a venture capitalist," he explained, emphasising the last two words. "I see new opportunities and invest in zem."

Last time Leborio had come across a self-proclaimed venture capitalist, it had turned out the investment was his own appeal to the opposite sex. After years of service under the kingpin of the underworld, Placido Pector, Leborio was promoted to head yoga instructor at the Lido Pool and Spa, where he was winked at, pinched in all the wrong places, and visually violated by a hungry heard of cougars. He preferred to think of that time of his life as the guru days. The Spanish guru guided the poor housewives of the city's elite down their spiritual path with his lunges and stretches. So much for being the protégé of a venture capitalist.

"We sell ze best silver in all of Morocco," carried on the Frenchman. "You really ought to see it. Tell you what," he said, still smiling through smoke-stained teeth, "you and your friend come eat at my 'ouse."

"What, now?"

"Yes, now." He held his hand out toward the door of the silver shop. "I welcome you in my 'ome." And then he shrieked at the top of his lungs, "Amal! Set ze table for guests."

"I thought this was your shop," said Leborio, taking a step back.

"Ah, shop, 'ome, is zere a difference? I told you I'm a businessman." The man grinned, showing his yellow teeth again. "I live to work and work to live. You are welcome! Come in! I will show you my beautiful silver," he said, pointing at the door.

"No, thank you," answered Leborio, this time sharper than before. "We've got to be on our way now."

The man pushed the brim of his hat higher up and squinted as he smiled. "I sell ze best silver in Marrakech. You just come and see." He added, "We've got a fan to keep ze room cool. And cold drinks. And zere is *interweb*."

Leborio looked up and, careful not to bang Snejana's head against the doorframe, unwillingly allowed himself to be guided inside. The shop was small but clean, and shiny silver artefacts glittered from behind glass cases. The dirtiest object in the room was the dusty plastic fan, droning like a coffee grinder from the corner of the shop.

Amal, the tall Moroccan man, was busying himself with the placemats. Leborio noticed his hands were very clean, and his skin was flaking at the knuckles. Probably the result of working with silver polish, thought Leborio, inspecting his own smooth hands.

"You can lay ze young lady over zere," said the Frenchman, pointing at a small wooden bench resting against the back wall of the shop.

Leborio turned to the bench and unloaded Snejana, placing her flat on her back. The cat had followed, hiding behind his legs. She jumped up on the girl's lap and curled across her tummy. The Frenchman snubbed his nose almost imperceptibly and looked away from the hairless creature.

"Do you need to wash?" he suggested, putting up his hands.

Leborio nodded. "But first I need the internet."

"Of course," said the man. "Over zere." He pointed at a Pentium computer whose yellow plastic carcase had once been white.

Leborio sat down in the wooden chair facing the computer and moved the mouse several times before the screensaver disappeared. Behind him, Amal chopped onions on a wooden board while the Frenchman impaled small strips of dark meat on a few wooden skewers.

"We make everything in zis shop by our own 'ands," said the host, turning on the gas stove by the refrigerator. He washed his hands and dried them on a linen cloth. "It's all after an ancient recipe, 'anded down to me by my forefathers. Zey were craftsmen too," he added. "From Marseilles. But zey lived most of zeir lives 'ere in Morocco. Ze only time a man from our family stays in Marseilles is when he's born, or when his sons are about to be. In zis way, we all have our French—how do you call?—citizenship," he explained. "I am ze exception, of course, because I lived most of my life in Marseilles and only returned to zis shop after my father passed." He counted on his fingers and decided. "Nine years ago he died. Bad liver from all the drinking."

Leborio nodded absentmindedly and unfolded the crumpled map to see the hotel name.

"Do you have a pencil?" He turned to the Frenchman.

"Of course," said the man, handing him a shiny case. "Open it," he smiled. "It's made in our shop from za best kind of silver. Very good quality, but for you I can make special price."

Leborio gave him a look and opened the case to grab a small pencil. He scribbled down the phone number to Sofitel Marrakech Palais Imperial.

"Maybe zis is not something you need," inferred the Frenchman. "Lucky for you, I 'ave exactly what you need!"

Intrigued, Leborio looked up to see the Frenchman lift up a silver teapot.

"Engraved by my own hand," he boasted, as Amal let out a single cough. "And my friend Amal 'ere," he added. Leborio turned to the computer again and carried on scribbling. "Of course, not everyone likes tea," continued the merchant. "I myself like tobacco," he said as he pulled out a sliver cigarette case. "And ze occasional drink," he tried, taking the silver flask out of his pocket. "Ze best quality in Marrakech. Perfect for gift too. For lady we have jewellery if you want." He shook a few bangles up in the air.

Leborio shot a quick glance at Snejana's inert body and continued to ignore him.

"Oh, I've got it!" yelled out the Frenchman. This time, Leborio folded the map, shoved it in his greasy pocket, closed the browser, and turned to face him. To his surprise, the merchant was holding a bejewelled knife, offering it to his guest with the humble generosity of one of the three kings visiting baby Jesus.

Without taking it from his hands, Leborio inspected the object with a sudden fascination. He'd always liked weapons, especially when they were ornate. Noticing his interest, the merchant flipped it on both sides.

"Silver gypsy dagger encrusted with semiprecious stones," he said with great pride. "Zis one belonged to ze king of ze gypsies."

"Which gypsies?" asked Leborio.

The Frenchman scratched his head. "Ze brave and colourful ones?" he tried. Seeing that his guest was not convinced, he added, "Ze ones zat play ze violin."

Raising an eyebrow, Leborio inquired, "Was anyone killed by this dagger?"

The merchant did not respond at once. He pursed his lips for a moment and measured Leborio from the corner of his eye. Then, he looked back to Amal, whose sharp chin descended in an affirmative gesture. The Frenchman opened his mouth only to make an indistinct sound:

"Mnyeah," he said, pulling the dagger close to his chest and freezing into an unusual grimace.

Leborio's nose wrinkled a little.

"Well, which one is it?" he asked.

"Which one would you rather it was?"

"Personally, I like a bit of history with my weapons."

Relaxing his face once again, the merchant stood tall, putting his arm around Leborio. "Oh, why don't you say so? Zis dagger has been used to kill many people. And animals," he added. "Ze gypsy king killed 'is cheating wife, 'er lover, six chickens, and a lame horse with zis dagger."

"That's all?"

"And zen he killed 'imself!" added the Frenchman, seemingly pleased with this last touch.

Leborio took the dagger in his hands by the handle. He ran his fingers over the double-edged blade. The metal felt cold against his skin, and for a moment, he tried to imagine what it would feel like to thrust it into a living thing. Glancing at the hairless cat, he lifted the knife into the air and closed one eye, like a hunter.

The cat looked up at him with humid eyes, and he lowered the blade. Under the hairless bundle, Snejana's tummy lifted and descended with every breath she took. Tempting, chuckled Leborio, looking at the blade in his hand. With one swift motion, he threw the knife across the room. The blade nailed itself into the target, causing the silver handle to waver from the impact. Amal gave the merchant a look, but the Frenchman took a step back and applauded.

"Very good! You are very good at zis!"

"I know," said Leborio, taking a few steps toward the small cupboard, where a half an onion was nailed to the wood. He pulled it out with the dagger and took a big bite out of it. "So," he said, licking his lips, "are we going to eat, or what?"

***

The three men were sitting around a knee-high table made of dark wood, sharing food from a carved bowl filled with meat and vegetable skewers dripping goodness over a hummus-like paste.

"Silver is only one of my businesses," said the Frenchman, shredding pieces of lamb off a wooden spike with his yellow teeth. "I'm also in travel and tourism. Always looking for tour guides, as a matter of fact."

Sitting to the right of his host, Leborio focused on the food, savouring the tiny dices of meat and vegetables impaled on the wooden spears and using generous pieces of bread to scoop sauce from the large communal bowl in the middle.

"I'm looking to 'ire one right now," carried on the Frenchman, leaning back against the doorframe. "A good tour guide is like an actor.

Tell ze right story, and you'll 'ave people eating from ze palm of your hand, tipping you, and telling zeir friends about it. I have to say zat with your natural charisma, you'd make a fine tour guide. My agency is very respectable, and my clientele is old enough for drinking. In fact, sings have been going so well zat now, we're expanding to ecotourism. It's ze sing to do right now. Got myself two ostriches from ze south, a tiger cub, a female elephant, and a sea lion and started my own safari tour, just outside of Marrakech. It's a day-long trip," he added.

"Wow, five animals. A veritable Noah's ark." Leborio looked up from his plate. "Sea lion?"

The man shrugged. "Sure. Why not? But exotic animals are not easy to come by in zis part of Africa. And looking after five of zem is no easy task."

"So how does this work? You take people in a jeep to see five animals in their cages?"

"No, no, no." He shook his head. "You've got it all wrong. I give zem ze real deal. We take groups on camels—after all, it is an eco tour—to see ze animals in zeir natural 'abitats."

"The subarctic waters?"

"Not necessarily. Seals love tropical places, as long as zere's water. I've been to California, and zere were plenty of seals around."

Leborio wondered if they were all married to Heidi Klum. The man took another sip from his silver flask.

"I've got a female, you see. Someday I'll even breed her for pups and expand my business."

Leborio smeared bread through the section of the bowl that was in front of him. "Breed her? What with? Have you got seals and penguins roaming the desert now?"

The Frenchman ignored him and continued with a grin on his face. "Michelle, our sea lioness, has her own tub in ze safari. Amal 'ere wakes up at ze crack of dawn, fills ze tub with water, and puts Michelle in it. Poor thing never thought she'd 'ave it so good. Lying in the sun all day, posing for ze tourists like a diva."

The man in the brown hat reached for the washing basin and held his hands out while Amal poured lukewarm water over them.

"Surely, the sea lion would be more comfortable in cold water," persisted Leborio, watching the Frenchman and his servant perform their hand cleaning ritual.

The host dried his hands on the towel provided and rolled up another cigarette.

"Tell you what," he said, spitting out tobacco through a gap in his front teeth. "Join us tomorrow and see for yourself."

"Tomorrow," repeated Leborio without a particular intonation. "Hmm. Tomorrow I don't have time."

"Phew." The man waved his hand. "Zere is always more time, my friend," he added, putting his arm around Leborio's shoulder yet careful not to touch the sweat stains by his pits. "We are in Morocco, remember? Zat means never having to worry about time."

As much as Leborio liked the prospect of rendering time irrelevant, he was anxious to reach his final destination and claim his inheritance. He shook his head and politely refused the man in the brown hat.

***

If Leborio had any inkling that Snejana would wake up to the sharp scratching of the hairless cat only to hear strange voices coming from a dimly illuminated kitchen, he would have been more careful with his words. He, however, had no suspicion that she was awake. He did not see her wave the cat off the reddened skin on her belly, rubbing the scratches with one hand and propping herself up with the other. He did not see the panic in her eyes as she wondered where he was. Did he leave her here? Perhaps he bartered her against a camel. It wouldn't have been the first time he tried to sell her off. Unnoticed by anyone, Snejana tried to sit up and turned to face them, but her wrists were shaking, and she felt very weak. Behind her, the clinking sound of glasses being knocked together accompanied the men's voices.

"Cheers! *Salu!*" said all three in unison.

"Zis is Moroccan whiskey, *mon ami.*"

"Tea?" said Leborio from his corner of the table. He hadn't left her. He was still here. She didn't recognize the other two men sitting with him. "I have to confess, I didn't care much for you when we first met. But you strike me as a very resourceful individual," he continued, stopping only to make a sloppy puffing sound.

The table had been cleared of dishes, although the lingering aroma of the food still wavered in the air. Snejana watched Leborio pucker his lips to a hose and suck in the smoke, as the glass water jar on a shisha pipe bubbled up like a volcano.

"I'm glad we came to an understanding," said the French man in the brown hat. "You'll 'ave to be very careful not to wake her," he added in a lower tone.

"I don't see how you can do it without waking her," objected Leborio.

"Oh, zat's easy," said the other man. "Amal will 'old her. He's very strong. Zen, ze two of you will 'ave to roll her in a carpet. Zis way, even if she awakes, zere's not a chance she'll be able to escape."

Concealed in the darkness, the girl moved her neck with difficulty, scanning the room for exits.

"Yes, Amal 'as very good technique," added the Frenchman, as he puffed on the water pipe. "He will teach you 'ow to roll her without waking her. Zen, when you're done, you will carry her together and throw her in ze water."

The girl smothered a gasp with the back of one hand. Grasping the hairless cat with the other hand, she stood up by the bed. Stealthily, her huge gray eyes bugging out of her head, she crawled along the walls and disappeared through a beaded curtain covering a gaping hole that could have been a door.

"What was that?" Leborio jumped, staring at the multicoloured murmuring beads.

"Just ze wind, my friend. Don't be so jumpy! *Asseiez toi,* sit down."

It wasn't until later that night that Leborio noticed Snejana and the cat had disappeared. It was clear to him this had been a purposeful act of disloyalty, brought about by the uncertain times they were currently facing. It was just like a woman, he thought, to run off at the first sign of hardship. Moved by proper motivation, any woman would leave behind the man she professed to love, in the same way rats abandoned ship before a calamity. He gazed at the empty bench where Snejana had been sleeping only hours ago. Submissive, dumb Snejana, who, like that hairless cat, was gone the moment she did not need him anymore. However little love was worth for a woman was why it could not mean any more for a man. Here was the confirmation of his axioms. A woman was only as loyal as her options.

Creatures were as fickle as their yearnings, and humans were no different. Why should they be any different? It was only fear of solitude that tied the weak into their pacts of conjugality. The Frenchman and Amal had fallen asleep with their heads over the table. Slowly, Leborio stood up and made for the door, wondering if Snejana had used the same exit strategy. Their circumstances were different, of course. He didn't owe the Frenchman anything. With that thought in mind, on his way out, he grabbed his duffle bag and the silver knife that had allegedly belonged to a gypsy king, and shoved it under his belt.

Surrounded by the dark curtains of the night, his thoughts wandered back to his oldest and most stubborn of friends and her idealistic take on all things human. Leborio once again saw her gaze, piercing through with the green amber depth of Indian mystics. She had loved him and betrayed him. On some level, all women were driven by their desires, slaves to their weakness and emotions.

He made his way through the convoluted obscurity of the Moroccan streets until he found a shiny telephone booth, strangely juxtaposed against the rusty stem of a streetlamp. If you wanted to know the true state of a culture, you needed look no further than their payphones. This one was a futuristic orange, with a triangular cover leaning above the blue stand of the phone, like a vibrant Gerber daisy petal. The only thing missing from this modern-looking phone booth was an actual phonebook. He grabbed the polished receiver with one hand and pulled out the folded map from his pocket. He dialled the number scribbled on it and waited for an answer. The servile voice of a man picked up at the other end, and Leborio asked for Ms. Blake.

"Blake who?" the hotel receptionist wanted to know.

"I'm not quite sure," replied Leborio in his best American accent. "This is an emergency, my good man. Her father has been in a terrible accident, and he only mustered up enough strength to tell me her first name and the hotel she was staying at in Marrakech. She's an only child, you see. The father has been muttering her name in his delirious state, and I fear she is the only one who can bring him out of his coma."

The receptionist apologized in a sudden state of panic and made the connection right away.

"Miss Blake Vos," he said. "Room 223."

On the other end, the phone rang seven times before a sleepy voice picked up and mumbled an irritated hello.

"Miss Blake Vos?" asked Leborio, nasally, this time with a tinge of French in his speech. "Is this Miss Blake Vos, room 223?"

"Yes! What do you want?"

"We are calling from reception. We are very sorry to wake you, but your credit card has been declined, and I'm afraid we're going to have to ask you to provide us with a different method of payment or vacate the room."

He waited a few moments, uncertain how the girl would process this information. She didn't seem too bright, especially at three in the morning.

"My credit card?" repeated the girl. " That's impossible! Run it again!"

"I'm afraid we can't do that. For security purposes, we have shredded your card number. Would you mind coming down to reception to sort this out?"

"Right now? Do you know what time it is?"

"Yes. We are very sorry, again."

"Can't I just give you the number over the phone?"

Standing in front of the payphone, Leborio made a joyous money-cashing gesture.

"Of course, Miss Vos. We can do that for you."

The girl dictated a series of numbers, complete with an expiration date and a three digit code. Leborio repeated it back to her and made her say it again for good measure. Then he apologized for the inconvenience and hung up the receiver. Moments later, he phoned the airport and ran the same credit card numbers to buy two one-way tickets to Franceville, Gabon. He would return the second ticket for cash and get some pocket money. Take *that*, Nigerian prince, thought the Gabonese landowner, with great pride.

"May I see your boarding pass and passport please?" asked the girl in the blue uniform behind the check-in counter of Afrair Airlines. She spoke in a robotic tone. She had long bangs that she had flattened against her high forehead with unmentionable amounts of gel in an unsuccessful attempt to press the curls out. The rest of her hair was tied up in a tightly wound bun right at the top of her head. She had sepia-coloured skin of an oily complexion, which, combined with her gelled hair, gave the impression that she had just crawled out of a swimming pool.

"Afrair Airlines," he said with a critical shake of the head. "Very unfortunate choice of name for an airline, don't you think?"

The girl looked something up on her computer without responding.

"It sounds an awful lot like *afraid*, don't you think? And who wants to be afraid on an airplane? It's not very reassuring. In fact, based on that name, if I were superstitious, I probably would not fly with your company."

"Boarding pass and passport," repeated the girl.

Leborio reached into his duffle bag without taking his penetrating gaze off the airline worker. He took out a bright yellow envelope and slowly placed it on the girl's side of the counter, leaning in with a deliberate smile. For the first time during their brief encounter, the young woman looked up at him, raising both of her thinly pencilled eyebrows.

"Place the documents in front of you, sir, and take a step back."

"You've got an interesting hairstyle," hummed Leborio in his most seductive tone of voice. "It's almost like your hair is…painted on."

"Sir." She raised her voice from the robotic tone into a nasal pitch. "If you don't step back right away, I'm going to press this red button here and call Afrair security. You don't want me to do that, sir!"

"No, there's no need for that." He stood back, a little startled. "Glad we sorted out what Afrair stands for."

"Now if you'd please take out your documents from the envelope," she said in a flat tone.

He obeyed reluctantly and placed them on top of the counter. The girl looked up at him with a weighing expression.

"Something wrong?"

"You have two boarding passes. Are you traveling alone?"

"About that," started Leborio, fixing his big, almond-shaped eyes on her. "When I bought these tickets, I was travelling with my fiancé. But she left me for another man, you see." He paused for effect and looked into the floor.

"Great shock," said the girl as she looked through the papers.

"Well, it was," he said indignantly. "The shock hasn't worn off yet. But you know what they say, time heals all wounds. This is why I was hoping you'd cut me a break and allow me to return her ticket, seeing as she won't be joining me after all."

"Refunds and date changes have to be made up to twenty-four hours before the flight," she said, reading the back of the boarding pass and pointing it out to him.

"I know, I know. But these are extraordinary circumstances. Haven't you ever been hurt by the cruel sting of love…Yasmen?" he asked, staring at her nametag.

"I can't refund your ticket, sir. It's against company policy. You can board, or you can step away from my desk."

"But Yasmen, there must be something you can do!"

The line behind him consisted of a single family and their multiple suitcases. The kids had become restless and were perching atop the luggage trolley, murmuring threats with a lisp. Feeling pressured by the young mob behind him, Leborio touched the girl's bejewelled hand in a final effort to soften her up.

"Sir, don't make me do it," she said as she pulled her hand away, her index finger hovering over the dreaded red button.

Deflated, Leborio took back Snejana's boarding pass and dropped his duffle bag on the scale.

"Did you pack your bags yourself?"

"I only have one bag."

"Well, did you pack it yourself?"

"Yes. I packed it myself."

"Would you like to upgrade your seat to legroom for an extra $50?"

"Are you kidding me?"

"I'll take that as a no," she said, stamping his boarding pass with great gusto. "Have a nice flight to Gabon!"

"Which gate am I going to?"

"We only have one. That'll be your gate."

He took a few steps back and dropped his bag on the floor, looking around to see if anyone had noticed the expedite manner in which he had been stamped off by the airline worker. But there were very few people around. The family standing in his place at the check-in counter was tying nametags to their suitcases, and aside from the short line behind them, there was only an in-wall ATM machine where a tall girl with very thin arms was counting up some cash. A mini plastic fan was duct-taped to the machine, angled so that a cooling breeze hit the faces of banking customers as they handled their transactions. Leborio stepped closer, attracted by the plastic fan.

The girl shoved a wad of money in the back pocket of her dusty jean shorts and turned to see him peering inches away from her shoulder.

"Son of a bitch," he yelled as the girl gasped, covering her mouth with both hands.

"You!"

"Yes, me."

Quickly scanning the area for exits, Snejana took a step back. Leborio grabbed her arm forcefully and pushed her into the nearest wall. Behind them, the lazy pace of airport traffic continued to drag on.

"Did you think I wasn't going to find you?"

"Let go of me," she cried.

"I'll let go of you when it pleases me, you treacherous twig. After everything I've done for you, after I've taken you to places you've only dreamed of seeing." He pointed at the small airport space with a flourish. "I fed you my own food and carried you on my back when you fainted. I turn around for one second, and you take off on me."

Pressing his thumb into her scrawny bicep until the skin turned yellow, Leborio fixed her with an angry look. She blinked vacantly a couple of times and then turned her eyes down in shame.

"I know what you've done for me, and I'm grateful. But you've also wanted to sell me a couple times. That's why I ran away. I don't want to be sold."

His eyes followed the line of her skeletal arm all the way to the prominent knuckles of her hand concealing a rectangular blue card. The passing shadow of a grin made the corners of his lips flutter as he spoke.

"Sold? I haven't tried to sell you since the Chinaman who sailed us down to Morocco. I thought we've put all that behind us."

"But I heard you say you were going to roll me in a carpet while I slept."

It was Leborio's turn to blink vacuously just before bursting into a fit of high-pitched hyena laughter. He let her arm go and put one hand on his chest.

"Roll *you* in a carpet? All one hundred pounds of you? No, my dear, there's no need for that. I think I can handle a scrawny, bony bird like you, even if you were to be struggling. We were discussing a three-hundred-pound sea lion named Michelle, who is the star of the Frenchman's eco park. She's a feisty one, and so to move her anywhere, they roll her in a carpet. Honestly, Sne, the way you think of me sometimes is downright disappointing."

The girl stared down like a scolded child, pressing her palms together. For a moment he thought he saw her pass the blue card from one hand to the other. If he weren't in the middle of a performance,

Leborio would have winked and smiled at the heavens for looking after him yet again. Moments ago, he was hopelessly struggling to refund the extra ticket to Gabon, and now he was an instant away from having his cake and eating it too.

"Even though you betrayed me by running away in our time of need, I never stopped believing in you," he said, magnanimously handing her the airline printout. "See? I got you a ticket."

She gaped at the paper, holding it up with one hand while still concealing the other.

"A ticket to Gabon," said the girl, with half a voice.

"Yes." He nodded dramatically. "Though I don't see the point in us going there now. I'll trade it for a couple of seats on the next flight home."

"We're going home?" Her face lit up.

"Well, yes. I'll take you home, and once I know you're safe, I'll find someone to return with. After all, I have an inheritance to claim. I might even stay to run my estate for a few years, get the hang of African lifestyle, and all that."

"Return? With whom?"

"I don't know, Big Bird. I'm sure there will be someone willing to join me on my venture."

"But it's not safe for you to go home yet," she said. "Placido Pector is probably looking to even the score with you."

It was true. The head of the mob in their city had surely placed a bounty on Leborio's head for having run out on his duties. He gently kicked his nearly empty duffle bag and fell back on it with the grace of Ophelia floating down the stream to her inevitable doom.

"Never mind that now. We shall go home for your sake. That is what you really want, isn't it?" His lips quivered enough for her to see it. "Your happiness is my utmost priority."

Snejana shifted her weight from one foot to the other, hesitating between leaning over to comfort him and holding her ground. He looked up at her from the corner of his eye. The hand holding the blue card was still wavering behind her. With a big sigh, Leborio rested his forehead on his knees and counted: one Mississippi, two Mississippi, three—

The girl gently tapped his Bedouin turban with her shiny fingernails, murmuring faintly, "There, there." Then she said, "I guess it wouldn't hurt to complete our journey to Gabon before heading back home."

Behind the dirty patches on his knees, Leborio grinned. The girl went on to persuade him. "You have to claim your estate and decide what to do with it. And then, once you have some money, we can return safely and find a place to ride out Placido Pector's fury. Perhaps we could hide in the mountains."

"Oh, what's the use? He'll find us anywhere we go."

"Then we can stay in Gabon longer," she volunteered. "We can live off your land. We'll grow vegetables and chicken. Easiest thing to farm. They practically grow themselves."

Silly girl, he thought. There would be no chicken in his future. The Gabon of his visions was all a great big desert filled with precious stones and camels. His fortune would be made out of mining for diamonds. There had to be servants on his estate, and those servants would do very well as impromptu miners. He'd seen a movie about African people mining for precious stones, and he knew he had it in him to run an operation like that. He would get them to sift through the whole desert, if that's what it took for Leborio Borzelini to reach his rightful destiny as a merchant of blood diamonds.

Seeing he was lost in thought, Snejana crouched down to his level and placed her head on his shoulder. The hand holding the blue card was now brushing against his calf. Judging this to be the moment he had been waiting for, Leborio reached out and took her hand into his,

C.R. Preston

raising it up to his lips in a gesture of affection. She clasped her hand around the edges of the card, but it was too late. His lips had touched the worn plastic.

"What's this?" said he, the picture of surprise.

Snejana let go of the card and began to whimper. "Please don't get upset! My mother said to use it only in case of emergency."

"You had a perfectly good VISA card on you all this time, and you let us starve in the Moroccan desert? You let me sell the shirt off my back to cross us over from Portugal, and all this time you had the means to get us anywhere we had to go? How could you?"

"It's not like that," she cried. "I was saving it in case I needed to get back home on my own."

With a dignified glance, he replied, "There's no *I* in team, Snejana. After everything we've been through, I thought that's what we were: a team. How could you betray me like that?"

"Please don't say that," she whined as she reached for his hand. "I never meant to betray you. I was just assuming you might leave me somewhere, and I wanted to have something to fall back on, just in case. I know now it was wrong of me to think that way."

Leborio said nothing and looked away from her into an imaginary horizon that did not contain a rowdy Moroccan family reorganizing their luggage to fit the weight restrictions. Desolate but proud, the former guru refused to be moved by her pleas for forgiveness right up until she offered to make it up to him.

"I'll buy you something nice. Anything you want. We don't need anything to fall back on. You've got us this far, and I know you'll look after me no matter what."

"Well, let's not get carried away," he said coldly. "I don't want you to lose your independence by relying on me to look after you. But if you insist, you can buy me a clean change of clothes."

With a confused expression, the girl accepted his offer, handing him the blue card.

"Over there." He pointed to a dingy store that aspired to be the duty-free shop of the airport. "We shall find clean clothes and something to eat."

They found more than that. Sitting on a wooden bench was the cousin of the shopkeeper, who offered to braid a head of hair at a very reasonable price. Leborio, who had always wondered at the aesthetic value of cornrows, decided to try it. An hour later, he left the store, with fully braided hair. He was wearing a purple silk caftan buttoned at the front and tied around his waist with a gold embroidered sash. Behind him, Snejana was dressed in a red wedding takchita adorned in gold thread. Her step rose a little higher.

"You look magnificent, my love!" she said, reaching for his arm. She admired her freshly manicured nails against his purple sleeve.

CHAPTER 2

WELCOME TO GABON

The flight had been short and uneventful. In the aisle seat, Snejana fell asleep with her head on the retractable food tray while Leborio stared out into the bouffant clouds as he put the finishing touches on his diamond mining business plan. He had decided he was going to offer his servants a three-day training seminar about sifting and mining safety procedures, followed by an immediate on-location practicum, where the naturally gifted miners could make an impression and be considered for a supervisory position. Once the diamonds started pouring in, he would only deal with direct clients from amongst the rich and powerful—and perhaps with Tiffany's—but none of those mall diamond chain stores, of course, and certainly not Costco. After all, he had standards.

From the airport in Franceville, they used Snejana's last bit of cash to board a small shuttle bus heading west to Bongoville. Through the dusty windows, they watched the motley urban traffic disappear, making way for the untouched vegetation of the equatorial rainforest. On either sides of the narrow dirt road, as far as the eye could see, trees sprung out of their curiously shaped foliage into the clear blue sky toward an unseen sun. The two travellers sat quietly for a while, watching the bumpy road unfold through a quiet sea of trees. Anything could have lurked behind the shrubbery and tangles of lianas.

"So when's the desert coming up?" asked Snejana. "I thought this place was a desert full of diamonds."

Leborio said nothing. Instead, he stood up. Holding on to the frames of the bus chairs, he made his way to the driver. He smiled gallantly at the corpulent lady splattered against two out of three of the courtesy seats and made a backhanded gesture to suggest that she'd move over. The lady smiled back, a little confused, and Leborio repeated the gesture. She shook her head in disbelief while she slid onto the next seat. He turned his back to her after he sat to face the driver and, without paying any mind to the road ahead, tapped the man on the shoulder with two fingers.

"Bongoville?" he enunciated. "Is it far?"

The bus driver greeted him with a friendly nod. Pointing his finger to the road, he too said, "Bongoville."

Leborio cleared his throat. Sitting a little taller in his seat, he repeated the question, this time adding a *s'il vous plait* at the end. The man shrugged, revealing a wide smile, and turned his eyes to the road again. Displeased, Leborio turned to the corpulent lady and gave her a look of frustration.

"*Français?*" she said sternly.

"Yes, yes," muttered Leborio. "I gathered that much."

The driver gave him another look and, deciding the time for communication had ended, picked up the wire to a rusted handheld microphone and placed it in front of a cassette player that had been duct-taped to his dashboard. He reached for a colourful tape, slid it in, and pressed Play. Immediately, Leborio recognized the beginning of Bobby McFerrin's classic:

Here is a little song I wrote.
You might want to sing it note for note.
Don't worry, be happy.
In every life we have some trouble
When you worry, you make it double
Don't worry, be happy.

The driver turned to Leborio and said, "English."

"Yes, thank you. I've noticed."

He stood up and made his way back to Snejana and the cat, who were waiting patiently at the back of the bus.

"Did you find out where the desert is?" she asked.

"It's coming up later."

The desert did not come up later at all. By the time the bus stopped, they had reached a clearing that seemed to resemble a South American rural settlement in that that it was quite underdeveloped and surrounded by tropical forest. The bus driver stopped the music and announced the name Bongoville a few times over the microphone. Within seconds of debussing, all traces of the journey were gone. The passengers had disappeared quickly between a mosaic of little streets and houses whose only common quality seemed to be impermanence. Separated by a narrow path of gravel, small abodes fashioned from wood bark, mud, or brick marked the way into the heart of the town. Leborio unzipped his duffle bag and unravelled the bejewelled silver knife from within a bunched up, dirty tank top.

Snejana gasped. "Where did you get that? It's so fancy!"

"Long story," he replied, shining it with the cuff of his sleeve. "It belonged to a gypsy king, and now it belongs to me." He tied the knife to his embroidered satchel and started strutting onward, like a peacock. Snejana put the cat down and followed Leborio along the road he chose out of the network fanning out in front of them. It wasn't necessarily the most travelled of the lot, but it appeared to be the widest.

Leborio walked slowly, like a man in an airport expecting to be recognized and picked up by someone holding up a sign. But no one came. A toothless old lady in a camping chair scrutinized him from her spot in the shade and then nodded in the general direction of the next earthen home, where another old lady with very shiny hair put on her reading glasses to see the white people better. Snejana smiled awkwardly, but next to the skinny hairless cat, she really didn't make for news. Her skin was gray from travel, and the elaborate fabric of her outfit had wrinkled from sweat and hours of sitting in narrow seats.

"Are we there yet?" she asked in an uncomfortable tone.

Leborio eyed some of the mud houses covered in palm fronds and grazed his fingers alongside the walls as if to test their transience. How many of these homes had been built within the last few years? As many as must have been destroyed, he thought. He could hear the sound of music coming from a radio and caught a glimpse of a television set through a door left ajar. It wasn't a flat screen or anything, but it was in colour, and the song playing on the radio had been a Western hit during that same decade. This wasn't a modern city, but it was far from being medieval. There were cars parked here and there. Some were old and rusty European imports that had been on their last legs for a few generations, while others were shiny, new jeeps and SUVs that could have been seen in any other modern place of the world. Without realizing it, he turned his head to check a Toyota Prado that drove right by him. The driver had his windows rolled down, elbow out, and dance music blasting. For a moment, Snejana's eyes followed the car longingly.

Around them, people seemed to go about their business peacefully and without hurry. In the shade of their front porch, a father was teaching his son to play chess. His voice carried through the afternoon quiet, enumerating something in a language that blended the heavy sweetness of African tongues and the grace of local French dialect. The child smiled at Leborio as he passed by and waved an ivory pawn at him. He waved back, watching his hand become one with the little white stain that was the pawn.

The deeper he walked toward the centre, the fewer mud homes he saw. Instead, there were big cement structures that reminded him of banks or governmental buildings. The downtown area was rife with them, as it was rife with well-groomed people in light-coloured suits. Opening a few buttons on his purple caftan, Leborio took a moment to assess his surroundings.

"Come," he said to Snejana as they walked up to a well-dressed man sitting on the steps of one of the cement buildings. He was browsing through the pages of a used issue of the *New York Times*.

"Hello," he addressed the man, who was wearing a whisper-beige suit. "Do you speak English?"

The man looked up at him over the newspaper and answered in a crisp British accent. "I do indeed."

"Oh, good. Well then, perhaps you may be of assistance. My name is Leborio, Leborio Borzelini."

The man nodded and raised an expectant eyebrow.

"You haven't heard of me, I see. That doesn't matter now. I am, however, the sole heir of the late Gigi Borzelini."

Again, the man nodded politely.

"Are you from Bongoville?" asked Leborio in a doubtful tone.

"Yes." The man smiled. "Born and raised here, although I did go to school in England for a few years."

"Well, my uncle was the proprietor of a large Bongoville estate, which in fact I am looking for right now. Have you any idea how I can find it?"

"A large estate in Bongoville? That's rather unusual. People don't own much more than a house in these parts. In fact, most people just move from spot to spot as it suits them."

"So you're telling me someone else could be living on my estate as we speak?"

"It's quite possible. What I can do is walk with you to...how do you say...*la mairie*?"

"City hall," guessed Leborio.

"Yes! I can take you to city hall and help you ask about your estate."

They followed the man in the whisper-beige suit down a smaller paved street and all the way up to a large cement building where the blown-up picture of a jovial African man in his sixties hung above the portico.

"That's the late President Omar Bongo," explained their guide. "This city was named after him."

"What do you know? One can do that in these parts," observed Leborio. He almost instantly started tailoring a city in his own name. In his view, Leborioville sounded too rural. Leboriopolis, on the other hand, sounded full of potential. A city of skyscrapers and stock markets. A city built on diamonds. And he was going to be the one to find them. With these thoughts, he found himself standing in front of a stout older man who looked at him with timid interest from behind a counter separated by a glass partition.

The man in the whisper-beige suit explained Leborio's predicament through a semicircular opening in the glass partition while the older man listened and shook his head sympathetically. "This is Monsieur Songoku, our notary," explained the kind interpreter, turning to Leborio.

Monsieur Songoku put his hand though the opening and shook Leborio's hand with a jovial smile. Then he turned to the other man and explained something in French, drawing a mysterious map on a piece of scrap paper. They continued talking and smiling until Leborio cleared his throat in an effort to end the pleasantries.

"So what did he say?"

"There is good news and bad news," announced the African man. "The good news outweighs the bad, I think."

"Well, tell me the good news first. I'm not sure how much more bad news I can handle."

"The good news is that Monsieur Songoku's daughter will soon be married to my cousin twice removed. They have been dating for almost a year, and he is a very good boy. Monsieur Songoku is happy."

Leborio's forehead crumpled into an incredulous expression. He turned to Snejana, acknowledging her presence for the first time.

"I don't believe this!" He pivoted back to the man in the whisper-beige suit.

The other man stared back at him with grave eyes. "Good news is good even if it doesn't have very much to do with us." His jovial face could not carry out a look of reproach for long, and he broke into a broad smile once again. "But I have more good news, and this one has to do with you. We know where your estate is."

Leborio skipped a little in his spot. At last, he could go home. "Well, where is it?"

"It's in the jungle, on the other side of Bongoville."

"The jungle? Surely, there must be a mistake. I was told this was prime real estate location."

"It was a decade ago. But things change very quickly in Bongoville, Mr. Borzelini. What is today's downtown could be tomorrow's shantytown. There's no way to predict how floods and urban planning will affect the face of the city. People here are used to moving all the time."

Leborio swallowed with difficulty and gave the man a sharp look. "If this was the good news, I'd hate to hear what you'd consider bad news."

Without further ado, the man announced, "The bad news is your estate was never claimed by anyone until now, so there is an entire village of people living on it. But wait, there is more bad news. You will probably have to evict them yourself, because Monsieur Songoku feels bad about doing it. He goes to church with some of the elders."

"But there must be someone who can deal with this! The police perhaps? I cannot be expected to move an entire village on my own. These people have no right to squat on my land."

The man in the beige suit shook his head. "They have never heard of you or your family, Mr. Borzelini. The people in these parts think that land belongs to those who look after it. That land you own has always belonged to people, because people have been the ones using it. And before people, it has belonged to the jungle. Never to a white man from—I'm sorry. I do not know where you are from."

Leborio thought about telling him but then decided he wouldn't have heard of the country he came from anyway. Not many people had heard of it and certainly not the people in Africa." I'm from Europe," he said. "Central...well, actually, Eastern Europe."

"Oh, Eastern Europe." The other man smiled. "Where in Eastern Europe? Poland, Serbia, Romania? That part of Europe is more beautiful. Like Africa. It has forests, animals, and nice people who are very clever in mathematics and engineering. And it has people who raise cattle and farmland too. You understand about the land then. You know the land must belong to the people."

"Yes, it belongs to the people who rightfully own it. In this case, me. How do I get it back? Perhaps the police should be involved. Where is your police station?"

"As town deputy, Monsieur Songoku is also in charge of police work."

"Good. Then he can call them for me."

"He is the police, I'm afraid, and he can't be in two places at once. Today he is looking after city hall. Yesterday, he was the police. He had to talk to Jumi the drunk about stealing chicken. This is the second time he's done it. Next time, I'm afraid he'll have to go help Monsieur Songoku for a week in order to pay for his crime."

"How about going to jail?"

"Jail?" repeated the man pensively. "Jail is for bad people. We don't have many bad people here."

Well, that's about to change by one, thought Leborio with smug satisfaction. "So how do I get my land back if Monsieur Songoku won't evict the squatters? Can we call the army?"

"Army?" The man scratched his head, puzzled. "There is an army in Franceville, I think. The Military of Gabon. They protect the president. They do not evict people in Bongoville. Like I said before, you will have to do it yourself, Mr. Borzelini."

Leborio sighed and raised his hands in a defeatist motion. "Well, then, take me there already!"

• CHAPTER 3 •

ESTATE OF TRANCE

They walked quietly for what it seemed like a very long time, Leborio leading the group with a look of indignation on his handsome face and Snejana with her head bowed down, wiping beads of sweat from her forehead and mumbling words of encouragement to the hairless cat. The only one smiling was the man in the whisper-beige suit, whose jovial expression hadn't been altered by the heat of the afternoon or by the disposition of his guests, for this is how he appeared to think of the man and the woman he was taking to the settlement in the jungle.

The man had a slight overbite that made his upper teeth stand out as if they had been chiselled in solid white marble. Leborio imagined how an overly artistic dentist could have sculpted a miniature of Mount Rushmore across his incisors. Personally, he would have chosen Bernini's work instead. But not everyone had impeccable taste. He wondered if anyone had thought of that before: tooth sculpture. Perhaps he could start a trend amongst the people of Africa, because it appeared they were all very eager to smile at strangers. Idle thoughts trailed off as they walked along the narrow path. Checking from the corner of his eye to see if the guide behind him was more inclined to make a right or a left, Leborio imposed a brisk pace on his party. They turned from an asphalt street to a mud road and then to a narrow trail marked by broken twigs and splayed vegetation, leading them far into the heart of the jungle. The ground was black and spongy, and most of the trees that sprang out of it, reaching for the sky, were entirely unknown to him. The air was humid with heat. They must have walked no more than a couple of miles, but to Leborio this seemed dangerously remote from civilization. The invisible trail ended into a vast, circular clearing sprinkled with bark and palm frond dwellings that were held together by mud and wooden beams. Leborio could count at least twenty of these homes.

"*Voilà!*" spoke the man in the beige suit. "This is your estate, *Monsieur* Borzelini."

A few older men dressed in nothing but rags tied at the waist were banging at a piece of wood close to the hearth that presumably marked the center of the settlement. They put down their tools and looked up to see the white travellers.

Snejana moved in closer to him, holding the cat in her arms. "Is this what you meant by black diamonds?"

Over to one side, concealed in the shade of tall trees, a few younger men with painted faces stared back at the group of visitors through puffy eyes. The bright white and red hues of the paint on their faces had dried out and had become wrinkled and smudged with sweat and drool.

"Last night was iboga night," explained the man in the beige suit. "Do you know iboga?"

"No. Is it a drink?" The men looked hungover.

"A root. Gives you visions and insights."

"So they're high." Leborio spun around, from the forest to the dwellings and back to the guide. His face grew redder by the second.

"This is unacceptable!" he started, lips trembling. "What kind of estate is this? It's just a forest clearing filled with...peasants...who are high. No, *peasants* would be an overstatement. These people are a tribe. How do you want me to live here with a homo-barely-erectus tribe? Do any of them speak English? Never mind that. How many of them speak anything at all? Clicking of tongues doesn't count as a language, you know."

The man in the beige suit looked past Leborio gravely, noticing the natives who were now coming out of their homes attracted by the commotion. He nodded at them quietly and made for the elder of the group, leaving the ranting white man behind him. With a respectful bow of the head, he greeted the elder and spoke to him in a tongue like no other Leborio had ever heard. The elder listened intently, paying particular attention to the white man's caftan. With its elaborate embroidery and unusual design, it must have looked like something worn by royalty to these people, thought Leborio, and he was glad to have picked it up. Most of the young men wore nothing but loincloths that had been dyed a crimson shade of red, while a few wore old jeans cut off at the knee. With the exception of the women and the elder chieftain, all villagers had naked torsos with skin that had dried from the sun. They all stood with their bare feet rooted in the dirt. From behind the male front, a few women peeked at the visitors, their curious faces more interested in the tall and thin white woman with flowing hair and sandals on her feet. The older matrons gathered the children nearby, making sure they did not misbehave.

The chieftain was the only man who wore a long brown shirt. It was covered with geometrical patterns that are so often encountered in Africa and that are thought to represent the mountains and rivers that give life to the ancient continent. When the man in the beige suit finished talking, the chieftain took Leborio's hands into his and bowed with reverence, as if to thank him. Then he stepped back and raised his voice, calling out a name.

"This is the elder of the villagers." The man in the beige suit turned to Leborio. "His name is Monsieur Juste Bamba. He will show you around your estate and help you communicate with the people. Everyone listens to him."

"But he doesn't speak English," murmured Snejana from behind Leborio.

"He does not. But his daughter speaks French and a little bit of English. Monsieur Juste called her just now. Ah, there she is." He gestured at a young girl, who approached them. "This is Léonie. She will be your interpreter."

"I am happy to meet you," said Léonie, curtsying respectfully to the two white people. She had a broad smile and very big eyes that rested with curiosity on the newcomers. Her white sarafan stood in stark contrast with the rustic decorum and the earthen tones of the huts.

Leborio checked his colourful caftan and stepped forward to speak with the girl. "And I am Monsieur Borzelini," he said rigidly. "I own this land and everything that is on it."

The girl continued smiling and looked him in the eye with warmth that made him feel uncomfortable. It was as if they were old friends for whom social conventions like the acceptable time one should make eye contact did not apply. He looked away from her to the chieftain, who was also staring at him with great curiosity.

"Well, it looks like you are settled," said the man in the beige suit. "I wish you a very pleasant stay. I will come to see you soon."

"Wait!" shrieked Leborio as the man made to leave. "What will happen to me now?" he asked, gesturing at the villagers with great concern.

The other man shrugged and placed a large hand on his shoulder.

"You will live on your land. Is it not what you wanted?"

"But these people," he started again, this time whispering, his eyes filled with sheer desperation. "How can I rule them? I don't even know if they're peaceful. What sorts of things do they eat?"

The man in the beige suit took Leborio's hand off his shoulder.

"Not people, *monsieur*, if that is what you fear. They eat what they grow, and there is plenty of it to go around. You will not hunger for anything. Do not worry."

Leborio wanted to ask where he would sleep, but by the time he thought of this, the man in the beige suit had disappeared through the forest, leaving him in a Mexican standoff with the natives, who were still motionless, staring at him. Uneasy, he turned to the chieftain's daughter. She too was staring and smiling.

"Léonie, right?" he said.

"I am happy to meet you," she repeated, in the same automatic tone that did not reassure Leborio about her actual fluency.

"Do you," he spoke slowly, gesturing at her, "know where my house is?" He put his palms together to represent the roof and stared back into her large, black eyes.

"Ah, yes." She nodded, pointing at the bark dwellings. "House."

Taking his head into his hands, Leborio turned to Snejana with an exasperated shrug. She dropped the cat, which had found shelter in her bony arms, and took a step closer to the girl.

"He is tired," she said slowly, laying her head over an open palm. "Sleep?"

"Ah, yes," said Léonie, still smiling. "Bed?"

Snejana nodded in relief. Following the chieftain's daughter, Snejana dragged Leborio by the hand through the crowd of natives. Behind them, Regina, the hairless cat, trembled and hissed as she struggled to escape the grabbing hands of the matrons.

They were settled into one of the larger dwellings, a house that had a well in front of it and a table made from a tree stump placed in the shade, by the door. There was a bed fashioned from wood planks; a thin, raggedy mattress; blankets; a metal bowl placed on a shelf of sorts; and a bar of handmade soap. The natives rushed to bring in an old mirror, which they put on the shelf next to the metal bowl. The reflective coating on the mirror was cracked and peeled, like the skin of a leper, returning the image of a flickering lamp nearby in dim shadows. There were dead insects all around and other living ones that surveyed the room in dizzying circles. The last thing Leborio saw before falling into a deep sleep were sun's rays penetrating the cracks between the thin twigs that formed the flat roof to his abode, reaching down through the mosquito netting, and playing across his face like the fingers of a benevolent deity. And then, the lights went out.

He dreamed of a bottomless lagoon with emerald waters, like the tiles on the Moroccan fountain. In his dream, he stared down into the deep and let the voice of the sea call out to him. He wanted to dive in and let himself be submerged into the green abyss. But he did not dive. Instead, he walked along the edge of the lagoon, allowing its swishing waters to tempt him with their song, all the while knowing that the gentlest of breezes would weigh on his precarious balance and push him in, into the place where he did not dare go. He felt a soft probing touch on his hand, giving him that dreaded push, and he began to fall toward the treacherous waters.

He let out a terrified scream before Snejana rushed to his side and woke him up. He was livid and drenched with sweat. Next to his pillow, Regina had arched her back like a feline warrior, ready to defend herself from this most unexpected reaction to a gentle cuddle.

"I was falling," he explained, catching his breath. "It pushed me, and I slipped..."

Snejana stroked his hair and pulled his head into her chest. "Hush now. You're safe," she lulled. "It was just the cat, licking at your hand. You're safe, my darling."

Leborio threw his head back and remained motionless, looking up at the ceiling in an attempt to control his breathing. His imaginary fall had been deceitful. He had been pushed. It was only a dream, he kept repeating. But anger stirred inside him, and an unnamed fear took hold of his heart. He reached into a hidden pocket and pulled out the crumpled shred of paper. *So long, your feudal highness.* Umberto must have thought he'd won. He must have thought he got her. They were probably together right now, somewhere on the patio of some fancy restaurant in the city he was from, a city with grand boulevards, high-tech billboards, and fashionable people. He folded the paper back and tucked it back in his pocket.

Above, he could see the fine mesh of the mosquito netting bunched up at the top of his bed, draping over him in a transparent rectangle—a wedding veil meant to cover him like a tent and protect him from the dangerous bites of tropical insects. Perhaps that was what got him in a sweat, he thought. Perhaps he had been bitten. Just as his heartbeat slowed down, and he began to feel his face cooling down, the wooden door squeaked ajar, revealing the slender figure of the chieftain's daughter. In one hand, she held a candle covered in a jar. The light flickered softly across her face, making her large eyes sparkle.

"Okay?" she lowered her head in a gesture of concern.

Leborio propped himself up on his elbows, revealing his muscular torso, which glistened from the sweat.

"Leave us." He waved Snejana's hand away from his head and watched her take the cat into her arms and sidestep the other young woman on her way out. He reached for his caftan and pulled it over his head slowly and deliberately under the girl's wide eyes.

"Léonie, right? Come in please," he urged her. "Take a seat." He looked about the room and noting there really were no seats, he straightened the covers on his bed with one hand and signalled for her to sit at his feet.

She smiled and nodded but did not sit down. "Yes, Léonie." She pointed to herself.

"Léonie, I am Mr. Borzelini. I have come from very far away to take back what is mine. This land," he added. "So what will your people do now that I am here? Where will you all go?"

The girl continued smiling and nodding, an expression of kind understanding beaming out from her luminous eyes. "I am happy to meet you," she said at last, causing Leborio to fall back on the bed and cover his eyes with one hand in a gesture of desperation. He was stuck here, in the heart of the jungle, deprived of his most efficient tool, his speech. Of course, there was Snejana, who could chitchat his ears off, and this girl, who could repeat the same sentence with a fairly good English accent if only he were French. He could not go back where he came from; he had nothing to go forward with—no money, connections, or women to fawn over him. All there was for him was this bark dwelling, these people, this tribe, and the feverish heat of the jungle with its insects, sweat, and its nightmares. Insanity! It was all insanity! He wanted to get out of there, to escape back to civilization, where there were luxuries, conversations, and air-conditioning.

His thoughts were interrupted by a soft touch on his forearm. She had sat down next to him and was now staring at him in silence through the transparent netting, almost apologetically. The smile was gone, leaving the corners of her lips to hang, defeated. When she didn't smile, her mouth wasn't so wide, he noted. It was actually quite a small mouth, like a heart-shaped bonbon. There was a patch of discoloured skin at the center of her lower lip that made her look like a painting. She looked saddened and disappointed all at once. But not with him. If she was not disappointed with him, then she could only be disappointed with herself, as they were the only two people in the wooden shack. Why should she feel so? Leborio tried to imagine that he was the wide-eyed daughter of a Gabonese chieftain and arrived at the conclusion that the only reason she should feel so unhappy was her inability to communicate as well as she might have hoped. Let's face it, her fluency in English left something to be desired. He imagined there had not been many opportunities for the young girl to prove herself to her father, and the all-consuming need to do so was something he understood too well.

But that was all done with now. He wanted nothing to do with his own father, except perhaps for having him watch wistfully as the mighty Leborio Borzelini returned home as a celebrated diamond merchant and landowner. Of course, given this recent setback of Gabon being an equatorial country with a full-fledged tropical forest, finding diamonds was going to take some time. It was also going to take a few trusted allies, preferably ones who knew the local landscape well. And who better than a gullible young girl to do Leborio's bidding? Of course, she did not speak English very well, he reminded himself. But he could teach her. She seemed to have intelligent eyes. He pushed the netting away, took her hand, and squeezed it in a gesture of encouragement. Then he lifted her chin with his index finger so that they now saw eye-to-eye.

"Leborio," he spoke, pointing at himself. "You are Léonie. I am Leborio."

"Name," she said, looking a little hopeful this time.

"Exactly! Those are our names. See, this is not so hard."

The sound of a broken twig somewhere outside of the door caused them to check themselves. The girl folded her hands on her lap, while Leborio leaned back on his elbows, once again at ease.

On the other side of the wooden door, Snejana froze in her tracks, glaring down at the piece of tree bark she had stepped on.

CHAPTER 4

TABLE FOR THREE

A few days ago, she was sitting across from Umberto and having dinner with him. Not as they had eaten a thousand times before, at his mother's table, gulping down whatever they could find in the fridge before they burst through the door to play out in the street, but as a woman and a man, dressed in their sleekest clothes, reading every small gesture with the anticipation a lifetime of familiarity builds. The waiter had taken them to a quaint table next to a wall from whence a painting of the Venetian Grand Canal at sunset hung inwardly, almost hovering over the table, like an impending secret. There were three seats at this table. Umberto felt uncomfortable with the third empty chair and asked the waiter to remove it.

"Leave it," said Iris. "I can put my purse on it."

Umberto smiled his half smile, the other half of his lips frozen. It was the first thing most people noticed when they met him. He had beautiful lips when his mouth was closed, but when he smiled, half of his mouth contorted into a grin of sorts. It hadn't always been that way. His faced had changed when they were only children, after the death of his airplane pilot father. It wasn't the only thing about Umberto that bothered the senses. His voice was unsuited to his otherwise handsome face. It came from somewhere deep inside of his being and was cavernous, almost muffled. He spoke slowly, and he thought as quickly as he spoke. But it didn't matter to Iris. She still saw in him the little boy with a full smile and a carefree voice.

They drank red wine and words started tumbling out as Umberto spoke earnestly about the state of affairs in their city and how he would change things for the better if only he would be given the chance. In fact, he intended to find a way to do so. She believed him. He was a man of his word, and his word was always defending a cause. Then he told her an anecdote that took too long to say, and by the time he got to the punch line, it had deflated like an old balloon. She threw her head back and laughed anyway, her full and hearty laughter ringing against the adorned walls of the restaurant. This seemed to please him, and he took her hand in his, quickly, furtively, as if they were committing a crime. And perhaps they were. A crime against their past, the long years of bicycles, rollerblades, secret attic incursions, sharing music, competing over who would hold their breath longest under water, and the years that followed, when she could feel Umberto's brown eyes resting upon her lips, full of wonder. There was no doubt that sitting across him at a grownup table in a romantic restaurant and letting him hold her hand felt a little incestuous. They both looked about them nervously, wondering if the couples at the other tables could tell. Tell what? That they were there together, despite the distinct and blatant feeling that they were not supposed to be.

They shared in the rush of defiance, both looking over to where the third chair stood, empty but for Iris's things. The crime was not against their past. It was against the man who had wounded them both, and as such, it wasn't really a crime. It was an act of deliberation. They would betray him by closing the circle of three into a private dance for two, a dance that ought not to have been danced by Iris and the cousin of the man she loved.

And dance they did. He spun her and held her; she locked her hand on the trunk of his neck and leaned back into a dip. Their feet moved lazily to the sound of summer music until their lips collided and locked into a salty kiss. He trembled a little. She sighed with the relief of liberation. Alas, the sweet taste of betrayal lingered on their tongues like honey. There was no going back. She knew this. But there was also no going forward. With a single kiss, she had broken herself free from the one she had always loved. She had betrayed Leborio by no longer belonging to him. But she knew now that she did not belong with Umberto either. Not because he was Leborio's cousin, but because between a man and a woman there should never be an empty chair.

She did not have the heart to tell him this right away. She would wait until later, when the right moment would soften the blow that was to be cast on his hopeful heart.

The next morning, as she walked into the colourful office of Private Affairs Investigators, her sole employee, Gretchen, was completing a Sumo-Sudoku puzzle at the front desk. The girl shoved the puzzle away, flustered, and mumbled an excuse.

"You don't have to hide it, Gretchen." Iris smiled. "There are going to be slow days, and on those days you may immerse yourself in whatever personal things you enjoy. As long as you do your job, I don't care what else you do with your time here."

The girl sighed in relief and shuffled through a stack of blank papers. She had an unusual sense of style, noted Iris, discreetly observing the grim accessories that gave her an air of tortured gawkiness. Angular blue-black hair framed her pale white face and curved around her oddly pierced ears like curtains behind their holdbacks. From the jet-black pair of tight pants that were topped with a studded belt to the stems on her neatly laced, graphic Vans, the girl looked as tightly wrapped as an Egyptian mummy—perhaps one that had died in a torture chamber of sorts.

"Here," said Gretchen, waving a yellow notepad under Iris's nose. She had taken down a new assignment. "That woman called about her missing daughter again. She's certain it was her daughter's no-good boyfriend. I still have their names and information, in case you change your mind and decide to help them."

Iris avoided looking at her. She hadn't changed her mind, though she had thought about it more than a few times.

"I couldn't find anything on him besides what the mother told me. I should also say that the mother is a famous healer. There's a year-long waiting list to see her. She's not one of those quack money-grabbers, but I imagine she must be successful. Money could very well be the motive behind her daughter's disappearance."

"Is this the first time she's ever gone missing?"

"Yes. She's spent the night at his place before but always called her mother to let her know."

"So maybe they decided to go on a spur-of-the-moment sort of vacation."

Gretchen shook her head. "I don't think so. Neither one of them has shown up for work. They work together, did I mention that? At the Lido. He's part of the animation team, and she works at the spa. The mother thinks that's how they met." The girl continued to stare in anticipation of a positive answer.

"No, Gretchen. We're not taking this case. End of story."

Her tone was final, and the girl resigned herself to completing the Sudoku puzzle, sullen as a death sentence. Iris sat behind her own large desk, pretending to read the paper. Words and pictures marched through her head like faceless soldiers forming a single giant headline. It read *No-Good Boyfriend, Leborio Borzelini, Abducts Young Girl.*

"What was the girl's name?" she heard herself ask.

Gretchen looked up, a glimmer of hope in her doe eyes. "Snejana. The girl's name is Snejana."

Of course it was, reflected Iris, conjuring a mental picture of the tall, thin girl she had met in Portugal. She couldn't have been older than eighteen, a child really, mesmerized by Leborio's tricks and shadows. What a way to lose your childhood, she thought, remembering all the years she had spent playing his games. Gretchen's voice brought her out of her trance. "I told the client that you would help her."

"Then call her and tell her I can't do that."

Iris noticed the thick black eyeliner the girl wore complimented the black frame of her glasses and made her look twice as serious. She couldn't understand young people's obsession with looking older. Didn't they know age happened to everyone equally and irrevocably?

The girl persisted. "May I ask why not?"

"No, you may not," she replied, a little louder than intended.

The tip of the girl's pencil rested atop the yellow paper in complete silence. Iris could see her upper lip trembling, although the light reflected in Gretchen's glasses, and she couldn't quite see her secretary's eyes. Overcome by remorse, Iris stood up and walked over to Gretchen's desk, putting her hand over hers.

"I'm sorry I yelled," she said. The girl listened politely, but Iris could tell from Gretchen's rigid expression that she was not forgiven. "I cannot take this case, you see. It would be...a conflict of interests."

These last words struggled to come out, leaving her spent. She went back to her desk and stared out the window at the boulevard whose name had yet again been changed. A group of high school girls in cropped shorts that seemed so much shorter than those Iris remembered wearing crossed the street and disappeared behind a corner. She knew where they were headed. She had turned that same corner countless times before on her way to school and just as late in the day. Some things never change. She smiled, thinking about the mornings she spent sleeping in and cutting class. And some things change too often, she reflected, trying to remember the new name for this street she loved so much. The boulevard, however, did not seem to care what it was called. It had been there from the time of horse carriages and crinoline skirts, and it would be there long after cropped shorts would go out of fashion.

"You know one of them?" Once again, Gretchen's voice brought her back.

"I know both of them," she replied, wondering if there was such a term as double conflict of interest.

The girl was still sullen, and Iris knew she had to give her more. "I know him a whole lot better than I should like to. As for the girl, she's a sweet kid. She doesn't have the slightest inkling of what she's in for."

"But you do."

She did. She saw the blueprints to his designs well before the rest of the world. She couldn't in good conscience let Snejana fall prey to him. Deep down, she knew she had to follow the yellow brick road all the way to the wizard's den, if only to pull the curtain of mirrors and smoke and set this young girl free. Yes, the curtain had to be pulled. And she was the only one who knew how. She picked up the yellow notepad as if it were a bad apple, bracing herself for the moment a big ugly worm would make its way through the rotten surface.

CHAPTER 5

MINERS IN TRAINING

The next day after he arrived at his inherited estate on the outskirts of Bongoville, Gabon, Leborio awoke to find a procession of villagers lined up at the door of his bark dwelling. There were seven men and three women, one of them carrying an infant tied to his mother's back with a sheet of cloth. The ten participants sang an upbeat folk song and followed in each other's footsteps, dancing to the beat of an unseen drum. Leborio searched the crowd that had gathered, hoping to see the man in the beige suit or the chieftain's daughter, Léonie. A few feet away, where the dirt was at its driest, stood the chieftain himself, Monsieur Juste Bamba, observing how the proceedings evolved. He seemed to be quite pleased with the song and occasionally tapped the long, carved stick he used as his staff against the ground.

"*Bonjour, Monsieur Bamba*," greeted Leborio, followed closely by Snejana.

The chieftain smiled at the guests and clapped his hands in the direction of the community matrons, who appeared right away, holding up a woven basket full of baked cassava balls topped with honey.

Leborio reached out and took one, nodding his head at the matron who had offered it.

"Is it good?" asked Snejana, leaning on his arm.

"It tastes like worn socks and honey. Want some?" He made a sound of enjoyment and nodded at the matron. Snejana nearly gagged and looked away. "It has the texture of carrots, or no, yams. But the taste isn't terrible. You should try it. Besides, you haven't eaten in days, have you?"

"I think I'm gonna pass. I'll wait until we get to the hotel."

"What hotel?"

"The one we're staying at." She raised an expectant brow.

Leborio put the remains of the cassava ball back in the basket and licked the tips of his fingers.

"I'm not sure what you think is going on here," he started, looking right at her, "but this is it, Big Bird. This is where we're staying. This is my land. I don't like it any more than you do, having to sleep in this bug-infested shack, eat mushy vegetables dipped in honey, and make conversation with my hands, but the fact is that this is my land, and these are my people. We'd better get used to it."

"Used to it? That's easy for you to say. They wake you up with drums and dances like you're some kind of god. They feed you and send you concubines—of course you're going to want to stay here! But I have news for you: these are not your people. When was the last time you had a good look in the mirror? You're a few shades off from being one of them, though you would never know it by the cornrows."

"Don't be racist, Big Bird. I've come to think of them as my subjects. This is not about skin colour; it's about my superior intelligence. It makes them look up to me—as it does most people. And... concubines? Really?" Leborio glanced at the heavyset matron holding his food basket. The woman smiled at him ever so sweetly, revealing a set of unusually long gums.

"Not this one. The one you were playing Tarzan and Jane with last night. The pretty one." Her eyes welled up, and her lip began to tremble.

"Léonie?" His eyes bulged out in indignation. "How do you know what we were doing? Were you eavesdropping? I knew it! I knew I heard your hooves dig into the dirt outside. We're just friends, you know."

"Yeah, friends who can't even speak to each other."

"Well, we're gonna have to change that, won't we? Over the next few weeks, my time will be taken by educational matters. And in the spirit of education, I will spend time with Léonie and help improve her English." Seeing that Snejana's gray eyes were about to pop out of her head, he added, "She is the only one who can help us, Big Bird. She shows potential to learn more, and she has her father's ear. We need to get her on our side if we're to get anywhere with these people."

"Our side? What side is that?"

"The side of success, of course. Can't you see it? We'll travel the world in our own private jet and do exactly what we want to do, when we want to do it. Money buys you that kind of freedom, you know."

He gave it a moment to let her imagination run wild. Whoever said you couldn't teach an old dog new tricks didn't try dangling a new bone under a pet's nose. Now that the promise of everlasting love had dwindled away from Snejana, the time had come to raise the stakes and promise her an entirely new sort of future.

Not far from where Leborio and Snejana stood, ten of the tribesmen were earnestly performing a ritualistic dance around the hearth.

"Just look at them," he said. "They're strong and able-bodied. With a little guidance, they're going to make outstanding miners."

"Miners?"

"Yes. We're here for the diamonds, remember?"

Just as the last word came out of his mouth, the drums stopped beating, and the dance came to an end. Monsieur Juste Bamba picked up his carved staff and said a few words Leborio imagined expressed his gratitude to his new master, the former Spanish guru. Then, as if by magic, all the men disappeared, leaving the women and children behind to tend to household chores. The only man left standing in the clearing was the chieftain, who was still smiling at Leborio with the air of an amiable tour guide awaiting questions or a tip.

"No, no! Where did all the men go? I need them here."

The chieftain studied Leborio's commotion with the utmost interest.

"I need the men to stay so that I can start training them! School. *École*. Do you understand *école*? I'm going to make a school." He pivoted in a circle, scanning for a good spot. Then he pointed at a place in the shade, where the settlement met the forest. "Right there."

The chieftain nodded with excitement, and bringing in his elbows, he began to hit his chest with his fists and make ululating sounds. Then, he used his index finger to point at the bushes where Leborio intended to commence the training of the men. Right in front of the shrubbery of the bush stood a tall tree, taller than all the rest that surrounded the settlement. Its thick trunk was marked by patterns in the bark that ran all the way up into the canopy, like veins running up the arm of a man in the prime of his life. The dense crown of the tree provided the shade Leborio needed for his classroom. And here were snacks for recess, he thought, looking down. At the foot of the tree there were some kind of nuts, some covered in a lime green skin, others rotted down to the brown nutshell. It was a Coula tree. He had read about these trees in his adolescence and knew they were native only to African countries close enough to the equator to have a tropical climate. The nuts were supposed to be very nutritious. He looked at the tree and nodded. This was going to be a good spot to have a school, provided the nuts didn't cause his pupils concussions on their way down.

"I know. It's very good news, isn't it? You're going to have your own school. A school for the trades, specifically mining. Well, there you have it."

The chieftain did not answer. Instead, he shrugged, somewhat frustrated with the communication breakdown, and retreated to his endeavours. From behind the tall tree, Leborio thought he heard movement. He looked back into the woods, feeling almost as if there was someone watching him. But there was no one there. The sounds of animals stepping over twigs and leaves, perhaps. Who knew what lurked in the heart of the jungle? His only chance for remaining safe were these people.

The excitement of the first day wore off, and by the second day, Leborio had had about enough of his monologue. It was clear to him that the real test of this endeavour was perseverance, not one of his strong suits. To go on for any considerable length of time without a change of scenery and stimulating conversation was something he had never had to do before. He would have to mime his thoughts to the natives, day in and day out, hoping they understood his meaning. Of course, the sorts of things he could communicate using body language had to be very basic and generally true. One could not mime gossip or manipulative lies. He communicated things such as the need for food, sleep, and utensils. He could also point at the sky above them and nod appreciatively. Talking about the weather was a universal conversational copout.

Even Snejana, who for better or worse was the only creature in a five-kilometre radius with whom he could communicate, was irritating to him. She refused to say much, instead eyeing him with a reproachful glare that was meant to say, "I could have been dancing in Ibiza." Her faithful companion, the hairless cat, always by her foot, admonished him in her own way by staring up at him and hissing. She too had a problem with living in the equatorial forests of Africa, where most creatures were larger than a mouse. Every once in a while , the cat would disappear behind the tall Coula tree that marked Leborio's school, into the impenetrable bush.

"Leave her." He raised his hand to stop Snejana from running after the animal. "Perhaps she's making friends."

As the days went by, he looked forward to his exchanges with Léonie, who, even though could not say as much as he would have liked, was at least always in a sunny disposition. During the day, she was mostly absent, but she brought him fresh clothes, food, and water every night just before bed. One time, when he woke up early, he saw her white sarafan disappearing through the forest and wondered where she was headed. But he had no one to ask. By the time she returned, he had other things on his mind. He managed to explain to her that he wanted to teach the men some things and got her immediate support in the matter. The next day, her father, Monsieur Juste Bamba, congregated the men and told them they were to go to Leborio's school just before sunset every day. Some of the men rolled their eyes while others clapped joyously.

"Men go school," announced Léonie with her usual broad smile, the rosy flicker of light playing on the fleshy hub of her lower lip.

On the first day of class, Leborio arranged his pupils in a circle around him and began drawing in the sand with a long stick. His first drawing was intended to give an overview of the course goal: mining for diamonds. He drew an engagement ring that was to represent the final product. Once the men recognized the symbol, they began to clap excitedly.

"Yes, we will get the diamonds out of the ground and sell them. I will become fabulously rich," confirmed Leborio, clapping back at them.

"They think we're getting married," pointed out Snejana, who had decided to observe, for lack of better entertainment.

Leborio stared down at his artwork. Realizing that the engagement ring might have sent the wrong message, he stomped the image with both of his feet. So much for being secluded in the forest, he thought, reflecting on the prevailing power of Western consumerism. These men could not speak a word of English, but they were all too aware of what an engagement ring was. He turned to Snejana, and with an icy glare, ordered her away. The men grew silent once again, visibly intimidated by his show of power. He could feel their eyes glued to his every movement, and his chest grew a little higher. It was as it should be. Leborio Borzelini imparting his great wisdom with various people of the world. And though he relished in this newfound attention, Leborio couldn't shake off the feeling that he was being watched by a spirit, some forest deity, hidden atop the luscious tropical trees. As with most other gods, this omniscient presence of the jungle made him feel uneasy.

With Léonie's help, he managed to convey the meaning of his teachings and began the practical component of fashioning digging tools and studying the soil. Here, Monsieur Juste Bamba was able to help. He took them to a spot where the earth was soft yet dry and told the men to start digging. Within a week, they had dug a hole that was ten meters deep and five square meters wide. Leborio would have liked to speed up the operation by keeping some of the men behind during the day, but his efforts to bring them to the digging hole were met with a smile and a firm shake of the head. They had other things to do. Everyone had their assigned responsibilities, such as gathering wood for the fire, going into town to trade for food and clothes, and fishing along a tributary of the Ogooué River.

At night, he fell asleep, exhausted from the day's work and from all the brilliant thoughts that swarmed around his head—thoughts he could not share with those around him because they did not understand his language or his mind. He would have given anything to sit across from an old friend, a familiar face, someone other than the tall girl who looked like an ostrich and her hairless cat. Their reproachful glares reminded him of where he was and how different from what he hoped it all had turned out to be. Alone in his bed, painfully aware of the noises coming from the jungle around him, he fell into a deep sleep plagued with fears and greenish-blue waters into which he never dared to dive.

One day, when he had lost all sense of the slow passing of time, Léonie brought him a leather pouch filled with drinking water for the night. She waved away the sheer bed drapes of the mosquito net with one hand, sat by the edge of his bed, and looked into his eyes with an intent expression.

"You have bad dream," she said without smiling.

Taken aback by Léonie's observation, Leborio looked past her and nodded. It made him feel uncomfortable that this young girl should know his troubles while he knew nothing about her. She touched his forehead again, the way she had done the first night they met, and shook her head with concern.

"Afraid?" she asked.

He wanted to use words and deceive her. But it would have taken too long to explain in words that she could understand. Her English had improved since his arrival, but it was still far from fluent. Exhausted, he told her the truth.

"Sometimes," he sighed. "I guess we are all afraid of something or other."

"Snake or big cat?" she asked, growling softly to explain the jaguar.

Leborio laughed. "No, no snake or cat. I dream of water. I walk along the edge of the water, and I want to dive, to jump, but something always holds me back. Then, I fall, and all I can think as I'm falling is that I could have just as well dived in of my own volition—of my own will," he corrected himself to make it easier for the girl.

From her bed at the opposite corner of the room, Snejana's gray eyes glowered in the darkness like two coals, charring slowly through the fabric of the draping night. Léonie listened quietly, seemingly unaware of Snejana's piercing gaze a few feet behind her. The chieftain's daughter remained silent for a moment. Then she lifted a finger in the air and told him: "You must jump. You look at water and you say, 'I am white man in Africa, and I am not afraid at you.'"

"Of you. I am not afraid of you."

"Of you." Her reassuring smile had once again returned. She wore no makeup and no adornments, and yet she looked so much like a painting. The natural slight discolouration at the centre of the lower lip created the illusion that it had been placed there by a brushstroke, made to glimmer and dance like the light in her eyes. She gave Leborio one last look of encouragement before leaving.

That night, Leborio did not dream of anything. He slept until well after sunrise and woke up to find Monsieur Juste Bamba sitting on a tree stump outside his door. He saluted the elder and watched him stand up to show a wooden bowl filled with a strange concoction. Monsieur Bamba put his fingers together, indicating it was for eating.

"Thank you," said Leborio, reaching absentmindedly for the bowl. But the chieftain slapped Leborio's fingers and placed the bowl out of reach. Then he proceeded to bow apologetically and explain something with great fervour. What Leborio could make out of his frantic waves in the air was that it was in fact meant for later.

"Just as well, Monsieur Bamba. I'm heading into town today, and I will be gone for a few hours. I figured I've spent enough time training the miners, and I need a break from the jungle. If you just show me which way to Bongoville, I shall return before nightfall."

The chieftain stared at him, seemingly somewhat alarmed by the mention of the town name. Then he shook his head vigorously, indicating he opposed the idea. He too mentioned Bongoville a few times while explaining something of great importance. Leborio gave him a friendly pat on the back, like that a teenage son gives his worrisome father, and went back inside. He emerged dressed in his Moroccan caftan with the sash tied around it and his silver dagger hanging like a Turkish yatagan. He walked up to one of the younger boys who was plucking a dead chicken, put out his hand revealing a coppery euro coin, and uttered, "Bongoville."

Happy to be paid, even in unknown and useless currency, the boy dropped his chicken and signalled for Leborio to follow him through the bush. He waved and mumbled a noncommittal greeting to Snejana, who was rubbing her eyes in confusion while the chieftain shook his head at her ominously. Through the trees, he saw the boy move as nimble as a jungle creature. How long, wondered Leborio, since I have moved like that? It wasn't that long ago that he had been the agile Spanish guru. Not that long ago, yet a lifetime away. The lifetime just before he had become the owner of this land.

• CHAPTER 6 •

ALWAYS START WITH THE MONEY

Iris phoned Umberto and told him what she had to do. She wouldn't normally disclose the facts of a case, but she knew she could trust Umberto to be silent. He knew Leborio as well as she did. Perhaps he might have an idea of where to start.

"Do you have any idea where he's headed?" he asked her.

"No. But if anyone can find him, it's me. You understand, don't you? That's why it has to be me."

"Would you still go if you knew where he was?"

"What do you mean?"

"I mean if you knew where he was at this very moment, would there be a reason for you to go? I suppose you could just tell the girl's mother, and she could go get her."

She weighed her answer. "If I knew where he was…I would still go, yes. I have to see the case to its end. Why? Do you know where he is?"

Umberto hesitated for a moment. "No, I don't. But good luck finding him."

"I leave first thing tomorrow. You do understand, don't you?" she repeated. "You get why I have to go. It's my job to see this case through. I want nothing to do with him."

She listened to his reproving silence, made her good-byes, and hung up the phone. Somehow, she couldn't shake the feeling that he knew more than she did, that perhaps he knew where Leborio was. But how was that possible? The last Umberto and Iris had seen of Leborio Borzelini was when they left him to outrun the Portuguese authorities alerted by Iris herself. She named him as the thief of the coveted Sophie Necklace, even though she was sure that he wasn't guilty. Not this time. He was not the diamond thief. But she gave him up anyway because of all those times he had seduced people, lied to them, and stolen that which they held most precious, be it a bracelet or a principle. Karma seemed to care very little about disciplining her favourite son. And so, Iris took it upon herself to put an end to Leborio's crimes and to remove herself from his hold. As a final act of betrayal, she chose Umberto. It was her way of yanking the Band-Aid off. She made sure that even if she weren't strong enough to stay away, he would never forgive her after this.

Her first lead took her to Morocco. A credit card had been used in the Marrakech airport shop to buy expensive clothing that most people wore for wedding ceremonies. That was the last thing the mother knew about her missing daughter. Inside the Moroccan airport shop, Iris opened up her old, worn wallet to show a small picture of a pubescent boy scotch-taped to the inner flap. The teenager in the picture was strikingly beautiful: doe-eyed and olive-skinned, with long waves of black hair framing a face captured just as it lit up into a hopeful and androgynous smile. There was nothing conclusive to indicate that he was in fact a boy other than a few handcrafted chains hanging from his neck. She had been carrying it with her from the day it was taken. Perhaps something more recent would have helped the women working at the shop identify Leborio. They looked at it and nodded with a smile, in the same way one does when shown pictures of a colleague's baby.

"No, no." She shook her head. " Have you seen this boy? Man? Well, he is a man now. This is an old picture."

She gesticulated muscles and height, waiting for telepathic imaging to kick in. It took longer than expected. At last, the women exchanged a few words and seemed to agree on remembering the same person. He was a tall and handsome white man who looked like Sean Paul, the reggae artist.

"No, no," repeated Iris. "I've known him for a really long time. He looks like this. Only older." She mimed a serious, more aged expression.

The women shook their heads in a synchronized but firm motion. One of them reached under the counter and pulled out a hair styling magazine for men.

"Before, he look like that." She glanced at the wallet picture. "Now he look like this," she said, pointing at a recent picture of Sean Paul's cornrows. "We know. We make the hair."

"Was he alone?" asked Iris with incredulous eyes.

"No, there was a girl. Very tall."

Iris started laughing, picturing Leborio prancing around dressed as if he were ready to receive his very own BET award. For the first time since she arrived in Morocco, she thought of Umberto. It would have been nice to share this moment with someone who could properly appreciate the implications.

"And do you know where they were going?"

The airport shopkeeper did not. But she knew a woman who could find out.

A few hours later, Iris met Farah, who was wearing a long, earth-toned skirt wrapped once over around her waist so that she could put her leg through. She also wore cowboy boots, which would have seemed a little extravagant to anyone else but Iris, who was well used to Leborio's flamboyant fashion statements. Iris took one look at this woman and decided she liked her. And if her sense of style was any indication, Farah was just the right woman to take on the daunting task of helping her track down Leborio Borzelini.

After listening to the shopkeeper's brief account of how she braided his hair, Farah checked the dingy monitor in the airport waiting area and walked up to the desk, where Yasmen, the airport clerk, was filing her false nails in anticipation of new customers. They exchanged a few words before Farah returned to speak to Iris.

"They went to Gabon."

"Gabon?"

"Yes. Gabon."

"How does she know?" Iris raised an incredulous eyebrow, looking at the airport clerk and her gel-wet, curly hair.

"She doesn't. We know your cornrowed white man left the shop Tuesday afternoon. That is when the plane to Franceville, Gabon flies out. This girl confirmed swiping his boarding pass. It means he went to Gabon."

Iris shrugged. Of course, it would be more expensive now that she had to fly out deeper into the heart of Africa, but money was not an object when one was trying to rescue a young girl from the sweet lure of corruption, especially when corruption had magnificent arms that clasped a woman's body as tightly as a cocoon and smelled musky, like ripened, fermenting fruits. A hollow flutter lifted from the pit of her stomach into her throat, and she made a sound like a high-pressure kettle.

"You all right?"

"Gabon is rather far," she said. It made no sense to her that he should want to fly to a random place like that. "I suppose I'll have to go there, then."

"Not so fast," spoke the woman guide in a firm tone. "You do not know where in Gabon. He could be in any number of places. You must stay here until you find out why he went there and where he needs to be."

Iris waved a dismissive hand. "You don't understand. I don't need to know any more than this. Cornrow man and I...we have a connection. I can...feel where he is."

"And could you *feel* he was in Gabon?"

"Well, no. Not specifically."

"Then you are going to need my help."

No ifs or buts about it—it was Farah's way. She spoke in clear and fluent language, as if she were the supervisor at a public service office referring upset citizens to governmental policy. Her accent was Arabic, but her confidence told of a different life, one where she had come to terms with owning a language she had not been born into. Iris wondered what her story was, but she knew better than to ask. This was not a woman one could make small talk with.

"I don't understand why we need to stay here. That poor girl could be anywhere in Gabon. In fact, they could have already left Gabon by now. It could have been their stopover flight."

"Nobody goes to Gabon to catch a connecting flight," said Farah, once again quoting procedure from an unseen book of laws.

"Well, he's not like everybody else. You'd be surprised at the kinds of things he can do."

She felt the older woman's quizzical gaze and blushed. Her eyes were ferocious with intelligence. She lowered her voice to sound less invested, smiled, and added in a neutral tone: "Anyway, I don't want to lose track of what's important here."

"What is that?"

"The girl, of course. We must find the girl. And if we want to find her, we have to choose the best course of action. Now, as an investigator, I—"

"I have a son, you know." Farah interrupted her as if she hadn't even heard a word she said. "My only child, not that I wish I had more. Children are a mixed blessing for a woman. They teach you things you don't want to learn, like unreserved love, disappointment, and fear. I love my son, but he is a constant reminder that I am not free to do as I please. This used to bother me when I was younger. Now, I have learned to accept that I will never be as wild as I'd like to be. Anyway, when it comes to my son, my skills are useless. I can guide a needle through a haystack and go back to find it after, but I cannot find my own son at the neighbourhood pub. It doesn't happen often, but he does not come home some nights. He goes off with a girl or travels here and there with his friends, as young people do. Every time, I think to myself this is it, I'm gonna read about him in the papers or have an officer come to my home to tell me he was killed in a bar fight or that he fell off some stupid mountain peak he was climbing. Despite my very best efforts, I am never able to track him down. And so I end up stirring on our couch, waiting for time to go by faster. I worry, you see. Naturally, he comes back unharmed. And do you know why I'm never able to find him?" She didn't wait for an answer. "Because I care for him too much. I let my personal feelings cloud my common sense, and I give into this bowel-shredding panic that renders my brain useless."

Once again, she spoke with ease and calm, as if before she wore wraparound skirts and cowboy boots, she had lived a life of comfort in some suburban enclave of the North Americas. Iris looked away, hoping the other woman would be as gracious as she was logical. And she was. The point did not need to be driven home.

"We have to figure out what he's looking for in Gabon. Everyone leaves clues behind. When we find these clues, we will know where to look for your missing girl."

"Where do you suggest we start?"

"We start with the money. Always start with the money."

CHAPTER 7

BONGOVILLE VISIT

After having spent nearly two weeks in the bush, watching pass-ersby from outside of Bongoville town hall made Leborio feel as if he were standing in Times Square. He stood proudly dressed in his caftan, his hair still braided in cornrows, almost expecting someone to notice him and applaud. People from all walks of life went by, some of them nodding politely and others making no eye contact at all. He noticed a man and a woman who looked to be British and followed their entwined silhouettes until they disappeared in the St. Hialire's Hotel, a small establishment that marked the intersection between the main boulevard and one of the narrower asphalt streets. Tourists, he thought with an air of superiority. What did they know of real life in Africa? They probably took pictures with smiling children and colour-ful artefacts and didn't even dream of ever setting foot in a genuine equatorial forest, much less sleep in it. Distracted thoughts fluttered like butterflies, taking him back to his cousin, Umberto, who was likely to be praying for him right now in some concrete European church, without a clue as to the adventures he could have been a part of had he been informed of his claim to Uncle Gigi Borzelini's estate in Africa.

Umberto was close in age to Leborio, and like his cousin, he had lost his father at a very young age, although the circumstances had been dramatically different. Leborio's father had left his family to join a gypsy caravan for the sake of an exotic but temperamental beauty, while Umberto's dad had found himself piloting a defective airplane—a one-way destination to the Pacific Ocean floor. The boys had grown up together but in so many ways apart. For many years, Umberto sought refuge in his Catholic faith, until his blind belief was put to the test of Leborio's enduring wickedness and had been found lacking. The last time he saw his cousin, Leborio had punched him right in the gut, causing him to temporarily pass out. It had only happened a few weeks ago, but so many things had changed since then, and Leborio felt ambivalent about the way things were left off. Someday, when Umberto could show he was a little more reasonable, Leborio planned to seek him and perhaps send some money from his diamond enterprise. By then, Umberto would have hopefully moved on from his incessant fixation with that woman. And here, Leborio took a deep breath, to calm his nerves.

The note made it back into his thoughts. *So long, your feudal highness.* He must have known about the land. Why else the "feudal highness"? Perhaps he'd seen the telegram in Portugal. Or perhaps it was merely displaced sarcasm. Who could know? There really was no way to be certain, not without directly asking Umberto whether he knew about the inheritance. And he could not do that. He couldn't risk losing the land, even if it meant Umberto got the girl in the end.

That ungrateful, stubborn, foolish woman! He couldn't even bring himself to say her name. Hovering over his shoulder like the ghost of justice to come, her face, her eyes, and her words were only as far as his next thought. Who could love a woman who constantly made him feel like the devil in church, like he had to say a dozen Hail Marys just for being himself? Not Leborio Borzelini, that was for certain. A woman's role was to bring good cheer, not to take X-rays of his soul and file it in a scrapbook. She and Umberto deserved each other!

Just at that time, he saw Léonie crossing the street with her hands in the pockets of her long white sarafan. He wanted to ask her about the man in the beige suit and find out why Monsieur Bamba had acted so strangely earlier that morning. Leborio waited for a few cars to get through and crossed after the girl, but by the time he turned the corner, she was already gone. A little deflated, he continued on the same path, lost in thoughts of Africa and its people. They didn't seem to be as complicated as the Europeans were, but there was a mystery about them that eluded him. And what was worse, he felt the answer was right under his nose. Perhaps it was the language barrier that kept him from truly understanding their meanings and nature. All his life, Leborio exceeded at manipulating people precisely because he knew their wants and needs and because he understood their motives. How could he do the same amongst these people when he knew nothing of how they saw the world?

He drew nearer to the sidewalk to make room for a passing burgundy Mercedes. It was an older, extravagant model, like those used as taxis in Mogadishu. As it came close to Leborio, the car slowed down until it reached a full stop. A tinted window was rolled down at the back, and he looked down to see the face of an African man who somehow looked familiar. He couldn't see the man's eyes behind a sleek pair of sunglasses.

"*Bonjour*," the man in the car greeted him.

"Hello."

"Ah, English." He smiled. He had a gap between his front teeth wide enough to fit another tooth in between. "I knew it! Welcome, welcome! How do you like Bongoville?"

Leborio shrugged. "It's okay, I suppose. I haven't been here long enough to form an opinion."

"You are visiting?"

"No, I own a big piece of land here. I am a landowner. Who are you?"

"I am sorry, I forgot to say. My name is Kodjo Mba Nze. I am a landowner too."

"Oh yeah? Which land do you own?"

The African man smirked smugly, showing the gap between his teeth. He reached into his suit jacket, pulled out a business card, and handed it to Leborio. The card said he was the president of Mba Nze Industries.

"I own all of it." He winked and waved his hand at the surrounding area. "Call me. My girl will take your information, and we can talk some business."

"What kind of business?" asked Leborio, with a quizzical look. But the window was rolled back up, and the car drove off, leaving a cloud of dust behind it.

He glanced at the card, wishing there was an Internet connection so that he could find out more about this Kodjo Mba Nze. Something about him seemed so very familiar. Perhaps he reminded him of the Frenchman he met in Morocco, or better yet, Leborio's old boss, Placido Pector, who by now was probably combing half of Europe trying to track down Leborio and make him pay for deserting his duties as second-in-command to the feared gangster. The problem with being a really bad guy, as Leborio saw it, was that there was always another guy who was worse than you were. He had no qualms with whatever means justified a glorious end, but in this case, the risks were too high. Leborio Borzelini was not willing to be a gangster because he was not willing to risk being killed or locked up. Instead, he would be a diamond merchant, legally using the unpaid labour of his subjects, the good people of the equatorial rainforest.

He retraced his steps back to town hall, where he found Monsieur Songoku reading the paper behind the partition glass. The notary seemed to remember him fondly; he put a hand out through the semicircular opening in the glass and shook Leborio's, murmuring a greeting in French. It took Leborio quite some time to relay that he was looking for the man in the beige suit, but alas, the word *beige* was of French origin so Monsieur Songoku got the gist of his meaning. After neatly folding his newspaper and putting it away, the notary came around the glass partition and locked it up with a key he kept in his vest pocket. With a cordial gesture, he signalled for Leborio to follow him outside.

Monsieur Songoku was a lot shorter than he looked from behind his desk. Though clean shaven, his five-o'clock shadow was beginning to come through in a salt-and-pepper shade. This was a man well past middle age, and yet here he was, working as the town notary and policeman. They walked for a little while, moving closer to one of the few apartment buildings that could be seen marking the horizon line of Bongoville, and passed a great modern structure that looked to be a soccer stadium. Monsieur Songoku didn't walk very fast, so the younger man took his time in observing these unexpected landmarks. This was a side of town Leborio hadn't seen yet.

They stopped in front of a concrete house, and the notary checked his watch before he rang the doorbell. A little boy opened the door, and right away, he sprung up to hug Monsieur Songoku, joyfully hanging by his neck like a baby monkey, almost causing the old man to lose his balance. Leborio watched the notary reach into his vest pocket, take out a candy with a colourful wrapper, and give it to the child, who stirred his feet with pleasure. At this time, the man in the whisper-beige suit appeared from behind the same door as the child, this time wearing a pair of beige trousers and a blue cotton shirt. He shook Leborio's hand and greeted Monsieur Songoku, exchanging a few words in French.

"What an unexpected surprise." He turned to Leborio after the notary had excused himself and left, presumably back to his post. "I see you've met my boy," he added, pushing the child forward a little. "Messi, say hello to the nice man." The child mumbled a shy hello and hid behind his father's leg, like a harem wife behind her veil.

"Messi?" Leborio looked up at the father.

"We live next to a soccer stadium." He shrugged, pointing at the landmark.

As if to prove his worthiness of the name, the child, who couldn't have been any older than four, ran to the cemented driveway and began tackling a football, one foot at a time.

"Come on in. Please have a seat! Can I get you a Régab?"

"What's a Régab?"

"You haven't had Régab yet? It is beer, our best Gabonese beer," he explained as he opened the fridge and reached for two bottles. He opened one for himself and one for Leborio, and without waiting to see if his guest approved, he cheered and took a thirsty sip. "Try it! Some might say it is one of the best ales in Africa."

Leborio was not an enthusiast of alcohol. In his view, drinking suited only two types of people: those who had a predisposition toward addiction and those who were socially awkward. His character was too sturdy for such nonsense, and he was too comfortable in his own skin to need alcohol for confidence. And why wouldn't he be? After all, he was the best-looking person he had ever come across and the closest to a genius he was ever going to get. Even so, one could make an exception, seeing as he was a guest in a man's house. It didn't do to refuse the drink. Leborio closed his eyes and took a sip. To his surprise, it was actually quite refreshing. A nice variation on the well water he had been drinking since his arrival in Gabon.

The room they were in looked to be the largest of the house. It had a television set that had been accessorized with a video recorder of sorts. Leborio hadn't seen a television set like that since the late nineties. On the wall opposite the window, there were bookshelves filled with colourful spindles. Some titles were in English and some were in French. By the door, he had noticed a poster of the Barcelona team holding up the Champion's League cup. He looked around to spot the traces of a female presence, but there were none.

"Do you live here alone with your boy?"

The man gave a lumbering nod. "My wife passed when the boy was only a year old."

"I'm sorry." Leborio lowered his gaze. "I thought you must have a big family in a house like this. It's a very nice home." He apprised the large room they were in.

"Do not worry about it. You could not have known. The house belonged to my family, and we lived here together—my parents, my brother, and my wife and me. She was a scientist, my Marie-Claire," he said with pride. "She worked to protect the animals in their natural habitat. That is a dangerous thing to do here, in Gabon. She was attacked by a gorilla that was frightened by the poachers. She lived for another day and then died. The internal bleeding was too severe. We got to say good-bye," he added, looking out the window at the child outside. "So that is good."

"I'm sorry," repeated Leborio, his dark eyes still scrutinizing the house. Above him, the ceiling rippled in the light. It was a high, whitewashed ceiling, adorned by a four-blade chandelier fan with a brass engine. There was a dark wood pattern on the shovels that framed the off-white inlay at the centre, and four lampshades made of opal glass seemed to attenuate the light rather than direct it. He hadn't seen a chandelier like that since he was a little boy. And even then, he'd seen it in a mobile home with an outer pattern like that of streaked furniture wood.

"And your brother? What happened to your brother?" he asked by means of lightening the conversation.

A shadow passed over the man's face and lingered there for a while. "My brother is not with me anymore. He…he is alive. But he has lost his way."

Leborio did not say anything. His thoughts turned to Umberto, and he wondered what his cousin—and for all purposes, his brother—said about him. Would Umberto tell strangers stories about how Leborio had lost his way? And would they ever see each other again? It was odd how at that very moment he missed Umberto, not in the way of wanting to see him, but in the way in which we miss people we can no longer fit into the vista of our lives and whom we nevertheless still carry in our hearts. He understood this man's longing for his brother and wanted to say something encouraging to him. But, alas, comforting people was a skill Leborio had never acquired.

"So how do you like your estate? Getting on well with the people?" The man's voice pulled him out of his daydream.

"Yes, I've taken an interest in their well-being. I am educating them. Just for a few hours a day, for now, but it's a start. They seem to enjoy it."

"That is kind of you, to teach the natives how to write. And are you teaching them English? How do you speak to them?"

Leborio imagined his pupils sitting on their tree stumps in the middle of the subtropical rainforest, writing down notes of his lectures and waiting for the end to ask questions in a posh British accent. Eventually they would need laptops, of course, which they would plug into their tree stump outlets.

"Oh, no. It's nothing like that. I teach them mining, you see. It's a very useful skill, far more useful to them than writing. What would they do with writing? The jungle has little use for scholars, I'm afraid. Besides, I don't speak French, and they wouldn't know what to do with English."

"Mining?" His host stared at him for a moment. "What do you expect to find in the earth of Gabon?"

"I don't know. Mineral resources, diamonds, whatever."

The word diamonds had been said under his breath, almost unintelligibly. Yet, the man had stopped smiling. He was staring at him quietly, watching him from under a cautious brow. Leborio suddenly felt uncomfortable. He sipped his beer in silence, waiting for his host to say something. At last, the man collected his thoughts and once again spoke, this time in a tone that seemed to be guarded.

"Do you know the difference between the Republic of the Congo and the Democratic Republic of the Congo?"

Leborio shrugged as if to say this was not something he would lose sleep wondering about. The man ignored him and proceeded to tell the story of the Congo.

"Like us, the Gabonese, they are descendants of the Bantu people," he explained. "But there are two Congos. One was lucky; one was not. The lucky Congo was colonized by the French and introduced to forced labour and brutal repression. The unlucky one was taken over by King Leopold II of Belgium, who paid his men commission to force the natives to produce rubber. King Leopold's men cut the limbs off the workers who failed to meet their quotas, cut the breasts off their women, burned their villages, beheaded those who dared not comply, and raped the females for good measure. The unlucky Congo was the inspiration for Joseph Conrad's *Heart of Darkness*."

"I've read it."

"Then you know," said the man, solemnly. "This was all for the sake of rubber. And do you know what happened to the unlucky Congo after the age of rubber ended? It became a supplier of blood diamonds, mined by modern-day slaves for the benefit of warlords and rich people. The mineshafts are dark, cold, and dangerous. The walls are unsecured and may collapse on them at any time. In fact, they often do, burying the men and boys alive. You would think such a dangerous job must be worth the effort. But the men very seldom find diamonds. When they do, they sell them for next to nothing and start over again, because this is the only way that these poor people can make an honest living if they don't want to fight for the warlord mercenary militias. So you see, anything found in the earth of Africa is more a curse than it is a blessing. Is this what you want to teach your pupils? How to mine?"

Leborio clasped his bottle of Régab with one hand, his knuckles turning pale under the pressure. He had heard of the so-called blood diamonds but had never really been bothered by it. So what if there were poor people somewhere in a faraway land who spend their living days squeezing down wet pits the size of water wells, searching for tiny pebbles that would fuel a war and feed their family all at once? They were abstract shadows with faces sunken in by hunger and hard labour, remote to him, like the extras in a film. Monsieur Juste Bamba's people were real. They were happy and well fed, eager to please their white landlord and learn what he had to teach them.

"My people quite enjoy learning about mining. I have to say they always carry a smile on their faces."

The door to the house cracked just a sliver, allowing little Messi to squeeze through as he chased a ball through the living area. He giggled at the guest and passed the ball to him. His father's eyes watched over him cautiously.

"Yes, we are a happy people," he said bitterly. "Always have been. No matter how many times we are struck down and enslaved by those who come to our land, we do not seem to learn our lesson. We welcome everyone with open arms only to find those arms bound by the very people we think to be our friends."

Leborio passed the ball back to Messi, and the boy retreated outside once again. "I don't want to enslave anyone," he muttered unconvincingly. "I just want to find a purpose for my land."

"A profitable purpose," said the man. "The land already has a purpose. The purpose of all land, everywhere around the world. It is the home of many people and animals that are quite happy to be living on it. There is no need to wish for more. And it does not matter what you hope to find, because you will not find diamonds in Gabon," he added, taking a sip out of his drink.

Leborio looked up, suddenly interested. "What do you mean I won't find diamonds in Gabon?"

"Gabon does not have very many diamonds. We are better known for oil. But I think you will not build an oil rig in the middle of the forest. Will you?"

"No. Not an oil rig," replied Leborio, after considering the question for a moment. Ever since he had received the news of his inheritance, Leborio had dreamed of changing his circumstances. And nothing held the promise of prosperity like the idea of finding diamonds. Who was this man to tell him he could not? It wasn't a question of mistrust; he seemed to believe what he said. But what did this man know about diamonds and their number in Gabon? It was only his opinion, nothing more. "So there are no landowners in these parts who turn a profit from the land?" asked Leborio, incredulously.

A fleeting shadow passed over the man's face, and then he shook his head. "The honest ones grow crops and make a decent living that way. But there are bad men too. "

"Who are these bad men that you speak of?" he asked, taken back by the other man's lack of appreciation for men who were not good. Here was a cultural paradigm Leborio was not prepared to accept.

"Poachers and loggers. They make their money from stealing what belongs only to the land, and they buy that land with the same money."

In the thin pocket of his pant, behind the dangling silver knife he had stolen from the Frenchman in Morocco, Leborio felt the sharp corners of a business card. It was the card given to him by Kodjo Mba Nze, the president of Mba Nze Industries. He had the unshakable feeling Kodjo Mba Nze knew something about making money at the expense of the land he now owned and decided this was a man he would have to know better if he wanted to be successful. Who in a position of real power could say they did not cross a few moral and ethical boundaries? Morals, like religion, were there to keep society from falling apart. They did not apply to visionaries and men of consequence. For Leborio, it would not be the first time he stepped over others to get to his dream. Only no matter how many people he had stepped on, his dream was still just out of reach. He imagined the soles of his best cowboy boots crushing the smiling faces of the tribe and for a moment felt the pang of an unfamiliar emotion.

"You should come visit me on my estate," he said to break his own thoughts. "We haven't yet developed the settlement, but I find it pretty cozy the way it is. We have the things we need, and the people seem to be content."

"Am I to understand you have decided to let them stay on your land, Mr. Borzelini?" The man's tone was hopeful.

"Why, yes, for now. They're a useful bunch. We'll see how it goes."

Leborio stood up from the table, and to his surprise, he found standing up after his very first couple of beers was not as simple as he would have thought. There was a lightness and pressure that danced inside his head and made him want to do something bold. He checked his caftan, smoothing out the wrinkles from sitting down, and thanked his host for having him over.

"You will come to see me, won't you? On my estate? You can bring little Messi too. The women will look after him, and there are plenty of children to play with."

"Yes, I will come," agreed the man, standing behind him, in the doorway.

Leborio shook his hand and started to walk away when a thought came to him. He turned and asked: "I never asked you. What is your name?"

The man's welcoming smile returned once again as he answered, "Jean. My name is Jean."

CHAPTER 8

AQUILA NON CAPIT MUSCAS

Iris and Farah took a taxi from the airport in Marrakech and cut through streets filled with colourful and identical shops. The taxi nudged its way through a flock of mopeds carrying neatly stacked families of four, and pedestrians butted into the streets with the confidence of SUVs. If there had been more time, Iris would have loved to stop and look for bargains, talk to the vendors, and see a snake getting charmed.

Every so often, she cast furtive glances at her companion, trying to figure out the woman guide's story. She wondered how she ended up agreeing to subcontract Farah's services. Iris was the type of investigator who could handle her own cases. But her intuition told her this hit too close to home and that she was going to need some help. Something about this foreign woman made Iris feel as if she'd just acquired a hidden weapon by hiring her. Whatever Farah's story was, Iris was sure it must have been an interesting one.

Farah was not beautiful. But she was statuesque. She had dark, leathery skin, not so dark that it reflected her African roots. Her high cheekbones made her look aristocratic. It was hard to tell where she was from—a place where the sun was both life giver and taker, perhaps. Her smoky, deep-set eyes were framed by a fan of crow's feet stretching from the outer corner all the way to her temples. But the feature that most stood out was her aquiline nose with its prominent bridge—it was both fearsome and regal at the same time.

Her long hair was as dark as her eyes, luscious at the root and burnt by frizz and wear at the ends. Iris could tell Farah had stained her hair black with layers and layers of colour that she had probably made herself from plants and roots. A single, thick, white strand peeked out from under the darkened mane, to tell of her age and vanity at once. She looked as frightening as the harbinger of death, and yet one could not look away from her.

Farah's house was on the fringe of the city. A woman dressed like the female version of Indiana Jones did not belong with the neighbourhood wives. There were trees and bushes surrounding the house like a finely toothed comb, making it difficult to see through. Farah unlocked the gate from three different spots, and they walked into a square yard where a skinny, middle-aged man was chopping wood on a wide tree stump.

"Mahdi, I'm home, *habibi*."

Mahdi smiled right from his eyes to greet them, and the two exchanged a brief but intimate look that told the man he'd better carry on with his chores. Farah was presently at work.

"Your husband?" asked Iris.

"No. My man."

As the older woman held the door open for her guest, Iris noticed the markings on the inner part of her arm, in the thin-skinned patch where her triceps and biceps met. The markings were blue, juxtaposed against the even brown of her skin like the tattoo of an old-time sailor. It read "Aquila Non Capit Muscas," and it was punctuated by a tiny drawing of a friendly black fly just above the last word. Iris had enough understanding of Latin to know it loosely translated to "The eagle doesn't hunt flies."

It was the kind of household where one took their shoes off. She watched Farah drop her boots in the doorway and took off her own navy espadrilles. She'd read somewhere that in Morocco, people ate off the floors with their bare hands, but the floors in Farah's house were not any cleaner than the ones Gretchen kept at the Private Affairs Investigators office. No food scraps or traces were present to confirm the myth. They placed the luggage in a corner, and Farah pulled a pot from the fridge and threw it on the stove. The faint aroma of cooking herbs, saffron, cumin, and coriander lifted off into the air and mixed with the smell of sweat and leather coming off from Farah's cowboy boots. She opened the fridge again and unapologetically popped the cap off a beer bottle.

"Would you like one?"

Iris shook her head out of habit and immediately regretted it. She also regretted not being able to change her mind about it and say, "Actually, I think I would like one." She couldn't think of the last time she'd had a beer in the middle of the day, just like that. It was probably because it had never happened. Beer was what potbellied construction workers had at lunch.

She sat on one of the large cushions thrown close to the wall. Half a dozen of these colourful bits of what could have been a couch lay tossed about the otherwise Spartan-looking room. Her eyes lingered back to the other woman's tattoo.

"What does it mean?"

Farah glanced down at her underarm and sipped from her cold ale, beads of condensation forming between the glass and her fingers. She did not answer. Iris watched her drink, hypnotized by the pleasure the other woman took in it. A mustard-brown fan twirled softly by the window, filling the silence with its constant droning.

"Is it always so hot in Morocco?" She tried again.

The other woman shot Iris a quizzical look as she lifted a foot into the kitchen sink and began to wash it with dish soap.

"Are you Canadian?" Farah asked.

"What? No."

"Then quit complaining about the weather. It seems to me you're uncomfortable with silence. You've got to learn to own your silence with pride. It'll keep you from getting yourself in trouble by shooting your mouth off." Farah patted her foot with a kitchen towel and pulled up the other one. "Oh, don't sulk. When people come to Morocco, they expect to eat off the floor, ride a camel, and have an epiphany in the desert. I'm giving you your money's worth, right here, in my humble kitchen. Don't know about the camel just yet. Maybe we'll get to ride one later." She threw the towel at Iris. "Wash your feet if you want."

"In the sink?"

"No. In my golden bathtub."

"I'm fine, thank you. I'll wait for my hotel room."

"Suit yourself, tourist."

"Are you always this rude to your guests?"

"No. Then again, I don't usually bring tourists into my home."

Iris was getting irritated. "It's a good thing I'm not a tourist then."

"Oh no? Then what are you?"

The answer didn't come as quickly as she would have liked it to.

"I'm an investigator looking for an evil man and my client's daughter, of course. That's why I hired you. Not to judge me for my reluctance to embrace the wild as you have."

Farah laughed. "You know nothing about me, investigator woman. But you can keep trying to figure out my angle. The more you do, the more you expose yourself to me. We'll find your client's daughter, don't you worry. As for the evil man, I'm sure you'll find yourself another one someday."

She felt the burn of indignation rise up her oesophagus at the speed of Diet Coke foam after a Mentos drop. Feeling transparent angered her. What angered her even more were other people's presumptions. Especially when they were right.

"Does the tough love routine usually give results? Probably, with rebellious teenagers. I've lived enough to know who I am, and I'm not gonna stand here and be judged by anyone."

Farah finished her beer in one shot.

"You already answered my question." She floated closer to Iris, close enough that the younger woman could smell her faint perfume. She smelled like essential oils, eucalyptus, and jasmine. "Pride. That is your weakness." Before Iris could snap back, Farah placed a manly hand on her shoulder. It was still surprisingly warm after having held a cold beer. "I'm not playing games with you, and I don't care how old you are, investigator woman. But I won't go into battle without knowing whom I have by my side. Now I know. You're too proud. I can live with that so long as you can. The thing about pride is that it invariably harms the sinner deeper than it harms the victim."

"Isn't that the way of every sin?"

"No."

Her answer was incomplete. Farah turned back to her hob stove and stirred the pot with a big wooden spoon. She disappeared behind a beaded curtain and returned with an earthen dish that she skilfully placed right in the hearth. Steam hissed and echoed from the fire pit. The heavy aroma of lamb, sweet fruits, and couscous filled the room.

"Most sins are vessels of pleasure with no other purpose than self-indulgence," Farah continued, as if a lesson had been learned. "Nothing wrong with that in my book. Pride is the burden of the fearful, the self-doubter who masquerades as the authority on right and wrong. It takes longer to boomerang back. Pride makes inverted ripples that draw back inward from big to small, until it whirlpools your soul into the deep."

She made a suction noise with her tongue.

"It's like that children's story I used to tell my son when he was little—the one with the boy who gets a piece of glass from a magical distorting mirror stuck in his eye and heart, and then he sees everything to be ugly and keeps his heart closed to the world."

"*The Snow Queen*."

"Exactly."

Iris felt a sort of fondness for Farah's unknown son. He was now part of a fellowship of children around the world who had been told the one story that prepared them best for what was to follow: love, betrayal, idealism, cynicism, quests, time wasted only to be written off as experience gained, and bittersweet endings. She and Tom used to read it together as children and shoot each other conspiring glances over the pastel pictures of the book, wallowing in the sweet drama of self-fulfilling prophecies. There is nothing more appealing and real than predestination to children who want to think themselves the centre of a universe created just for them. And what child doesn't think the world revolves around him? It is the sense of all-knowing invincibility that makes dependence on hope unnecessary. It is what makes childhood so difficult to recreate. How do you unknow that there is no Santa Clause? How do you unknow you can be rejected? How do you unknow you are only one of many? The end of Eden must have come with a thundering realization of our own inconsequential need for hope.

"And what if the piece of glass allowed him to see the world as it really is?"

"He didn't need a piece of magical glass for that." Farah's lips were tight like her skin. "Growing up would have done the trick."

She tried to remember Tom's face as a child, before she became an investigator and before he became Leborio Borzelini. It seemed like a lifetime ago, when they had been so very happy in each other's company. She remembered his eyes, nose, and mouth but could not put them back together. Like lost pieces of a puzzle, they no longer fell into their rightful place. His face was gone, save for the picture in her wallet. And so was childhood. Her memory of it was just that: a memory, no longer to be trusted as truth.

All the bridges we cross constantly crumble behind us.

"Time to eat," she heard Farah say. Iris turned to see her crouching on one of the cushions on the floor, in front of a funny-looking ceramic dish that tapered at the top. "Here's the authentic Moroccan experience you paid for, investigator woman."

CHAPTER 9

MUST MAKE LOVE SOON

After leaving Jean's house, Leborio found he had no trouble tracing his steps back to the center of the city. He went over his conversation with the man in the beige suit, now simply known to him as Jean, and decided he had to meet with Kodjo Mba Nze, who seemed to be the only person he had met since his arrival in Gabon who had an interest in turning in a profit.

He walked back to where he had last seen the Mogadishu Mercedes. All along the street, there was nothing but dirt and heat. There was not a trace of the burgundy car or the driver. He would have to use the business card and set up an appointment. As he started to walk back, once again, his eye caught a glimpse of a white sarafan. This time, the girl was carrying a stack of folded clothes. He ran after her without thinking and caught up in a few paces.

"Hello! Léonie," he called out. "What are you doing here?"

She shuffled her feet uncomfortably and pulled the folded clothes closer to her chest, as if to cover herself.

"I…come see mother people."

"Your mother's people live in Bongoville?" He followed by her side.

"Yes. Mother, she Bongoville lady. When young, she meet my father and make love. Then, move to the bush."

"She fell in love with your father, you mean," he corrected her. "Making love is quite a different thing. I suppose you know nothing about that, do you?"

"No," she shook her head. "Not fall love. Make love. Now my turn. My father wants that I must make love soon."

"Like get married?"

"No. Married later. Make love first."

Leborio forgot to walk. "Really? To whom?"

"I must find man I like. In Gabon, first you make love and have baby. Baby is for you and only you. When married, man takes baby. If man is no good, you must leave. If you leave, you leave baby. No baby for you. Understand?"

"I think that I do. You're saying children that result from a marriage go to the father. The mother can only keep the children she's had prior to being married. That is a very odd custom, Léonie. Very odd indeed."

"It is Gabon way. I must make love soon and make my baby."

"And do you have a man in mind?"

She shook her head. "Man must be clever and fast runner. And man must have school."

"So you want someone athletic and educated. Interesting criteria." He watched Leonie moved her lips to imitate the words he said, seemingly fascinated with the new sounds. "And have you found anyone?"

"Maybe. Every day I come to Bongoville, and I look. Today I meet school friend. School friend very big man now. Makes machine to find...*comment s'appelle pétrole*?"

"Oil," supplied Leborio.

"Yes, oil. Much oil in Gabon," she explained. "This is good job. But I don't know if he is good man."

"Does that matter to you? Is it important that he is a good man?"

"*Mais bien sûr*, yes, yes. I must have good baby. And good man. If man is good, I marry later."

"But you can have two men," suggested Leborio with a wink. "One for the baby and one to marry. You should go for it. It's the law."

Léonie stopped from walking and gave Leborio a very solemn look. The smile had altogether disappeared from her lovely face. Though it was very probable she had not understood the joke he made, she appeared to be bothered by the wink. Clearly, this was a serious matter for her. Leborio apologized and continued walking by her side in silence for a while.

"Father must be not happy," she said suddenly. "Today he want that you take iboga. But you are in Bongoville."

He remembered Monsieur Juste Bamba chasing him with the bowl that very morning. "Iboga? What is that?" he asked.

"*Une plante.* Men must take." She stared at him intently, as if to convey this was not negotiable. Then, with softer eyes, she tried to set his mind at ease. "Sometime women too. I take before."

He had heard of such plants and their hallucinogenic effects. Primitive communities such as these deemed the high as a sacred experience, a way to communicate with the gods and connect with the animal spirits. Back where he came from, such a plant would serve to connect one to the vivid vision of Mickey Mouse himself. Leborio despised such people. He despised their music, their constant grinding of the teeth, and the dumb expressions on their faces. It was difficult to reconcile his perception of what drugs were with the spiritual angle these people took to iboga.

"Why must I take it?"

"To know your heart," she said, pressing the stack of folded clothes closer to her chest.

Her answer was final, and he knew better than to ask her again. Iboga was a rite of passage in these parts, and if he wanted the respect of his own subjects, he had to partake in the custom. After all, how bad could a plant potion really be? He was a trained spiritual leader—granted, he had trained himself—and indubitably, he was the most intelligent person he had ever come across. If anyone could handle a hallucinogenic experience, it would be him. Nah, Leborio wasn't going to let this worry him. He was going to wield iboga to his will.

"You mentioned education before. Did you go to school, Léonie?"

"Yes." Her face lit up again. "I have one year, and I am teacher."

"You'll be a teacher in a year? That's fantastic! And here I was, trying to teach your people while all the while you were qualified to do so. But there's one thing I don't understand. Between looking for a father for your baby and picking up clothes for the villagers, when do you have time to go to school too? Do you go to school every day?"

She shook her head and explained she had to stop going to school for now. Her father wanted her to get on with her personal life before becoming a teacher. He believed that once she finished her schooling, she would care more about her pupils than about having her own children. Now was the time to become a mother. They sat down on a wooden bench. She told him about her school and how much she loved learning; the young people of Gabon who were juggling tradition and the natural desire to be part of the world at large; her French ancestors from her mother's side, who had raped the women of the village and burned their homes over their heads; and the questionable geographical borders that had been drawn over the cultures and people of equatorial Africa. The French and Belgian colonials suddenly and brutally separated people from the same kin and overnight found themselves citizens of the Congo or of Gabon. That was why many of these people still spoke the same language today. She spoke about the

French with piety, as if speaking of a civilizing god whose reasons for enslaving a people, raping its women, and beheading its men were higher than her and her understanding. He caught her meaning, if not always her words, and taught her new words, such as "ruled" and "borders," and watched her mimic his pronunciation.

"Who ruled your people?" she asked after a while, perhaps wanting to practice the new word in context.

Leborio was surprised by her question, first because of her assumption that every people had to have had a ruler, and then because he realized this was actually true. His people, if he could call them that, though half a world away, had been, at one time or another, the docile pawns of many great powers, powers that had brutally raped and pillaged villages on their way to other helpless countries. The Romans, the Ottomans, the Greeks, the Austro-Hungarians, the Russians, and now the Americans all left their brutal imprints on the moral landscape of the country. And so it was that innocence turned to corruption, modesty turned to greed, and good nature turned to a virtue only to be had in stories and foreign films. Why did human beings have this unstoppable need to expand and seek the happiness of others, a happiness that only behoved the people of the land? Leborio knew the answer all too well. He felt it, as if it were his own invention, that ephemeral quench of an everlasting and all-consuming thirst for more. The only thing standing between him training the forest people to mine for diamonds only to exploit them for his own profit and calling himself a humanitarian was his overall fondness for the tribe and a general predisposition toward benevolence he was currently experiencing.

"Can I trust you with a secret, Léonie?" he asked. The girl made a serious face, watching him with her immense black eyes. "I am looking for something in the ground, you know, where we dig every day. I'm searching for something very precious. Do you know what it is?"

Léonie smiled and waved her hand dismissively. "Pffft," she said. "You look for diamonds. Everybody look for diamonds."

"What do you mean 'everyone'?" he asked a little weak at the knees. "Other people know about this? Have you told anyone?"

"No, not me. I don't know, and I don't say. White men always look for diamonds in Africa. They think diamonds grow in trees. In Gabon, no more diamonds. No more gold too."

"Why didn't you say something, then? If you knew it was pointless to dig, why didn't you say something?"

She looked at him like a mother teaching her child matters of simple logic and answered:

"When you dig, you are happy, no? Happy is good. Then you must dig."

CHAPTER 10

HERR PUTZIFFER

The best thing about Farah, as far as Iris could tell, was that she had contacts—lots of contacts. She seemed to know the right person in just about every place. This extended from getting the freshest cup of coffee at any roadside joint to tracking down untraceable transactions on the black market. In a matter of hours, she had already tracked down the man who was most likely to have purchased a stolen piece of art or jewellery that made it into Marrakech.

Herr Putziffer was a private collector who ran a luxurious art gallery out of his riad, just outside of Marrakech. He was a German Stasi general who had conveniently taken a trip to Morocco before the Berlin Wall fell and forgot to return. He brought nothing with him, save for a small fortune amassed during years of torturing it from enemies of the state and accepting bribes.

Iris knew that Leborio's modus operandi when it came to making money was very predictable: find a wealthy woman and relieve her of her jewellery. Back in Portugal, she'd set him up to take the fall for the disappearance of a diamond necklace valued at an extremely high price. She hadn't really confirmed that Leborio was the thief, but at the time, it seemed like the right thing to do—get him for a crime he hadn't committed to punish him for crimes he got way with. And who knew? Perhaps he really was the one who'd taken it. One thing was for certain. If Leborio had anything to do with the stolen Sophie Necklace, or any other jewels for that matter, this was where he would have brought it.

Looking at Herr Putziffer, it was hard to believe he had ever amounted to anything else than a pensioner. Like most vicious men, he had aged into a meaty blob with pulp features and very little hair. The body adapts to survive; he looked like a retired merchant and inspired nothing but sympathy. The only thing that gave him away was his smile, false like the grin of a hyena, glimmering with gold caps and saliva.

Sitting across from Herr Putziffer, Iris eyed the opulent artefacts adorning the gallery. In no particular order, there were elephant tusks standing by a Greek urn filled with Japanese Geisha umbrellas and sculpted walking sticks, a red cross encased in a glass fixture hanging like a chandelier from the crimson ceiling, and fragments of Egyptian scrolls framed over silk tapestries that draped like curtains over the grainy inner walls of the riad. In another glass casing, there were jewels and crystals that had enough sparkle to reflect the light around the room like a colourful constellation. There were some paintings too, but as far as she could tell, they were not by anyone she knew. As if this cluttered collection was not unusual enough, the only pieces of functional furniture were a wicker desk and the three matching armchairs they were now sitting in.

And then she saw it. The light was shining on it from four different fixtures, just like in a museum. There, right behind Herr Putziffer's wicker desk, stood a colour lithograph of an ethereal red-haired beauty resting her head over a shore rock, staring into the water like a translucent fairy, her body glowing with fluidity. Behind her, a zodiac in Art Nuveau pastels bejewelled with twirling flowers left no doubt it was an Alphonse Mucha. She held a white chess pawn in her hand, barely, as if at any moment she could open her tiny palm and drop it in the water.

Iris wondered at the meaning.

"It's an original, you know," spoke Herr Putziffer solemnly. "I brought it with me from Germany."

"It's exquisite."

Farah seemed to watch the exchange, unimpressed. She made no effort to conceal her dislike of the German even as she related the reason they had come to see him. Leaning back in his generous wicker seat, Herr Putziffer listened, interlocked his sausage fingers, and rested his elbows on his side of the desk, like a law clerk passing good advice.

"I don't know what to tell you." He smiled, but only with his lips. When he didn't speak, his convex stomach lifted with the wheeze of his breathing, shiny and hard, like a Bosu exercise ball. "I deal in art, not jewellery. Perhaps you should try my friend Monsieur Lacroix. French fella. He owns a jewellery shop in the city. Here's his business card. You can tell him I sent you."

He looked away from Farah and stretched over to the corner of the desk to pick up brandy and a glass from a shiny silver tray. He waved the decanter at the two women.

"Drop of brandy?"

Farah, who had not picked up the jeweller's business card, continued to fix him with her piercing gaze. He turned and showed his teeth to Iris. The yellow patches in the white of his eyes matched the yellow of his teeth. Once again, she thought of how easily the body betrays the nature of our souls. One needed only take the time to read these scattered clues. "Monsieur Lacroix deals mostly in silver, but every once in a while, he'll carry diamonds and emeralds…"

Farah raised her hand to silence him. "I have no interest in speaking with your jeweller. I'm here to find the man who sold you a stolen diamond necklace. The necklace is still here," she said, scanning the room. "I can feel it in my bones, and my bones have never failed me so far. Understand that what happened to that necklace is of no interest to me. I don't care if you display it on a velvet cushion in the front windows of your riad, and I won't be going after your potential buyers. I'm only here for the seller. That is, if you cooperate. Otherwise, you'll find that I invariably live up to my reputation."

"I'm not aware of your reputation, madam." He put the decanter down, trying to appear confident. Beads of sweat sprung through his pores like hatching fish eggs. His smile was still there, yellow and sticky, but the corners of his mouth had dropped a little.

"Oh, but I'm aware of yours, Herr Putziffer. You wouldn't be where you are if you didn't make it your business to know who's who in this town. And outside of it," she added, casting an impassive look through the large windows from whence an undisturbed red dirt road stretched into the distance. "You know of me, and you know what I can do."

"Madam forgets this is not some kind of trinket shop in the Sux, and I am not a bargaining rat. I am—"

"An interrogating rat who used to torture innocent people for a living. I stand corrected. Your new life doesn't do much in the way of redeeming your soul, not that I expect you to care about that sort of thing. I would, however, think a man with so many secrets and so much to lose wouldn't want a careless and unstable enemy like me."

She sat back, making it obvious she had no intention of leaving before she got what she came for. "Give us a name and a sense of direction, and we'll be on our way."

Herr Putziffer shifted uncomfortably in his wicker armchair. His breathing sounded like a shutting valve now, wheezing with every mouthful of air. He reached into his desk drawer and pulled out an inhaler. He pursed his lips around it for a dose and looked up to see Farah's unyielding gaze. It didn't work.

Deceit mutated ever so slightly.

"Funny how our short-term memory holds on to useless bits of information only to have it handy when our friends ask for it. May I think of you as a friend, madam?"

He grinned without waiting for a reply.

"There was a man, some days ago, who, as you say, had heard of my reputation as a collector of beautiful things. He came to see me about a necklace he wanted sold. The details escape me, naturally; I only deal in objects that are sold by their rightful owners. But I do remember he was renting a place near the Medina."

He scribbled down an address and pushed it with a stubby index under Farah's nose. From where she sat, Iris could see the apartment number was underlined. When the right pressure was applied, Herr Putziffer had an outstanding short-term memory.

"I don't need to tell you ladies that I trust you'll keep my name out of it. One does not stay a successful businessman by making enemies. I prefer making friends." He cleared his throat, glaring meaningfully at the older woman.

Farah's thin lips flared out with let's-get-out-of-here urgency, and she asked him to call her a cab. The women stood up to leave.

"One more thing," said Iris, as she wavered in the doorway. "What did this seller look like, Herr Putziffer?"

The German broke into another slimy grin, his rivery eyeballs racing down the younger woman's blouse.

"Oh, you'll have no trouble finding him. The man's a giant, if I ever saw one. A giant from some Eastern European country. Come back and see my Mucha any time you please, young lady. Any time at all!"

CHAPTER 11

SUNSHINE IN A FEEL-GOOD BAG

His dreams had changed. They happened less frequently now, and they were harder to remember, but the uneasy feeling was still with him. The bed snapped under the weight of his stirs and threw him on to the floor, where he whacked his head against the ground. He woke up in sweats and lay there with his eyes shut, trying to commit his visions to memory.

He'd been walking down a deserted road for a long time, playing with a key hanging on a black leather string tied up around his neck. The key had a blade that ended in a heart-shaped bitting. Heart-shaped! He'd never wear something like that. He yanked the whole thing off, and threw it in the dirt.

Further down the road, he reached a crossing. To the left, he could see a house with green shutters, surrounded by a high wall and a gate. Somehow he knew the gate could not be breached. It was made out of solid metal and only a tiny heart-shaped opening in the lock allowed for the sunlight to get through. He could have used a heart-shaped key right about then.

He looked to the right. The short path ended with a fence. Through the cracks in the fence, some kind of round gems glistened in the sunlight. Diamonds! Well, this was a no-brainer. He started walking in their direction. But the closer he got the less of them he saw. In his dream, he hopped over the fence with little difficulty. He landed on a haystack and found himself surrounded by a pride of ostriches, craning their necks over him and wobbling their heads blankly. He climbed off, keeping away from the curious creatures, only to find himself in a yard full of oversized birds who all had Snejana's face. Their eyes sparkled, not with the glimmer of intelligence, but rather with the vacuous twinkle of contentment. From far away, blinded by the light of the sun, one could easily mistake them for precious gems.

He ran back to the fence, with the certainty that dreamers have when they get stuck in the eerie world of their imagination, knowing he could no longer climb back out to the road where he came from. He could no longer move any of his limbs because he was now a compact colourless figure, almost tubular and definitely faceless.

He was an ivory chess pawn, just like the one the little boy held on Leborio's first day in Bongoville.

The last thing he remembered was staring out to the house with the green shutters, whishing he'd never thrown the key from around his neck—that, and an ostrich pecking at his perfectly spherical head.

He woke up panting, drenched in sweat.

He was alone in the room. Snejana must have awakened already, and the cat was probably with her. Light bled through the cracks in the low wooden ceiling, revealing tiny dust constellations floating in the air. Outside, the women of the tribe were feeding the livestock, one of them humming an upbeat song. He washed his face in the small ceramic basin by his bed and looked up at the old, cracked mirror the natives had presented him with a few days before. His unshaven cheeks were drawn in, and his coal-black eyes were sunken into his head, framed by dark circles that gave him a ghastly appearance.

"I am a white man in Africa, and I am not afraid of you." He repeated Léonie's mantra, his breath fogging up the glass as he said it. All the while, his eyes never left his reflection in the mirror.

Some time went by before Leborio came out of his dwelling and into the clammy air of the early hours. He had come to understand the changes in the weather that occurred from morning into midday rather than from one day to the next. The only trace of the early rainfall was the humidity that imbibed itself into the rest of the day with the sticky, musky persistence of tropical climates.

Snejana was jerking about by the edge of the clearing where Leborio had designated his classroom space, moving her awkward body in a vertical serpentine to the beat of a man's drum. Her face was painted a little, two red stripes across her cheeks and a white one down the bridge of her straight nose. She moved just outside of the beat, confident in the power of motion over rhythm, like an incongruous flash mob of one. Two of the native men watched her, smiling and clapping.

Leborio lashed out instinctively, pulling her out of sight by the arm. "What the hell do you think you're doing?"

The natives, who were no longer smiling, looked away into the trees, proving that feeling uncomfortable around couples who fight is a universal reaction.

"Let go of me! What did I do?"

Taking a deep breath to calm himself down, Leborio whispered an explanation. "I am their landlord, Snejana. Their *lord*. Do you know what that means? It means I do not paint my face and dance for them. They do it for me. It's been the natural hierarchy of respect between lord and vassal since feudal times, and if you knew anything about history or the world we live in, you'd know that much. God, how can you be so stupid?"

Under the weight of this last insult, Snejana stood very still, as if to consider the question for a moment. Then, without any warning signs, she started sobbing the way she used to do before they came to Africa. Small rivers of tears made their way through the red paint on her cheeks, washing out the colour all the way down to her pointy chin, where they hung in limbo, waiting for another tear to add to their weight and help them fall. Leborio hated when she cried. He took no pleasure from yelling at her now. It was a little like having your adversary knock himself out in the middle of a fistfight—terribly unsatisfying and anticlimactic. Most men wouldn't have had the heart to pursue a fight when there were tears involved. But he was not most men. He saw right through cowardly manipulation and rose to the challenge.

"They think you are my woman," he started in a secretive tone. Snejana looked up at him through the tears. "And as my woman, you have to abide by the rules of…" He wavered. What rules were they? Feudal rules did not have the modern, cosmopolitan ring that Leborio wished to inspire. He remembered the lyrics from a song he used to like while he was going through his carefully disguised adolescent phase.

"As my woman, you have to abide by the rules of master and servant. I am their master; they are my servants. We don't dance for the help. Got it?"

He knew all too well his words would fill *his* woman with wifely pride and waited for the girl to wipe off her eyes, smudging the leftover paint with tears and stretching it along her cheekbones like some kind of primitive blush.

"But they're having this ceremony for us. They've been rehearsing since we got here."

"Ceremony? What kind of ceremony?" He pictured a large wooden throne, like that of his ancestors, when a crown would be bestowed upon his head, perhaps together with a cape and other appropriate regalia.

"I don't know. An initiation into their community, I think."

"Nonsense. We've been a part of their community for a while now.

It must be a ceremony to acknowledge my supreme rule over them. Like a coronation."

"Whatever you say, my darling," she conceded, gently touching the paint on her face.

As Leborio guided her through the door of their bark house, his eyes met those of Monsieur Juste Bamba, who had been standing outside of his own dwelling all along, watching Leborio with concerned eyes. Leborio waved a polite greeting, but the chieftain did not return it. That evening, by the fire, he saw Léonie have a spirited discussion with her father and knew it had something to do with him. He waited until the chieftain went back to his abode and made his way next to his daughter.

"Everything all right?" he asked.

Léonie looked away, almost unwilling to talk, but then her open nature took over, and she told him how her father did not think Leborio was a good man. Monsieur Juste Bamba had seen him hurt his woman.

"She's not my woman." Leborio cut her off.

Léonie's big black eyes opened incredulously, as he went on explaining.

"Snejana is my friend. Her mother is a witch, a very dangerous witch. You understand that? Yes? Good!"

She didn't seem convinced. He looked around for something he could offer as proof, and saw the cat coming out from behind the Coula tree.

"You see that cat Snejana brings with her everywhere?"

Léonie nodded.

"It used to have hair. It was the most beautiful cat in the world," he added longingly, trying to buy himself time to think up the next part of the story. "Her mother, the witch, made the hair fall."

"How?" asked Léonie.

"She used black magic."

Léonie covered her mouth with her hand to suppress a gasp. In Africa, black magic was no laughing matter. Leborio continued his story.

"When Snejana saw this, she ran off from home, afraid of her mother's magic. She had no money, no family, and no friends. I took them both in, out of the goodness of my heart. She is like a sister to me. And sometimes, older brothers have to look out for their sisters to make sure they don't do anything stupid. You understand this, don't you?"

Léonie nodded earnestly. The familiar smile had returned to her face, the little discoloured patch playing upon her lower lip as she told Leborio that she knew all along he was a good man. She'd even told her father. She touched his cheek with her small hand, in an unexpected gesture of affection, and then he watched the shape of her white sarafan disappear into the night. For a while longer, he did not move at all. His heart was beating a little faster, and his body hardened with anticipation. He looked up to the Coula tree and walked up to sit at its foot. Its branches reached out into the night, colossal and majestic.

His eyes held their shape for a while, until the branches were lost, like supple hands, moving quickly, shaping fantastic images through the tapestry of stars, as if they were weaving a dream. One could sit there for hours, trying to spot the obscure silhouettes playing against the night sky, guessing at their meaning. It was at the feet of such trees that imagination was conjured and stories were told, passed down from elders to youth. If you were wise enough to listen and hear the thumps drawn in from the sap of the tree, you would spew its riddles on the youth of your kin and open their eyes to the wonders of the world around them. The Coula tree was no ordinary tree. It was a tree of dreaming and imagination.

For the first time, he thought about the loggers that Jean had spoken of. They cut down trees like these, trees that provided food and protection for a community who in return protected it from the evil men with axes. This sort of symbiotic bond was present everywhere around him. It was what the tribe was doing in the jungle. The jungle protected the people, and the men kept other men, who did not love the jungle as they did, at bay. He too was part of it now, master to his people, who in turn were there to keep him safe. He closed his eyes and fell asleep at the foot of the tree, dreaming of the jungle, his people, and Léonie.

His mining school continued, despite the warnings he'd received from Jean and Léonie. There might not have been any diamonds left in Gabon, but there was nothing else for him to do during the day, so he taught the men how to sift through the soil they were digging out and how to say things like *hello*, *big*, and *small*. The sound of his own didactic voice made Leborio feel confident and powerful. His superior mind was all that he needed to make his mark amongst these people.

At first he had worn his caftan to impose respect, but in the tropical heat, it became clear that respect came mostly from keeping cool and comfortable. He walked about the settlement and the school with a bare torso, as all the other men did. He was a little taller than most of them, and his shoulders were framed a little wider. His skin had darkened from the sun, making Leborio feel enigmatic and dangerous.

Of course, that was not how the natives perceived him. The women continued to giggle every time they saw him, while the men nodded and smiled, like children to a teacher. This transient sense of safety amongst the indigenous community was not always shared by Leborio. In fact, any feeling of comfort he fostered disappeared a few times every day, when the sounds of someone else's weight sinking into the dry leaves made him painfully aware of another presence. Every once in a while, he glanced over his shoulder, into the jungle, where he could swear dozens of spirits invisible to the eye were watching him.

"I am a white man in Africa, and I am not afraid of you," he murmured, looking out.

"Big. Big," chanted one of his pupils and pointed into the bush behind them.

"Yes, it's a big jungle." Leborio nodded.

The natives looked at one another and shrugged. They did not seem in the least frightened, so Leborio carried on with his lecturing and miming. Sometimes he recited lyrics from songs he remembered to pass the time. His hands mimed "rope," but his lips delivered Freddy Mercury's soliloquy from Bohemian Rhapsody, told in a neutral, instructive tone. Only Snejana recognized what it meant. From her spot on the bark house veranda, she joined in with an exuberant "Galileo, Galileo, Galileo Figaro, Magnifico," until the captivated faces of the natives and stern glare of the teacher rendered her voiceless.

Every day, just before sunset, Leborio sat back in the dirt, his magnificent arms around his knees, his eyes fixed on the changing sky above him. As if observed by a time-lapse camera, scattered clouds disappeared like the waves of an ocean made of molten lava under the bleeding light of the sunset, until all that was left behind was the dusky gray of the tropical sky during rainy season. This was his favourite part of the day—the part where the light of day gave into darkness and Léonie returned from her excursions into town. His heart skipped a beat, seeing her white sarafan sway through the pathway leading in from the jungle, and he stood up to greet her with a wave.

They talked by the fire for some time, as they did almost every night, until they were the only ones left awake, and the fire began to give out to the ashes. She told him stories about her mother's people in Bongoville and about the upcoming presidential elections. They elected a president every seven years, and the time had come to vote again.

"Who will you vote for?" he wanted to know.

"Everybody vote Ali Bongo Ondimba."

"All of you? Then what's the sense in voting?"

"He is son of old president Bongo. He is good man."

"How long was his father president?"

"More than—how do you say this number?" She scribbled the number forty in the dirt.

"He was president for more than forty years? And his son was president for seven? This sounds like a monarchy to me. It sounds like the king has passed his crown down to his son. Aren't you worried about him taking over? Aren't you worried about the freedoms of your country?"

He looked around, searching for another man to back him up, but everyone was gone. It was just the two of them.

"He is good man," repeated Léonie simply.

She touched his hand and looked into his eyes as if to set his mind at ease. Without thinking, he lifted her hand to his face and pressed it against his lips. She blushed. He could feel her breath hasten against his jaw as he drew nearer.

"Leave her be," warned his mind, knowing it all reeked of tragedy.

"Go after her," pushed his blood, boiling with the urgency of desire.

The mind, in its vast experience of such affairs, was right; but the flesh was easily corrupted. He cupped her burning cheeks with his hands and put his mouth to hers. Her kiss felt moist and cool, dizzying and soft, the way he imagined his last breath before death to be. He took her smell in with trembling nostrils and opened his eyes to see her face transfixed, eyes closed and lips swollen. He kissed her again, this time drawing her closer, until his hardened body began to ache with wanting. She squealed from the pressure of his arms around her, but her lips remained entwined to his, as if she was willing to take this pain with the pleasure. The more he hurt her, the more he wanted her. Through the blur that had become his vision, he caught a glimpse of her white sarafan and remembered he did not want to harm the girl. He let go and took a step back.

"You're so beautiful," he heard himself say.

Léonie stared at him, spellbound, her black eyes illuminated by a vibrating glow. He wanted this to be the end of his story and knew that it would not. How many more beginnings did he have left in him? Beginnings were just as powerful as the end, and just as heartbreaking, precisely because of the knowledge that they too had an end, as everything does.

"You remind me of someone I once knew," he said, again, without thinking.

Léonie came closer to him. She pulled him to her once again. He looked away, but this time, the girl turned his face to her with a gentle but firm touch of her small hands and forced him into another kiss. He wanted to resist her and did not know why. Part of him wanted to lift her up and carry her into the woods to lay her down on a bed of tropical leaves, and part of him wanted to get away from her and this intoxicating feeling. Her kiss made him long for something he dreaded, as he dreaded those ever-watching eyes in the jungle. With one swift jerk, he pushed her away.

Taken by surprise, she fell under the weight of confusion, her body making an almost imperceptible muffled sound as she hit the ground. She did not fall hard. But she looked up, desolate, like a child when she first falls, sitting there, crouched in the dirt by the dying fire. She wasn't crying, but she might as well have been. Looking at the shape of her, bright and small, her big eyes staring up at him without understanding, Leborio stepped forward against his better judgement and lifted her up in his arms. She received him as if nothing had happened, as sure of him as she had been the moment they first kissed, and he knew then that she would give herself unequivocally and without the false coyness of young girls who teased men like him into committing. They looked at one another for a moment and knew there was only one thing they could do. Silently, he carried her off into the darkness.

He could have skipped along the clearing the very next morning. The sun was up in the sky, tropical birds were making cawing noises in the trees, and the sweet smell of fried cassava filled the air.

"This is a good day," he said to Snejana, who followed right behind him, holding the cat under her arm. After all this time in the jungle, her skin had remained tissue white. Only a few patches of redness at the top of her nose and forehead set a contrast to her translucent skin.

He grabbed a freshly made patty from the stone dish by the fire and kissed the cheek of the matron who had cooked it. The woman spat in the dirt from being startled and then giggled like a little girl, raising her arms up in the air to mock being cross with him. Leborio gobbled down the succulent treat and started toward the school. Still behind him, Snejana frowned in confusion.

"What's the matter with you? You look like you've won the lottery."

"What can I say? I always get lucky," he replied.

Right away, he felt bad about it, not because Snejana might have caught his meaning, but because of Léonie. What he said had made her sound cheap. And she wasn't. She was good, pure, and generous. Suddenly, he was filled by complete and utter remorse, the kind that shatters the heart into a million retched pieces. To want, to have, and to destroy—this was the vicious cycle of his nature. Had he always been that way? Who could remember? He was what he was. Every one of his synapses was now wired in this way. It wasn't a question of *if*; it was a question of *when*. Not now, he thought, not soon. Right now the sun is shining, birds are singing, and there is a kind and beautiful girl whose heart belongs to me.

It caught him by surprise to find more than a dozen men dressed in ceremonial attire waiting for him in the clearing he used as a school. Monsieur Juste Bamba was sitting on a tree stump, rubbing some sort of plant leaves and bark into a tin bowl, pressing the concoction against the walls of the dish with a wooden pin and turning it into paste. A young boy stood behind him, pouring drops of water into the bowl as he stirred. The chieftain looked up and saw Leborio staring at him. He nodded and uttered a few words, showing him the bowl and signalling with the pin that this was edible.

"You take iboga?" He heard her voice and turned to be greeted by her warm smile.

"Léonie. You're here."

"Yes." She returned his affectionate glance. They moved away from the group of men, behind the communal cuisine—a kitchen hut filled with pots and pans.

"I do not go to town today," explained Léonie, gesturing for Leborio to sit next to her on one of the bamboo resting beds. "Today is special. Today we take iboga."

"What is iboga?" Snejana stepped forward from behind Leborio, her voice scratching his ears like a piece of sharp chalk on a blackboard.

As welcoming as always, Léonie turned her attention to her and told her iboga was a magical potion that connected her people with the ancestor spirits and helped them find answers to questions they dared not ask.

"Everyone try iboga at least one time to know their heart," she added, looking back to Leborio.

He didn't look convinced. It was Snejana's comment that sealed the deal. "We will not try this iboga." Her thin lips pursed, haughtily.

One sharp glare from Leborio rendered her quiet. "Of course we will try it. If Léonie says it's good, then it must be good."

"But it's a drug!"

"Cocaine is a drug. This is all natural stuff. Haven't you heard what she just said?"

"Oh, I heard what she said," said Snejana, hands on hips, like a disgruntled wife. "Is this the coronation you had in mind? Getting high with the natives?"

Never underestimate the dumb, thought Leborio, staring at Snejana in disbelief. Just when you think they know their place, they will find ways to surprise you.

"You're welcome to go back to sleep if you don't want to try it," he said.

Her gray eyes flickered with suspicion. "I might just do that," she sneered and started walking back to their bark bungalow, sulking. He would have liked nothing better than to grab her by the hair, drag her to Mr. Songoku's counter, lick a stamp to her high forehead, and ship her home with the first postal donkey—or whatever the locals used to deliver large parcels. Aware he was being observed by the chieftain's daughter, he watched Snejana perform the innerved swagger of a cheeky teen and kick the firewood in her way before she disappeared from sight.

Relieved, he turned to face Léonie. Her round face was just as kind as ever, though she was giving him a look, the first one he had ever seen her give. He waited for her to speak up, but she said nothing. Another woman in her place would have felt entitled to say something, to set him straight, now that they found themselves intimately and undeniably linked. Not Léonie. She folded her hands over her white sarafan and watched him in silence.

"She's annoying," he started. "She follows me around everywhere like a Greek choir, lamenting and crying about this and that, exaggerating every little gesture into the tragic ending of something or other. I'm not even sure I understand what the hell it is that she wants. I'm sorry." He sighed. "I'm using words you don't know yet. I know you mean well, but Snejana is a big girl. She will survive all this. Looking hurt is just her way of getting people to do her bidding. You know how some animals play dead to fool their predators into walking away?"

Léonie conceded, her head rising slightly with interest.

"Well, she's like those animals. She will play hurt until you do what she wants. Do you understand? We call that manipulation. There's a new word for you."

She mouthed the new word, unconvinced. "It is true. Animals look dead. But they only do this because danger. Is danger for Snejana?"

"Of course she's not in danger. I've been looking after her for a long time now. I am like her older brother, you know."

"Yes. You say this before."

"Said," he corrected her.

"Said. You said this before. But, if she not fear, she not play dead. Do you understand?"

He rolled his eyes and nodded reluctantly, not wanting to argue with her. Who cared about Snejana? She was like a parasite, living around a stronger organism and drawing the livelihood out of it.

"When will I see you again?" he burst out, grabbing her hand in his.

She shook her disappointment away. "In the jungle?" she asked, simply.

There was not a trace of deception in her manner—no false modesty and no pretence. She understood his meaning, because, in his very words, he was seeing her now—literally. She knew he had asked if they could be together again, the way they had been the night before. What was extraordinary to him was not that she knew this. It was that she did not bother pretending that she didn't.

"Yes. In the jungle," he said.

"Tomorrow night."

"Why not tonight?"

"Tonight you take iboga. Tonight you cannot come," she said with finality. "We meet tomorrow. Tomorrow I go to the river to wash my body. You can come there too."

Suddenly he did not feel as cavalier about the sacramental herb. He wanted to ask more about what exactly would happen if he took iboga, but the mental image of her body bathing in the river distracted him. He leaned forward, grabbed her by the waist to pull her closer, and kissed her with such fervour that once again she groaned in pain.

"Tomorrow! Not here." She stood up. "My father see."

"And why not? Why shouldn't he see us? I am the owner of this land. He should be honoured that I chose his daughter."

"He think you are bad man."

Once again, Leborio reflected on the meaning of the phrase. It seemed to him that on this little patch of earth, a man was either good or bad. It was as simple as that. People were built with some intrinsic scale for measuring a person's heart and could tell good from evil. Leborio knew he was not what people called a good man. But why, he did not know. On the whole, he approved of his own decisions, even of the means that justified his ends. Yes, they might have been unorthodox, but they served a greater purpose: that of fulfilling Leborio's grand, if yet unconfirmed, destiny. Who were these people to divide men into two kinds only, good or bad, and determine that he belonged to the latter? And what did they base their judgements on?

Where he came from, flaws would be narrowed down and reasons properly named, even explained. Yes, fathers would almost always dis-like their daughters' suitors, but they would focus on a specific cause: the boy was lazy, reckless, or dishonest. Monsieur Juste Bamba had simply decided that Leborio was a bad man, without rhyme or reason.

"And what do you think, Léonie? Do you think I am a bad man?"

He liked saying her name. It sounded primal and green, like the name of an animal fledgling, perhaps a lion cub or a fawn.

"I think you are not man," she said with a playful smirk. "A man must try iboga." And then, more softly, she added, "There is good inside you."

She touched his forehead with her small hand, as if to brush away a migraine. It felt soothing and agonizing at the same time. It was soothing because it reminded him of when he was little and he would await his mother's touch before sleep, and it was agonizing because it clashed against the twists and folds of his dark soul. And yet, if he had to do it over again, he wouldn't have changed a thing. More than anything, Leborio wanted to shine. He wanted power and an important place in the world. These were not things one got from being charitable. What would he be without his dauntless ambition, callousness, and gall? Who would he be without cruelty and charm? The answer was there, lurking inside of him. It stopped him dead in his tracks and sent cold shivers up his spine. When all was said and done, all that was left of him without all that was a frightened boy, terrified of ever growing up.

Later that night, he barely recognized his mining disciples, painted as they were. It reminded him of the first day he arrived to the settlement. Red and white pigment covered their faces and torsos, and the women participants had painted their faces white. Some of the older boys were keeping the beat of a tribal dance on the wide brimmed drums made of animal hides and hollow tree stumps. The same hides used for the drums were used to cover the loins of the men, though some appeared to do a far better job than others. Monsieur Juste Bamba was presiding over the ceremony along with a few of the elders. Their loincloths were looser than the other men's and adorned with a few totems—dried chicken feet, roots, and every once in a while, a shrivelled sort of fruit that resembled a giant raisin and was very inopportunely hanging from a rope around the waist area.

The women wore rags fashioned from painted materials and turbans over their heads. Together, men and women formed a circle around the hearth where the tribe's fire was burning and began to dance to the rhythm of the bongo drums, keeping the beat with their feet and voices. At the center of the circle stood a few ceramic bowls smudged with a greenish brown substance that looked more like a paste and seemed to have started to oxidize.

Iboga, Leborio thought, suspiciously.

Once the dance ended, some of the men dipped their fingers in the bowls and licked off the goo. Children drank a similarly coloured broth. One by one, the villagers sat in the dirt and beat their hands to the ground, keeping the beat of the drums around the fire. He surveyed the commotion from afar for a while before coming closer to the hearth. If Leborio was going to be a lord to these people, the focus of the ritual had to be deflected to include and celebrate him.

The drug seemed to manifest itself in a musical fashion, increasing the men's ability to keep a good beat. It all looked safe enough. But one could never say for certain until running a real-life experiment. His eyes fell on Regina, who was watching the commotion from the safety of Snejana's underarm. If it was good enough for scientists, it was good enough for Leborio Borzelini. The disclaimer for a number of movies came to mind: no animals were hurt in the making of this film, possibly because animals very seldom complained about being hurt during the making of anything.

With one swift move, he grabbed the cat from under Snejana's arm, and warding the screaming girl off with one hand, he sidestepped a few natives and pushed the cat's face into the ceramic bowl. The animal arched her back, convulsing under the weight of his hand, and hissed like a bat in a frequency too high to fall on human ears. It was too late. Regina's white nose had been smeared in the greenish brown potion. He let go of both the cat and the girl. The cat drew away and licked her mouth and paws with a tiny pink, flickering tongue. Leborio watched her with interest, warding Snejana's slaps and punches like a bison waving off flies. The animal finished licking herself clean and circled into a resentful pretzel a few paces away from the humans. Her bald, wrinkly skin glimmered in the moonlight like the hide of a tiny gargoyle with peach fuzz. She was upset about being pushed into the iboga bowl, but other than that, she displayed no symptoms of hallucinations.

"You suck, you know that?" huffed Snejana, surrendering to his superior strength.

"Well put, Big Bird. I do. I know I do. Thank you for putting up with my experiment."

He let go of her hands. The girl straightened up the wedding takchita she bought at the airport shop in Morocco. She hadn't worn it since the first day they arrived in Gabon. But tonight was a special occasion, and she had wanted to look festive, in case Leborio would decide under the influence of the drug that he wanted to take up with her again. His apology was a good omen. She couldn't remember him ever having apologized before. She nodded magnanimously and checked in the direction of the cat, pressing her thin lips together in contempt, as if to say, "Yes, my dear creature, he is a brute, but he is *our* brute."

The brute daubed the wooden stirring pin around the walls of the bowl and lifted it up. He smelled it and grimaced.

"Ugh."

"Why take it if you don't like it?"

He cast Snejana a brief glance. "I don't suppose you know who Octavian was, do you, Big Bird?" He did not wait for an answer. "He was a nobody, a boy really, who, by virtue of his wits and cunning, transformed himself into the first real Roman Emperor. In an age of turmoil and power struggles, he climbed to the very top of the Roman Republic and rode it as if it were a brazen mare until he broke her to his will. And how did young Octavian achieve such a thing? By making small, incremental changes until he had the people convinced that he was one of them. 'Please help us rule the empire, oh, great Octavian!' the people would ask. And he would coyly turn them down until they begged. In the end, of course he would comply to be the despot stirring the helm of the Republic—if Rome could still be called that. He came to be known as the great Augustus, had an entire month named after him, and rebuilt the city of Rome after his own mind."

"Do you want a month of your own?"

"Maybe. My point was that it isn't enough to own this land. I must make the people want me to rule them. And to make a successful entry into the upper echelons of a kinship, I must become one of them by mastering the most sacred of their rituals. But don't worry, Big Bird. I was once a guru, remember? My mind is trained to surmount more daunting things than a jungle herb. I will dominate iboga."

"I know why you're taking it," she said, waiting a moment before giving him the answer. "It's because of her. Léonie. You're trying to impress her."

For someone of limited understanding, she certainly had a knack for sniffing out the competition. Leborio's noble tale of Augustus's rise to power had not swayed her proprietary instincts. Oh, it was like casting pearls before swine. She wasn't worthy of the tales he spun. He waved a hand dismissively and touched the wooden pin with the tip of his tongue.

"Yuk! It tastes like analgesic. I'm not taking it to impress Léonie. I'm taking it to impress her father."

She stared at him, confounded. "Why do you want to impress her father?"

"So he will approve of me."

"Isn't he your—what's that word you used, the feudal word?"

"Vassal?" provided Leborio. "Yes, he is my vassal when it comes to this land. But I am his vassal when it comes to his daughter."

"So you are doing this for her! I knew it! You and your lying tales of Italian emperors." She slapped him over the head and hit him with both hands until he raised one arm to fend her off, and she yelped from the pain of crushing against his solid forearm bone. "I knew this day would come. This precisely why I wanted to keep the emergency VISA! I knew one day you'd leave me for a younger lover. After I followed you here, to the end of the world…to live in the jungle like savages—"

"Oh, Sne, you're wrong about Léonie," he said, trying to console her. "You're both the same age."

She began to cry. A few feet away, the hairless cat made a playful leap at its thin tail, paws conducting a passionate concerto. Seemingly intrigued with the instability of the appendage, she began what was to be a very long and circular chase.

"Oh no." Leborio took another lick from the wooden pin and

squinted at her like a man in need of glasses. "I think I judged this too rashly, Sne. Please promise me you'll stop me if I should start chasing my own tail."

"It's not your tail I'm worried you'll be chasing."

"*Touché.*"

He began to stumble, feeling his way through the night with waving arms and reaching hands. He staggered away from the fire toward the edge of the settlement, close to the tree line from whence the dreaded noises of an unknown presence came in the daytime. There was nothing in his path but air and darkness. He put up his hands, fingers spread out like antennas, sensing the currents of a light breeze, the minuscule drops of humidity caught in the air, invisible to the eye. It was as if he could touch atoms and light them up with the tips of his fingers. It was as if he could stop time. From the jungle around him, he could hear whispers, spilling in front of him like waves of brightly lit energy, splashing against the opaque canvas of the night and breaking into beautiful patterns. He watched with his jaw open. It was so vibrant, so real. His body began to quiver, one with the motions around him, and suddenly he felt terrified. He tried to speak, but all that came out was a whimper.

"Leborio! I'm talking to you. Leborio, come back!" He heard Snejana's voice rising from a distant dream. "Come back this instant!"

The sound of her voice screaming somewhere behind him made him feel more terrified. The more she called out to him, the more he tried to get away from her. He increased the pace of his wobble, feeling the trees and the bush with his hands, like a blind man.

"I won't come after you into the jungle. I'm frightened. Please come back!"

Soon, her voice disappeared, giving way to nothing but the swishing of trees and the rustling of night creatures. Leborio squinted—his eyes were almost useless. Somewhere ahead of him, he made out two little glimmering spots, like two fireflies. If he could only get to the light, he would see. How simple a task that promised to be and how daunting a feat it really was.

Finding the light.

Seeing.

Seeing what?

He saw things all the time. He saw everything. What else was there to see besides everything?

Seeing didn't seem that important when one could do it. But it seemed like the very thing he needed now that he couldn't see.

Yes. Everything was too much to see. He just wanted to see one thing. The thing he most wanted to see.

The specs of light got dimmer and dimmer. Leborio reached out to them, wavered, and tripped on a fallen branch. He felt every inch of his fall—his body levitating weightlessly in the musky air and then the impact with the moist ground, violent, like a tear. He would lie there, motionless. He would wait, or die, or both.

The realization that he was most likely going to die sent him into a state of repose. Only his heart fluttered like that of a rabbit, a dimming echo in the cavern of his chest.

There wasn't going to be a Leboriopolis, after all. He wasn't going to be powerful, wealthy, or adored. He was just going to be dead.

If he could have moved, he would have chuckled at the irony. Instead, he took another breath. All his life, he had wanted so much. Money, power, beautiful women, respect, adulation—all things he could do without at this very moment. Of course, if he were allowed one final request, only one, he would have asked, simply for life. Life seemed to be the only thing worth having.

As he lay dying in the heart of the Gabonese jungle, splattered on the ground like a starfish, Leborio made an edifying observation: the purpose of life was, plainly put, living. Right before he closed his eyes, he wondered if anyone had thought of this before. His last thought was to wonder if death had green eyes too.

CHAPTER 12

THE GAULOISES MAN

Mahdi stood up first, quietly rinsed his dish, and left the kitchen, unnoticed. Farah, who had poured herself another helping, stirred the caramel-coloured broth in her bowl, making a grinding sound with a metal spoon. Another twenty-four hours like this, and Iris might just decide to go back empty-handed. She'd known this case was a bad idea from the beginning. She should have listened to her gut feeling instead of the nagging pleas of her assistant, Gretchen.

Stir, stir, stir. Farah sipped from her spoon, making a slurping sound with her tongue. She had no table manners or she cared very little to mind them.

"Too hot?" asked Iris.

Farah looked up, bemused, but did not answer. The slurping sound got louder.

Iris cleared her throat.

Farah continued to slurp.

"Would you like me to take you to a disco tonight? Maybe meet a man?" Farah asked.

"Why would I want to meet a man tonight?"

"So I can eat in peace tomorrow."

Iris chocked on her broth.

"It was just a thought, investigator woman," said Farah.

"I have a man. And stop calling me investigator woman. I don't like it."

Farah smirked without looking at the younger woman. "You don't have to have a man to get a man, and there is nothing wrong with it. It's just as natural as drinking water. If you'd had a nice tall glass of water, you wouldn't mind being called a woman. You'd love it."

Iris put her bowl down, and let out a loud huffing sound before she found her words. "I came to find something," she stared, "and you're supposed to help me find it. That's why I hired you—not to sit around your living room and behave...unprofessionally."

Farah laughed. "Behave unprofessionally? How could I possibly do that without an actual profession?"

"You're a woman guide."

"That's a character trait, not a job. I just happen to get paid for it."

Iris stood up and began pacing around the room. The only lead she had was what Herr Putziffer had reluctantly given her, the giant from an Eastern European country. The giant was none other than Kim, the bouncer who followed Leborio through his adventures in Portugal. Somewhere along that trip, Kim had parted ways with Leborio and Snejana, and now she knew why. Kim had stolen the Sophie Necklace and had gotten away with it, courtesy of her commitment to her personal vendetta against Leborio. From now on, she would only trust hard cold evidence and ignore this intuition nonsense that prompted her to accuse Leborio of a crime he happened to not have committed. Not that Leborio didn't deserve it. Chance was a one-way street, and if you walked it long enough, you were bound to reach its end.

"We have to go back to Herr Putziffer's riad."

"Fine," said Farah, without questioning her sudden decision.

They both knew they had hit a block in their search, and the longer they waited, the farther their enemy was getting and the harder it became to find the girl. Herr Putziffer's riad was as good a place to resume the investigation as any other. She could tell him she came back to see the Mucha. He'd invited her to do so whenever she wished.

They took a taxi back to his place, crossing the city under an amber sunset. The road to the riad was empty but for another moving dot ahead, a blue cab that left a descending trail of dust for the women to swallow. Farah ordered the cab driver to pass the other car, and soon they were making their way ahead, raising sand clouds for the blue car behind. They pulled into the spacious C-shaped driveway of the resplendent riad, and Farah reached for the money to pay their fare when she was interrupted by a firm knock against the backseat window. A middle-aged fellow dressed like a cowboy looked down at her. She rolled down the window and held her arm up by the frame of the roof, showing off the black fly and its Latin name in her tattoo.

Gallantly, the man tipped his hat and greeted them in Arabic. For a brief moment, Farah and the cowboy stared each other up and down. In that briefest of moments, he had seen the markings on Farah's underarm and was now thinking of its meaning. Iris could tell. She could also tell Farah enjoyed this. The crow's feet around her deep-set eyes shrunk with satisfaction.

He mumbled something in French, tipped his hat again, and made his way to the front door.

"He looks like the Marlboro man." She elbowed Iris with a girlish giggle, as if they were two friends checking out the men at a bar. "Or the Gauloises man, I should say. He's French."

"What did he want?"

"He said to drive more carefully. We nearly sent his cabbie spinning from the dust."

Iris shrugged, about to make a remark about the pot calling the kettle black, when the lightbulb turned on. "French you say? Do you know him?"

"No. But I can tell from his accent. It was straight from the motherland."

Herr Putziffer's servant had left the front door ajar, so they slipped in unnoticed. They waited a moment for her to return. They could hear Herr Putziffer's greeting voice coming from the main floor gallery. He was with the Frenchman.

"Come." Iris grabbed Farah's arm and pulled her into an adjacent wardrobe just in time for the servant to miss them. She crossed her lips with her index finger and shushed.

Farah nodded skeptically but did not make a sound. They both moved in closer to the wall, inches away from the door to the gallery. A chair was pulled and backs were slapped the way men do to show they're friends.

"Lacroix, *mon ami*, what brings you by? My item is not ready to be sold until next week, you know that."

"Yes, yes. I'm not 'ere for ze necklace." The two women exchanged glances.

"How did you know?" mouthed Farah under her breath.

"Putziffer said the jeweller was a Frenchman. I had a feeling this might be him." Then the younger woman signalled she wanted to listen. Inside, Herr Putziffer was treating the other to a glass of brandy.

"Why are you here then, if not for the necklace?"

"I'm 'ere for one of my own items," said the Frenchman.

"Oh?"

"Remember ze knife I bought from you last month? Ze gypsy knife with ze emeralds."

"Yes, of course. Beautiful piece!"

"Yeah, well, it didn't 'appen to show at your door, did it?"

"No, of course not. Why would it?"

"It was stolen from me, you see. And because you're ze best paying buyer, I thought—"

"You thought I'd hold out on you like that." Herr Putziffer made a tsking noise with his tongue. "My friend, if your knife showed at my door, you'd be the first person I'd call. After all, you're my best paying buyer too. And the most discreet. No one would ever think to look for priceless jewels in that dreadful shop of yours."

The Frenchman wasn't amused. "Look, if it does show up 'ere, will you do me a favour and call? Discreetly, of course. Don't want to spook ze bastard."

"Who am I looking for? Did you get a good look at him?"

"Did I ever? I let 'im spend ze night under my roof. 'im and 'is girl. Zey looked a little parched and soiled but overall of good stock. Expensive belt and a nose that was turned up so 'igh zat it probably overlooked *La Tour Eiffel*. Business has been so dry, I thought I'd turn some profit from 'aving ze man work for me at ze eco tour. Strapping animal, zis man was. Eastern European, from what I could tell, but 'e could've been from Greece too. Straight from fucking Olympus. Ze most magnificent arms I 'ave ever seen on a man, and I'm not ashamed to say it. Pretty in ze face too. Would 'ave gone easy on ze ladies' eyes. Better zan zat old grumpy seal of mine. Anyway, zey took off, ze bastards, in ze middle of ze night. Amal and I were sleeping and didn't 'ear a sing. Ze next day when I woke up, ze knife was gone."

"Did you phone the police?"

"Ze police are nothing but a waste of time. I know where 'e was 'eaded, but 'e's gonna need some money to get zere."

"Back to Europe?"

"No. Get zis! 'e was going to Bongoville, Gabon, to claim—'ow do you say...*l'héritage*?"

"Inheritance?"

"*Exactement!* Inheritance of land—'e was gonna dig for diamonds and the like. Zat was what 'e hooked me with, ze diamonds. Can you imagine having a contact like zat?"

Herr Putziffer broke into a fit of laughter. "My dear Lacroix, you've lived in Africa twice as long as I have. And you're a jeweller. A successful one. How is it that you don't know where diamonds come from, my friend?"

Lacroix went silent for a moment. "Where do zey come from?"

"Many places, but wherever they come from, it's not Gabon. Sure, if you want oil, timber, or black market gorillas, that's the right place to do business. But if you want diamonds, I'm afraid—what was the name of the place again?"

"Bongoville."

"Bongoville, Gabon is not a...gold mine of diamonds, if you will." Herr Putziffer continued gurgling through his nose. The two women moved ever so slightly to give each other can-you-believe-this glances.

"Very well, laugh if you must, Otto." So, Herr Putziffer had a first name. It was the women's turn to muffle snorts. "But make sure you keep zis between us. Ze last thing either of us needs is a reputation for being naive. Every thief in Marrakech will try zeir luck with my shop, and guess who's going to be next? Your riad. So keep your eye out for ze knife, and for fuck'sakes lose some weight, man. You're as fat as a pig. Who am I gonna do business with if your heart gives out?"

"You worry for me, Lacroix? That's touching. Be sure I'll let you know if your precious knife shows at my door." Farah nudged Iris to show her the servant disappearing up the stairs. Behind them, Herr Putziffer's voice dimmed into the background as the Frenchman spoke. "By ze way, what do you plan to do with the diamond necklace?"

"Funny you should ask. I'm trading it to an ex-KGB official for his villa in Sardinia."

Sardinia, Marrakech, Bongoville—there was a world of mobility to be had in crime. It used to be that only the rich could afford to travel at a moment's notice, from one exotic destination to another. But now, courtesy of low-cost airfare, planes were filled with pimply Erasmus students representing NGOs, aspiring models with sunglasses the size of saucers, and girls with Hello Kitty cameras dressed in over-sized Avril Lavigne T-shirts. Also, occasionally, aboard the very same planes, ordinary thieves and their respective investigators flew across continents at an easily traceable speed, stopping to be checked at the appropriate gates in a septic and humourless fashion and declaring the value of their purchases just like everyone else. She wasn't looking forward to flying to Gabon now. She had just become accustomed to Morocco and its dazzling flavour.

Quietly, they made their way outside, where the Frenchman's blue taxi was drawing circles at the gate. They jumped in, and Farah gave the man directions. He protested a little until she waved a bill under his nose. So much for loyalty to customers.

As if reading her mind, the older woman spoke: "I know you said money is not an object, but I want you to know I will charge you a fair price."

"For what?"

"For Gabon. We'll have to take a couple of days before we fly out there, and I will have to bring my son on the trip. It is going to cost extra, but it'll even out once we get there. The cost of living is much cheaper than in Marrakech."

"Why don't we bring your boyfriend too? I'm sure he'll get lonely without you here. He can babysit your son while we…investigate."

Farah shot her a quizzical look and said something in Arabic to the driver. He rolled his eyes and turned a corner through what appeared to be a street market of sorts. The vendors waved colourful merchandise at the car, smiling at the white woman in the back seat. Again, Farah spoke to the driver, this time in an imperative tone. The car picked up speed, leaving the vendors behind like passing visions of another world. Iris felt carsick. It happened when she tried to keep up with the scenery, so she leaned over the driver's seat, looking forward through the dirty windshield.

"Taxi drivers take the main roads at this hour because they know the traffic is bad when people come back from work," said Farah. "You end up waiting in the cab with them and paying twice the fare. But I'm sure you knew that, seeing as you don't need any help from me. My son, Diya, is a few years younger than you are. If you believe in coincidence, he played soccer for the FC Bongoville for a number of years. He knows the town and its people and understands their dialect of French. Though if I'm entirely honest, he doesn't yet understand the workings of human exchanges. I suppose all young people are either idealists or cynics."

"Young people can't be cynics. They don't know enough about the world."

"You're right. Cynicism is what happens after idealism fails, and for some that marks the end of an age. I guess it depends on your definition of youth. At any rate, he falls under the first category for now. This is why you need me. Can't have two idealists running around a Central African country, looking for a cynic and a pubescent girl."

"He's not a cynic."

She tried saying his name, and once again, it remained stuck at the back of her throat. Farah looked away to conceal an all-knowing gaze. There were lines around what used to be a dimple in her cheek. If Sophia Loren had spent a lifetime in the Saharan desert, she would have looked just like Farah.

"Idealists often pass themselves for cynics," she said. "The same is true in reverse. You cannot catch a fox if you're planning to trap a coyote."

Aside from basic physiognomy, Iris couldn't think of what was so different between a fox and a coyote. They were both thieves who preyed on smaller creatures. Perhaps the difference lay in their escape strategies.

"Coyotes live in packs," spoke the woman guide, as if she'd heard her thoughts. "Foxes are solitary creatures."

CHAPTER 13

BROTHER KING

He woke up with the taste of bile in his mouth, unable to tear his eyes open from the discharge that had dried his lashes together. His tongue felt inflamed, pulsating in his mouth like a dying fish out of water. He groaned to call for help and thrashed his body about, feeling his surroundings against his sweaty skin. I am dead, he remembered wistfully. I have surely gone to hell, and this must be it—a blind, thirsty, helpless state of being, where only the mind was left to wander a chaotic unknown.

"Shhh," he heard, feeling a moist towel against his forehead. He moved his weight away from the hand wielding it. "Shhh. I am here."

It was Léonie's voice, and for a moment, he felt terrified, thinking that she had died with him. He felt her hand, gently lifting up his head, supporting it from the neck to touch his lips with the wet towel. He puckered his mouth, sucking the water out of the fabric.

"Not too much. Too much is not good for you."

She wiped his eyes with the same towel, and blew over the candle to dim the lights so he could open his lids. He fluttered and squinted, like a newborn. The smell of wax from the candle made his head hurt, and he groaned again, hiding his head into a handmade pillow.

"Shhh. *C'est fini.* Iboga very strong. More strong first time."

Iboga. He remembered now. He had taken iboga and had died from it. But he was not dead. Léonie was here, taking care of him. He had stumbled into the jungle, looked death in the eye, and made his last plea to be spared.

"Alive," he uttered, feeling a thousand needles pierce through his dried up throat.

"Yes." She gave him more water. "Alive, *mon amour.* You are very brave."

Slowly, he began to swallow, and his eyes adjusted to the darkness until he saw her shape above him, contoured by the light rays piercing through the wooden beams across the roof. An angel, he thought. She was an angel.

"You go jungle. Snejana call help. But I cannot find you. Great Brother King save you. He put you on back and bring here."

"Brother King—" he muttered.

"Gorilla. From behind school trees. Your school."

"A gorilla…a gorilla carried me on his back?"

"Yes. He carry you back from jungle and put you down when he sees our people. They bring you to Snejana, but she cry and cry, and then we give her iboga tea to sleep. After, I come to help." Then, her voice grew softer, almost timid, "I…I think something bad happen to you, then I cannot forgive me."

"Myself."

"Myself. I cannot forgive myself…" She didn't finish the sentence.

Leborio propped himself up on his elbows. His head was still throbbing, but some of his strength had now returned to him. She looked so desolate, sitting there, next to him, on the edge of his bed, hands grasping onto the wet towel on her lap, tears falling out of her big, black eyes. He lifted her chin with his fingers until their eyes met, and he took the towel from her hands and wiped her tears. Léonie closed her eyes, opening to his touch like a flower to the sun, and before he knew it, he was undoing the ribbon on her white sarafan and removing the arm ruffles from her shoulders until she was left naked before his eyes. He cupped her breast with one hand and pulled her over him with the other, reaching up her thigh until her legs came ajar, curling around his waistline, pulling him closer. Her skin was soft but firm, her tongue was sweeter than he'd ever tasted.

"*Je t'aime*," she kept repeating, whispering his name with piety.

They made love right there, in his bed, covered only by the sheer white of the mosquito netting, unhindered by the sounds of the village going about around them or by the possibility that at any given moment someone could walk in on them. When at last they fell onto each other, breathless and drained, he held her to his chest and kissed the top of her head gingerly. She let out a long sigh of relief to have him close and safe, or maybe the sigh was from sheer exhaustion.

"What colour were the eyes of the gorilla?" he asked, out of the blue.

Léonie looked up at him and laughed. It was strange he should ask that, she said. This gorilla was very special. It was the only gorilla she had ever seen to have green eyes.

***

Even crouching on all fours, the animal was taller than the man was. A flash from an old King Kong movie he'd seen as a child ran before his eyes, a great big gorilla, holding a blonde woman in his hand, keeping her from falling off from the top of the Empire State Building. The ape had fallen in love with her, and it had made him human-like. This gorilla was not as big as the monster from the movie. But to Leborio, who had never seen such an animal up close, it seemed gigantic nonetheless.

"Come," said Léonie, taking a step closer to the gorilla. "Touch him."

Leborio stood there, rooted in his spot behind the bush, under the wide canopy of the Coula tree, his black eyes fixed on the beast, appraising him with suspicion. The two males stared at one another ready for the primeval battle of survival, every muscle tensed, every vein throbbing with anticipation. Léonie was right. This gorilla had green eyes, impenetrable and deep, as if they had been made of steel. Without having seen them, he knew these were the eyes that watched him through his days and the feet that cracked twigs in the shrubbery behind the great big tree where his school was. This was the forest deity he'd long suspected.

The longer he stared, the harder it became to look away. The strength in the beast's eyes petrified him. Leborio had never in his life been truly terrified of another's presence. He knew the ape was a male long before he heard Léonie refer to him as one. He knew to the depth of his core that he was standing in front of a natural overlord, a true alpha male, proof that he was not—nor would he ever be—a force of nature, but rather a man, a fluky perversion of nature, with no claims over it beyond the arrogance and affectation of a spoiled child. How cruel that it was this monster who had been his saviour, who had carried him on his back through the jungle and into the safety of Léonie's arms. Knowing this twisted the knife of his impotence even further. Locked in this strange exchange with the male gorilla, Leborio felt himself weaken at the knees and thought of the madman in Edgar Allen Poe's story, who was driven to murder by a single blue eye. He too wanted to do away with the beast, to return the world to the reassuring illusion it had been before this day.

He lifted his hand slowly, until it settled on the silver handle of the gypsy dagger tied to his sash. He could almost hear the breath coming out of the animal's wide nostrils, a roar away from shattering Leborio into little pieces. The smell was pungent and sour, like that of human sweat, and for a moment, Leborio was not entirely sure if he wasn't the one emitting it. He waited. The gorilla did not strike, although his eyes never left the man in front of him. And just as he prepared to pull the dagger out of its sheath, a tiny white shadow slithered by the foot of the beast. Both man and animal looked down to find Regina, the hairless cat, purring softly against the gorilla.

"Look!" giggled Léonie. "The cat likes him."

She bent down to pet the cat, but it gave a loud meow and moved away, circling the sturdy legs of the beast, who brought them closer together, as if to protect her.

"They are friends."

Regina peeked out from behind the trunks of the gorilla's legs and slowly emerged to sit over its great big feet, ogling the humans with a spiteful look that seemed to say, "Do you know who my daddy is?" The gorilla's curled fingers grazed over the skin of the cat, gently.

"Indeed," muttered Leborio, relaxing a little. Weakness was his specialty. "They seem to be friends."

"See? You can touch. He is friends with your cat."

"She's not my cat."

Léonie raised her hand, slowly, to touch the beast. Under the tender stroke of her hand, the gorilla's stance softened. He breathed out loudly, a sigh of indulgence, and licked away the spittle at the corner of his great big mouth.

Weakness made the world ripe for the taking. He was nothing but a colossal pet now, tamed by the touch of a woman, just like the beast in the movie. Leborio took a step forward and then another, until he was close enough to touch the gorilla. He put out one hand, holding the gypsy knife with the other, and made for the animal's forehead.

"No. Don't touch Brother King there. Head must be tall. Touch hand if you want."

Leborio glowered at her. "What if I don't want to touch his hand?" Where he came from, a hand touch meant friendship, even if it wasn't a shake.

"Touch here." She pointed at his chest. "But be careful. Female touch him there."

Unwilling to try mating signals and meaning to get it over with, Leborio touched the gorilla's hand instead. At once, as if awoken from a sleep, the beast moved swiftly to take a hold of Leborio's wrist with his own enormous hand. Leborio shrieked and lifted up his knife, wielding it in the air like a sword.

"No!" the girl cried out. "Stop!"

Unaware of the weapon hovering about him, the beast brought Leborio's hand closer to his face. He was going to bite his hand off. The knife might not even be enough to stop him. After all, he was so big, his teeth so massive—his skin felt as thick as armour. Nothing but bullets could penetrate it. Caught in the clasp of the gorilla, the man cowered, computing the ways in which to hurt him more efficiently. Closer to the heart perhaps or under the armpit, where the skin was softer. The animal paid no mind to the man's struggle. His powerful hand pulled Leborio closer, as if he were a weightless toy, waving him around a little.

When his hand was close enough to his nostrils, he began to sniff it. He took his time smelling the man's skin. His dark, wrinkly face looked patient, almost peaceful.

"He wants to know you," said Léonie. "You don't need knife here. Brother King is friend."

The gorilla seemed to have lost interest in the man's hand. He let go of it and swung his arm about his body to pick up the cat and throw it on his shoulder. Leborio fell back on the soft, damp ground, panting from relief and exhaustion, his right hand still clasping the silver handle of the knife. He stared up at the patch of sky above him. There were almost no clouds, just a fine white film stretching over a portion of the sky that was away from the sun. In it, symmetrically elongated ripples, like those the currents make in shallow waters, culminated in a translucent brume that was just at the very beginning of grey. The calm before the calm before the storm, he thought.

"Good cat," Léonie whispered, petting the hairless creature perched atop the gorilla. Even though her hand moved calmly over the skin of the cat, the young woman's eyes were steely with anger. She turned her back to Leborio.

Propped comfortably in between the wide shoulders of the beast, Regina was now staring down at Leborio with the smug look of the protected. He was certain this was payback for the other night, when he had shoved the cat's face in the iboga bowl. Brother King knuckle-walked the tiny rider and made a clicking sound with its protuberant mandible, like a father playing horse with his child and teaching it to speak. After a while, the cat became irritated with the motion and let out a nasal meow of protest. The gorilla stopped abruptly. Leborio saw the small claws of the feline scratching the dark fur of the beast as if to prepare a fluffy nest and watched Brother King settle down peacefully, careful not to disturb the cat.

Yes, thought Leborio, weakness made great beasts into cattle. A long time ago, a clever ape figured out what weakness meant and used it to rise up on two feet, to heard and harness the world around him and own it from the safety of a cave. He was never going to be this gorilla with its threatening stature and inexplicable gentleness. But he was that first ape who saw the great beast's weakness and learned how to exploit it. Looking at the hairless cat, Leborio realized he knew just how to overcome this ignominious encounter. He didn't quite know when, but the cat would deliver him the beast.

CHAPTER 14

IN THE DESERT

Farah sidestepped an animal carcase and dropped her leather satchel in the orange sand.

"We might as well stop here. This looks like a good spot for the night."

Iris complied, mostly because she was tired of walking. She watched Farah pull out a few twigs and small logs from God knows where at the bottom of her bag and then have a sip of water from the leather water pouch she wore strapped across her shoulder. Tomb Raider had nothing on Farah.

"It's a bota bag," she said, waving the water pouch. "The Spanish brought it over centuries ago. You should get one from the market when we go. I'd give you this one, but it was a gift from my first husband, and it has sentimental value. Did I ever tell you about my first husband?"

She didn't wait for an answer.

"I met him in Venezuela. I used to live there, you see. He was handsome like the devil, and he loved to ride motorcycles. In those days not everyone had motorcycles, so it was a real treat to be taken on one. He let me ride it by myself sometimes. I remember it used to make me tremble with fear and excitement. Nothing like that fresh taste of adrenaline you get in your mouth when you first probe at the boundaries of your world. You think you're being cautious, but it turns out that's really the most reckless you'll ever get to be. All those nights spent flirting with speed and heights and depths, they go by so fast. Thirty years later, you can't even remember what you did, only the way you felt, because you haven't felt that way in decades. You tell yourself it doesn't have to end, that you'll jump out of a plane some day. And who's to say? You might even do it. But the fall lasts as long as it lasts. Nothing stays fresh forever. One day the freedom caged in the pit of your stomach fizzles out the moment your feet touch the ground, and you realize that the only way to keep it alive is by planning your next jump as soon as you land. It's just a matter of time before you know the choice is simple: you can either join a circus and become a stuntman, or you can accept that life is not meant to be lived on the edge of things."

"And how is life meant to be lived?"

"Between them or beyond them. In wide spaces where you can wander."

She sipped from the bota bag again and let out a sound like the one that follows the first burn of a stiff drink. "Anyway, these water pouches are neat inventions. Leather lined with sap to prevent liquids from seeping through. They're quite simple to make and a lot more effective keeping water cold than regular bottles."

"What happened to your husband, the motorcycle rider?"

"He crashed—into a beautiful French ingénue. An exchange student. He left me for her and then left her for her sister. What can I say? The man had short attention span. That's probably why he was such an adrenaline junkie. I used to sigh with relief that we didn't have any kids. It would have complicated the split. But now I think it would have been nice to have something other than this bota bag to remember him by. It makes no sense that we should miss the people we're ashamed to have loved, but we do nevertheless. Once in a while, I think of him and say I miss that old bastard and the way he used to make me feel all neurotic and breakable. Oh yeah—there was a time when I was all those things."

Iris hadn't taken the time to observe her companion until now. The people we hire are often reduced to mere soundboards for our purpose: a construction worker will quote us prices for materials and labour, a hairdresser will listen to our vacation plans, and a deli server will nod politely to our dietary updates. It was true that a woman guide was a less defined profession, but Farah's role so far had been to keep Iris moving to her destination. This was the first unaccounted-for day they had spent together, and Iris had not the slightest clue why that was. Here they were, in the bone-strewn, dune-waved wasteland of cowboy movies, two women in no particular rush to get back to civilization. One was telling stories by an unlit fire. The other was half listening.

"What the hell are we doing here, Farah? We're in the middle of the desert, away from any visible signs of civilization."

Farah pulled her long skirts up, revealing a bandana she had tied like a garter around her surprisingly firm thigh. Tied to the bandana was a tiny pistol, which she unfastened with one hand. Her eyes fixed on the gun, Iris stiffened in her spot. The woman paid no mind to her.

"We're not in the middle of the desert. The desert is a vast space, investigator woman. We've barely touched the edge of it."

With her finger on the trigger, Farah set the crumpled paper on fire.

"It's a lighter," gasped Iris.

"Of course it's a lighter. What else would it be?"

"It looks like a gun."

"Things aren't always what they seem," said the woman, pushing the burning paper under loose twigs and wood, watching the flames grow. "You should know this by now if you are to be an investigator woman."

Investigator woman, thought Iris, sounded like some sort of witch doctoring title, just because of the gender delimitation. She liked to think there was no difference between men and women, at least not beyond the fractured individuality that separates and unites at once each human being from another.

"Investigators don't carry guns. Or lighters shaped like guns."

"I do not know what investigators do. I am a woman guide, and I like to light my own fire," she said, pressing the trigger on her lighter to spark up the tobacco in her pipe. "Why do you mind so much being called an investigator woman?"

"Because my gender shouldn't make a difference."

"But it does. You are a woman. And women are…magical. They can be lionesses and gazelles all at once. They can bring thunder and sun to the sky. They can soothe just as they can destroy. There is no fiercer force of nature than a woman, the giver of life. You should not be afraid to reach deep inside yourself and find that dormant goddess that is just waiting to break out."

Listening to her, Iris inhaled the pungent fumes of Farah's pipe. No, this was no ordinary tobacco.

"See that shape on the horizon? It may not look like much from here, but it's a canyon made mostly out of limestone. And it's my biggest foe in life. My son, you see, likes to climb. He'll climb anything that gets him closer to the sky above, even if it is a fifty-foot piece of crumbling sedimentary rock. That's where he is right now, sleeping under a canopy he's pitched, waiting for dawn to start moving back home. We'll catch him then. Out here, he's more likely to concede."

"Concede to what?"

"Coming on this trip of yours. To Gabon. He hates to go anywhere with me. You know how young people are, embarrassed to be seen ten feet from their mothers. But if I know my son at all, one look at that pretty face of yours, and he'll be ready to join us."

"Whose son is he? If he isn't your child with your first husband, I mean."

"He is my second husband's son. But that's a story for another night."

"Jesus. How many husbands did you have?"

Farah smiled. "Enough to not run out of stories by the camp fire."

Nothing was said after this, as the two women lay back in silence, staring at the sky above them. Stars flickered like diamonds against the dark velvet of the celestial fabric, tiny and impermanent, perhaps already dead, somewhere at the edge of our galaxy. Iris had forgotten all about the stars as she lived in a city of yellow clouds and light pollution. But here, in the desert, she could really see them and almost felt the planet spinning under her, a lonely spec of life in an infinite universe. There was something comforting in the other woman's presence, fluid and female, strong but not abrasive. In moments like these, periods were synchronised.

"Is that really necessary? Bringing him along?" Her tone was not affected, but rather subdued, like that of a child asking why the covenant of an intimacy must be broken.

Farah told again of the hardships and dangers of Central Africa. She mentioned something about Joseph Conrad and recited the piece about the horror. Iris listened to her voice, seeing her words off like fleeting bird shadows against the night sky. If her mother ever told her bedtime stories as a child, this is what they must have sounded like, a little louder than a whisper, keeping the cadence of a dance between darkness and imagination. She closed her eyes and drifted off for a while, into a vision of herself floating down the stream of a muddy brown river, alone in the empty shell of a hollowed-out tree trunk that glided through the heart of an unnamed jungle. The river was fearfully silent, and all around her, she could hear humming tropical insects and fluttering bird wings announcing some unseen cataclysm. She wanted to jump out of her little boat and swim to the shore, but who knew what monsters lurked in these murky waters? It could be alligators, snakes, or currents that whirlpooled down into the secret womb of the river. She had no choice but to drift with the wooden dugout, downstream, always downstream, until somewhere in a distance, the faint throbs of a waterfall began to send their humid haze like smoke signals into the air.

Paddles. She needed paddles to take control of her boat and steer it to the shore before she'd be sucked into the fall. Frantically, she searched the boat, to no avail. Her hands were too small a surface to oppose the tumultuous force of the water.

***

By the time she woke up, Farah had cleared away all traces of their spending the night there. Iris nodded good morning and pulled her hair back into a ponytail. The desert had a different landscape in the day, with a half disk sun rising over the dunes like a record in a jukebox and the milky mist of dawn lifting off the remains of greyish darkness. Her mouth tasted of toxins and thirst. She hated not brushing her teeth first thing when she woke up.

Farah took a sip and handed her the bota bag.

"Here. Have what's left of the water. He shouldn't be long now."

And he wasn't. Despite the open vastness of the sand dunes, he snuck up on them just about undetected. Farah saw her son first and yelled out a savage desert sound. He didn't holler back. No more than a silhouette nearing in, he waved and made his way over fast and steady until he perched his walking stick at the top of their dune, his face beaming like Edmund Hillary. Too tall to be a soccer player, but too athletic for a layman, Farah's son had shiny, fair hair and dirty cargo pants. He looked nothing like his mother. He was robust like a Bavarian, friendly and approachable, with one of those faces you feel you've seen before. She decided instantly she was going to like him because he smiled with his eyes instead of his mouth.

"*Farah.*" He said her name with the guttural *h* and glottal *r* of Arabic pronunciation. Then, he gave his mother a bear hug.

"This is my son, Diya."

He put out his hand and switched to English. "Pleased to meet you." His accent had a tinge of British posh, like that of an Indian man who was educated at Oxford.

"And this is my client, Iris Bendal. She's investigating a criminal, and I'm helping her find him."

"Are you a policewoman?" He said woman just like his mother, swirling the word in his mouth, as if he tasted a full-bodied wine.

"I'm afraid not. A private investigator."

Diya's eyes were almost blue or should have been to match the brightness of his face.

"And guess where this criminal is hiding?" Farah didn't wait for him to answer. "In Bongoville."

"Gabon?"

Mother and son exchanged a meaningful stare, unaware for brief moment of the younger woman's presence. She could see the shape of Farah's eyes on his face but nothing else. He had a snub nose that wrinkled at the root when he laughed, and lips that were small and red, cherry-like. A few dunes away, a group of students appeared out of nowhere and headed into another dune, backpacks strapped to their bare torsos. Diya examined them, breaking the soundless shell of familial communication. The students waved. Iris watched the exchange with interest, trying to guess if they all knew each other.

"The desert is like a small village where all living creatures greet or eat each other. And I've already had breakfast." He waved back.

She pretended to stare at her feet so she wouldn't have to wave, while Farah continued to press her son for an answer.

"Fine. When do we leave?" It felt like a concession but for his eyes—they betrayed an unwavering, sunny disposition.

"Right now."

"I'll need to go home and shower first."

Hours later, they were above the clouds, flying toward the heart of the continent. Farah slept in her window seat, with the blinds on and a soiled waterproof hat over her eyes. Iris caught Diya up on the case, leaving out the part about having known the criminal they were pursuing for the better part of her life. He listened intently, rediscovering colourful words as she said them and nodding at them as if they were old friends. The more Diya nodded, the more she spoke, until she felt her cheeks burn with his brightness.

"You sound older than you are," he said. "I like that. It means you've not been afraid to live. Who says you have to wait? And until when? You see, where I live, there is plenty of life. The streets are always full in Marrakech. Tourists come and go so often that it makes the old city look multicultural, and even the desert is buzzing with small, unnoticeable beings. I get to use three languages daily. Yet looking at someone like you, I feel…rural. You've probably lived in a dozen places and tried a dozen lives. That's what I want to do!" he said, casting a glance over to his sleeping mother. "I want to live everywhere! And at the same time! There's just so much I can do, so many things I want to try."

"Why don't you?"

"I'm just not…I don't…There are certain…*expectations* of me. I can't just pick up and go in the same way I pick up and go climb my rock."

"You'll find that the effort required for either is not proportional to the consequences. You just have to pick up, and inertia will take care of the rest."

"So let me ask you this: have you ever done anything reckless? Anything that changed the shape of your inner landscape forever?"

"Are you asking for my story or my advice?"

"Can I ask for both?"

"No, you may not. Yet, at least. But I can give you my advice. Making a decision is the hardest part. What follows is as easy as a snowball rolling down a hill. Make your decision and roll with it. There are no right or wrong answers if you only get to pick one."

She knew right then there was a question she did not want to ask. Like a young girl who sees the tan line on a man's ring finger but chooses not to know, she looked away from his luminous face and kept on talking to fill her own thoughts. There was something about the way he listened, intently, completely absorbed, soaking in her words as if they were wisdom.

"You know, I've never seen a snowball," he said.

"Really? But you speak English so well. I thought surely you must have lived—"

"In England? I get that a lot. No, I lived with my father in the Belize for a few years after Farah left us. You'd think I picked up a perfect accent while I was playing cricket with the local Brit brats, but we mostly spoke German at home. My father is German."

That explained his Bavarian stance. She'd never thought the Germans an attractive people until now.

"Your mother left you?" she whispered, checking to see if Farah had heard. Under the wide canopy of the Jacques Paganel waterproof hat, her breathing lulled away like the purr of a cat.

"Oh yes, she did. My father was too soft for her. Though if you ask, she'll say he didn't care enough, that he was too complacent. Strong women find the quirkiest means of explaining their inability to stand boring relationships, as if they have to justify why they wanted out of something that was no fun. She left to marry a Canadian. I know— you're probably wondering why an intelligent woman like Farah would marry again. The explanation lies in her upbringing. We don't credit culture enough for our choices, I think. Every woman in Morocco knows that the net worth of her intelligence is measured by how well she guards her reputation. Reputation is everything in Moroccan society. And you can take the girl out of Morocco, but you can never take Morocco out of the girl. It took her a very long time to let go of the illusion of herself and live her actual life the way she intended." He cast an affectionate look at his sleeping mother. "We both learned a lot from her struggles."

"You're an unusual young man."

"I certainly hope so. It would be dreadful to be usual. Think of the disappointment it would cause Farah."

"You call your mother by her name." It was more of an observation than a question.

"She calls me by mine. Why should I not call her by hers?"

"I never thought of it that way. Are you two close?"

"We admire each other, I think. But we are not dotting familials, if that's what you mean by close. She wasn't one to tuck me in at night, and I knew better than to ask."

"She said she used to read you stories."

"Story. Yes. She read me the same story about seven times before she left for Canada. In retrospect, she was probably feeling guilty knowing she would leave and wanted to do something nice for little me."

"You know, when your mother told me she used to read me *The Snow Queen* to you, I knew you and I would get along. That was my favourite story growing up."

"Not mine. I'm sorry to disappoint, I liked *The Three Little Pigs*. I found the moral a lot more useful. And Aladdin...because of his gadgets—he had a magic lamp and a magic carpet. If you think about it, magic carpets preceded airplanes by centuries. Sadly, we can't credit *Arabian Nights* with the vision. You might not be aware of this, but the story of Aladdin was not part of the original manuscript. It was actually added by an eighteenth-century translator, a French Orientalist named Antoine Galland. Galland might in fact be the author of Aladdin altogether. No one knows."

She watched him light up with enthusiasm when he spoke—as if it were possible to light up even more. She could have asked. She should have asked. But she didn't. She was aware that sunlight from some tiny airplane window reflected off his apricot skin right onto hers, making her glow with the aura of mornings in the Swiss Alps. His brightness was infectious.

"Clever." The word got out of her mouth before she could shut it.

"What's clever?" Farah tipped the waterproof hat away from her face.

Iris sat up straight in her seat and folded her hands in her lap like a boarding school pupil. "The French. The French are a clever people, it seems." She turned to Diya. "So you got the gist of the case, I hope. Do you have any questions?"

Diya shook his head. His eyes were still smiling, only this time with a vague twinkle of amusement.

CHAPTER 15

A DEAL WITH THE DEVIL

L éonie had prepared him a satchel with food and water. She was going to take him into town herself. He hadn't said why he wanted to go, and no one had asked him. All the better. Snejana had disappeared with one of the women and he didn't feel like looking for her. She'd been learning how to make lotions from natural ingredients the native women found in the woods. Overall, she seemed somewhat aloof since the iboga incident. Perhaps she had reached some sort of primitive realization, the kind that even a basic creature like her would be able to draw. Perhaps she was so overjoyed at seeing Leborio alive again that she decided to forgive and forget and maybe even felt generous and inclusive in her revelation. A supercilious grin changed the configuration of his scruff. To have two or more understanding women by his side, to train them to overcome provincial sentiments of possession and exclusivity in favour of a Leborio-centred convivial system. Only Léonie's grave face scouting the overcast sky above them brought him out of his daydream.

"Rain will come," she said starkly.

She had been unusually quiet ever since the knife incident. The only time she spoke was to practice the simple future construction Leborio taught her. What did she want him to do, face a massive gorilla unarmed? It was enough that the animal had humiliated him, saving his life without discretion and then dangling him by the wrist like a keychain. He wasn't going to let the beast maim him too. Other than her anguished protest in the jungle, Léonie had not brought it up with him again. She continued helping him with his teachings, bringing him water and food every day. But there was something remote about her now. Her smile had faded, and on a few occasions, he caught her studying him when she thought he wasn't looking.

"Then we'd better hurry," he replied eventually, using an unusual modal to bamboozle her.

But the girl did not ask for an explanation. They picked up the pace and walked together in silence. She was leading him through a trail he hadn't seen before, one covered with foliage that seemed to spring right out of the ground like a luscious green carpet. They were climbing plants that had evolved to spread beneath his feet, growing horizontally rather than vertically, covering the soil and feeding off its riches. It was amazing how life twisted and turned over backward, so it could be. He took her hand in his, and she allowed him to do so without showing any emotion. The lack of emotion did not arise from concealment, but rather from her lack thereof. She hid nothing behind those huge, black eyes. She looked the way she felt. And right now, it was hard to tell how she felt.

The way through the jungle was not as short as he remembered it and walking in silence did nothing to make it shorter. By the time they reached town, the rain started pouring all at once. It was the way of the African jungle, where the rain came down like a bucket of water over a garden patch. They ran for shelter under the eaves of the church. He was already drenched and so was Léonie.

"I will not wait," she said, examining the clouds above. "Rain will not stop soon. I will go to Mother's people now."

Her white sarafan was sticking to her, transparent and wet, revealing the ripe, dark skin underneath it. His eyes were drawn to the ribbon at the front, which only a few days before he had unfastened feverishly. He wanted to cover her with a jacket to protect her from the prying eyes of other men. For some reason, Kodjo Mba Nze popped in his mind, and he shook his head at the thought in horror.

"You should cover yourself." The words had slipped out before he could stop them.

Léonie looked down at her sarafan and shrugged. "This is water. It will dry."

And with that, she disappeared around the corner of the church. He didn't follow her. A little space would do them both good, he thought, taking in the humid air of the town and savouring the sour smell of asphalt, which he had taken for granted all his life. One does not miss the building blocks of modern civilization until one is forced to live in the jungle for a few weeks. He thought about the dozen different cell phones he used back home, one for every day of the week, assigned according to mobile plans and lovers. He would call the brunette from the iPhone because he had an unlimited plan, and she liked to talk. He would e-mail the blond from the Android because the phone came with a one-month data plan trial, and the touch-screen keypad was easier to use. He hadn't touched a mobile phone since he took a picture of an American teen in Morocco nor had he thought about it until just now.

He walked into the first eatery, a slight place with plastic tables impaled by Coca-Cola umbrellas with earthed bases that helped stabilize the weight. *L'Arbre de Bois Bistro*, he read on the carved wooden plaque above the cash register. It meant The Timber Tree Bistro, though there was nothing *bistro* about it. Behind the food counter, a middle-aged woman was cleaning scales off a fish the size of a man's palm. Her hair was tied back in a turban, and she was wearing a red apron with crab fish cartoons. He gagged from the smell of seafood. Leborio had always hated seafood and its tangy odour. It made his stomach churn and rebel, and he was ready to retch the contents of his small breakfast. He felt the acids coming up his oesophagus at intervals, swirling in his mouth, stinging his glands with vinegary flavour. His airways closed down for a second before he cleared his throat to make himself announced.

The woman looked up at him and put the fish down in a metal bowl. Struggling to ignore the smell, he asked if he could use the phone. It was one of many phrases that started with *puis-je*, which as a boy he had learned in school and which he might have forgotten all about if not for Léonie's diligence in teaching him French words. He wasn't sure he had asked the right way, but the woman seemed to understand him. She nodded amiably, wiped her hands on her apron, and reached under the counter, pulling out a crème-coloured phone with a very long and curly chord. She handed it to Leborio with both hands. He wondered if she'd ever seen a smartphone.

He dialled the number, and after a few rings, the voice of a woman greeted him in French. She had an attractive voice, like that of temptresses on television shows or of adult telephone line encounters. He responded in English and was relieved to find she could speak it also.

"I'm looking to speak with Kodjo Mba Nze."

"Monsieur Mba Nze is very busy," she purred. He was not going to be in the office over the next week. Could she take a message?

No, she could not. But the assistant could help him. Kodjo had a trusted lady assistant he was supposed to ask for, he said, mentioning nothing about the *girl*.

"Trusted assistant?" Her voice smiled and her tone librated. "That is me. I am the only woman here. Wait one moment please. Let me see if I can get him."

He waited longer than one moment, exchanging glances with the heavy woman behind the counter. She adjusted her turban coquettishly when she thought he wasn't looking and concealed her calloused hands in the folds of her apron. He could tell she liked him. But then again, so did most women. It was still nice to acknowledge this, here, in Africa, where he no longer knew if women looked at him because he was handsome or because he was different.

The phone was taken off hold, and he heard the roar of the wind on the other end, followed by a loud *hello*. It was Kodjo himself, and it sounded as if he were aboard a convertible with the top down. Leborio greeted him and recalled their meeting a while back.

"Yes, yes. I remember you. You own the land close to the river."

"I do."

"Wait where you are. I will be there in ten, maybe twenty minutes."

Leborio looked around confounded. As far as he could see, there was nothing but the rain coming down in sheets, washing streets and the homes where the citizens of Bongoville lived.

"How do you know where I am?"

"It says on my phone. You are at *L'Arbre de Bois Bistro.*"

Call display was but a distant memory, along with television, music, and fashion. He wondered if there were new styles being worn out there. Not one to dress according to the trends but rather impose his style upon those around him, Leborio wore clothes too remarkable in cut and pattern to ever go out of style or that ever truly fall under a certain fashion. People admired him, his carriage, confidence, and good taste. And good taste did not yield to the whims of ever-changing fashions. It remained there, ruling over what endured. Good taste could not be taught. Either people had it, or they didn't. In the end, be it in a month, year, or decade, it vanquished the absurdity of fads just by being there, absolute and confident, just like Leborio.

Contrary to his first impression, it was a pleasant place to pass ten minutes, maybe twenty, especially in the shade, where the scent of fishy humidity became bearable. The rain stopped, and under the umbrella, the burning sun could not stretch its glowing tentacles to darken another uncovered patch of his sinewy skin. He ordered the only thing he trusted: tea. The woman reached to a pot of boiling water on the stove and poured some in a cup with a wooden ladle, placing the cup on a saucer with a tea bag and two cubes of sugar. He took the cup to one of the tables and sat.

He was good taste, he thought, looking at the woman behind the counter who was still observing him admiringly, just as the women at the Lido had done before. He had mastered good taste to such a degree that he made gaudy look exquisite. Who else would be able to pull off cornrows and still look ravishingly handsome? He treated dress like a costume. Just as with anything else in life, the point was to amass power from it. And power did not come from dressing boring, although most heroes of the epic tales were dressed rather poorly, in his view.

It was the villains who knew how to dress. The secret, he had discovered, was in choosing one object—just one—that fringed on ridicule and making it the centrepiece of one's costume. It was strange that none of the women he had cared for had been born with the same innate sense of style. His mother dressed because she had to, paying little thought to what she threw on. All his life, she seemed austere and grungy, like an impoverished princess who lost interest in her title and awaited nothing more than the passing of time, for which she did not see fit to dress in anything better than a sleeping T-shirt and a long, hippy skirt.

His first love was by far the most terrible of all. She dressed too trendy, with no logic to the outfits that she wore. One day, it would be a pair of jeans and a Diesel shirt; the next day it would be a designer handbag and that could almost pass for good taste were it not for the gold hoop earrings she would pair it with. Her sustained efforts at looking modern irritated him. It was as if she had not found her style, as if she was constantly struggling to overcome an inherited lack of taste. Her new escape, the chiffon dress, looked well put together at a first glance but was in fact a simple strategy to mask the genuine puzzlement of one who did not have the slightest clue how to put top and bottom together. It looked suburban, and he saw through it. Even so, he had loved her through the ugly purple skirts of their childhood and through the chiffon that expressed her newfound womanhood. What fabric best expressed betrayal? Velvet, he thought. A tough material to love. Who knew what she would wear the next time they met and if there would even be a next time?

He rested his head into his hands, over the rising hot vapours of his cup. The bitter taste of tea sediment lingered on his tongue, and he pushed the sugar cubes around his little plate with the teaspoon.

A strange, hollow feeling, dull like a toothache, commenced in his chest and made its way up to his throat, where it lingered and swerved like a serpent stuck in a small box. The smell of fish in the bistro no longer bothered him. Love, he thought, was such a strange word, even stranger when used by him. He thought about Léonie and how he cared for her; he thought about her white sarafan, the uniform of a young girl who had been unspoiled. No, there was no one in his life to have the good taste of his carriage. Yet there were a few he would have cared for, despite the questionable layers they chose to hide behind.

Such were the thoughts floating around in his head when Kodjo Mba Nze walked into the bistro. He was dressed less formally than on the first occasion they had met. He was wearing just a blue soccer jersey that carried the French insignia—a white rooster. Leborio, who did not particularly care for soccer, wondered if Gabon had a good soccer team.

"Here you are," the man in front of him said by way of greeting. He smiled, showing the wide gap between his teeth.

They shook hands and sized each other up, Kodjo from under a pair of designer sunglasses, Leborio from under his monobrow. The matron at *L'Arbre de Bois Bistro* watched them both, wiping away, stuck in some sort of ominous loop. Behind her, a large pot spilled at a steady pace, bubbling over with fish heads that were almost disintegrating into a vaporous paste. It looked like a wizard's cauldron brewing a dark magic spell that filled the air with heat, humidity, and the stench of death.

"Do you know her?" asked Leborio.

Kodjo took off his sunglasses and threw them in front of him, on the table. "No. But she probably knows me. Everybody in Bongoville does," he added with pride.

"Is this where you grew up?"

"Yes and no. I grew up here when I was very young. Later, I became a man in the Congo."

Kodjo did not seem to be too eager to discuss the time he spent in the Congo. He took a sip from Leborio's tea without giving it any thought. Leborio had never been one to share his food or drink, especially with a man who didn't even bother to ask if he could have some of his tea. If this had happened back home, in Europe, Leborio would have broken the man's teeth against the teacup. Being that the other man was his only hope at becoming rich, Leborio cringed just enough to make him uncomfortable by European standards. But here, in Gabon, social subtleties were like a different language whose translation eluded him. He could not afford to be any more obvious.

"No sugar," noted the African man. "How can you drink tea without sugar?"

"I don't believe in sugar. It's an unhealthy way of making things taste better than they really do. Sugar is to food what illusion is to the mind."

"As you say. Chitchat is for the women," said Kodjo. "Why don't we get down to business? You have land. I want to buy it."

Leborio smirked and took his cup back, placing it on the saucer in front of him. "My land is not for sale, I'm afraid."

"Everything is for sale. There must be something that you want, something I can give you in exchange for this land. How about a nice house on the beach, close to Libreville? Everyone wants to be close to the capital. That is where things happen, you know."

Leborio shook his head. "I came here to get away from civilization and its plagues. There is nothing you can offer me for this land. I am going to keep it. That is not why I called to see you."

Kodjo's eyes glowered from behind his eyebrows. Leborio could see the man's large fists closing in on themselves, like the carcass over a slithering mollusc. Outside the door, two massive men were eyeing their master for a signal.

"There is something else I can give you," continued Leborio, "something I know you will value more than the land itself."

For a moment, the man watched him with cold, black eyes, deciding what to do about him. Leborio met his gaze, calmly sipping from what was left of his tea. After a while , Kodjo waved his men off with the back of his hand and signalled for the woman to bring him a drink.

"And what is this thing I value more than the land itself?" he asked with a quizzical look. His black eyes surveyed Leborio as he spoke.

"I'm going to guess its resources. Especially the living ones. We've got birds and animals, and we have more trees than you can possibly know what to do with. I will not give you all of them, of course, but I think I can spare a large portion of it."

"And why do you think I'm interested in this?"

"Call it a hunch." Leborio had the distinct feeling words were not going to work in his favour when it came to this man, so he kept it short. "Well, are you or aren't you?"

Kodjo nodded with reluctance. "Yes. I am. But not in your trees. Or your birds. I have an interest in animals—gorillas. I have killed most gorillas in this jungle. But one troop still lives, and I believe it is hiding on your land. Find them for me and let me take them. If you do this for me, I will pay the full price of your land and let you keep it."

Leborio did not say a word for a while. He weighed the offer and thought about the gorilla that saved his life. To sell out an endangered species and make lots of money in the process, or to play out this misplaced champion of the forest fantasy he seemed to have embarked on? After all, the blasted beast was the only creature ever to cause Leborio to slightly urinate himself from fear, and that was not something he was willing to live with, especially for as long as the troop lived on his land. Since when had he become Robin Hood, the protector of under-creatures? It was enough he tolerated the tribe on his land. Keeping the gorillas safe was not his business. Besides, Kodjo would probably sell them to a zoo, or a private collector, like the Frenchman from Morocco.

"Why do you want to kill the gorillas?" His question sounded like an afterthought.

"A little for the business, but mostly for the pleasure." He looked Leborio right in the eye as he spoke. "Some people are willing to pay good money for a dead gorilla."

"Dead gorillas? What would one do with such a thing?"

"Let's see. The meat is a delicacy, the hands make unusual ash-trays, and the bones are used by witchdoctors. Yes, the market for dead gorillas is very good. Sometimes, I keep one alive, the stronger one, and sell it to the richest man. Rich men are more vicious," he explained with a sadistic smirk. "Life in captivity is worse than death for the alpha males."

"You seem to have strong feelings *vis-a-vis* gorillas."

"I do. They're a danger to human beings. The way I see it, it's us or them."

"Couldn't agree more," said Leborio. "Are there many people killed by gorillas in these parts?" he asked, recalling Jean's story and his own recent encounter with the beast that saved his life.

A shadow passed over Kodjo's wide face.

"Not many," he said, moving his jaw in a single, embittered grind. "The mother of my child was killed by a gorilla."

Another woman, thought Leborio. He didn't know much about

science, but he had a strong feeling that gorillas knew not to mess with human males. The more he thought about it, the more it made sense. The gorillas had killed at least two women who had been the wives of men he knew. And a gorilla had carried Leborio on his back and brought him home unscathed. Perhaps it was because the animals instinctively realized the value of a man's life over the life of a woman. They seemed to be quite intelligent creatures, after all.

Kodjo made a funny noise squirting saliva through the gap between his front teeth. "She was unlucky. But not as unlucky as the gorillas. Think about my offer, Englishman, and let me know soon."

"I'm not English."

He stood up from the table and casting a last glance at Leborio, put his hand out. "You drink your tea like an Englishman. An Englishman on a diet."

Although he wasn't a tall man, there was a caliginous determination in his expression that commanded submission. Ordinary men would no doubt obey a man like that. But Leborio was no ordinary man, and he did not feel afraid but was rather intrigued by him. Kodjo Mba Nze was definitely an interesting character. He wasn't yet certain that he wanted to do business with him. Even Leborio had standards when it came to annihilating species. Maybe he could sell off only one gorilla—Brother King—and rid himself of the blasted ape. Léonie would never forgive him, of course. But perhaps she wouldn't need to know.

Hesitating for a moment, he shook the man's hand back and felt like Faustus after having struck a deal with the devil, only his cause seemed to him less inspiring of a tragic play. There was no hero that he knew of who sold his soul out of sheer jealousy of a more powerful being. None but Milton's Satan.

CHAPTER 16

EXTRACTING THE CARROT

"What you need to know about Bongoville," said Diya, "is that everything is either good or bad. Most of the natives are thrifty with their words. They will not waste them by describing shades of in between. If they can't describe something or someone simply, then it probably does not belong in Bongoville. Why am I telling you this? Because our friend, the kidnapper, will probably stand out like a sore thumb. It shouldn't be too difficult for us to find him."

Kidnapper sounded a little harsh, seeing as Snejana hadn't really been taken but had very likely willingly followed Leborio out of naiveté. Iris had been naive once too and had yielded to the powers of seduction much in the same way. She hadn't followed him to the end of the world but rather ran off to the other side of the ocean to make sure she would not lose herself in him. Her pride had saved her from sharing Snejana's fate and moved her forward on a path she had yet to discover.

"That's all well and good, but where do we start looking? This place is much bigger than I expected," said Iris, eyeballing the immediate nooks and crannies of the town unravelling around their hotel. Her haystack definitely had gotten bigger and more urban. However odd the juxtaposition between mud-walled, thatched-roofed homes with outside latrines and cement block houses like the ones they'd seen flying over Fraceville. This was a municipality with an infrastructure and communities, consignment shops, cafes, hair salons, and news-stands.

"Where there's a town, there is always a town hall and a filing system." She decided she wasn't going to let the size of the place get her down. Her eyes met Diya's for a moment. His eyes were uncovered by sunglasses and lit from within. He was as beautiful as a child.

"I don't know about the filing system. I believe he's on policing duty today."

Farah, who until now had been studying the passersby with palpable curiosity, turned to face her son. "Do you mean to say the filing system is a person?"

"Yes. Monsieur Songoku has been the town notary, mayor, police, and filing system for longer than most people here have lived. They say every year the town hall hosted an election, and every year the people of Bongoville would vote him in. They got bored with participating in the elections and just decided to drop them all together and have Monsieur Songoku run the town for as long as he's able. Truth be told, he's been doing a fine job until now. No reason to mess with a good thing."

"So where can we find this Monsieur Songoku?"

"Hard to say. Police day is not a good day to look for him. We might have to wait until tomorrow."

Iris shook her head, dissatisfied. "Time is of the essence in these… kidnapping scenarios." She still had trouble saying the word. "Please tell me you thought of some other way to do this today."

Diya's Teutonic shoulders folded in with disappointment, not noticeably, but enough to suggest he would have liked to impress Iris. Just because a young person's eyes aren't always glimmering with optimism doesn't mean they're not still flushed with life.

"I agree." Farah seldom did. "Diya, my duckling, can you take us to the local tavern?" The diminutive started small and rolled out of her lips to grow impending like a sentence. She tipped the brim of her wide, waterproof hat over her eyes low enough to hide them from her two very uncomfortable companions.

Diya's shoulders dropped, and he said nothing as he led the way. The three followed each other in silence, too uncomfortable to make small talk. Voices of children echoed from a massive soccer stadium they passed, and Diya gazed through the gates nostalgically.

This must have been where he had played, Iris thought. Iris didn't want to get caught seeking his eyes once again, so she looked away, across the street, where in the pebbly stretch of road in front of a cement house a little boy was bringing a ball down, trapping it with his foot. The boy saw her watching him and tried even harder, showing off his skill move by move. She smiled politely and looked away. People trying too hard had always annoyed her.

They shared a pitcher of beer and eyed the tavern for a chatty regular. But it was slim pickings at that hour, and in the end, they agreed their best bet would be the barkeep himself. Diya walked up and ordered an elaborate mixed drink. He returned with a story about a mining school in the forest and a white man who was digging for diamonds.

"That's him," Iris said and got up from her seat.

Farah looked up. "Where are you going?"

"To catch him, of course." She fixed her hair behind her ears and looked at her reflection in the window. Wild auburn curls twisted around her face like skinny snakes.

"Didn't you hear my son?" Farah stressed the last word. She had never called Diya her son in his presence before now. "Your friend is playing Che Guevara to an entire tribe of people. First we take a close look at the land documents and see what we can learn. "

"What does the land have to do with the girl I'm paid to find?"

"Look, I get the impression the girl is here on her own will. To bring back the girl, you have to pull the wizard's curtains, and at this moment, his curtains are his land. Let's wait and see what we find at the city hall archives. Besides, if you don't want to spook them, we're going to need to catch them when they're alone. Tomorrow is another day, investigator woman. Now, sit down and finish your beer. I don't know about you two, but I'm growing fond of this Regab ale. It reminds me of this organic brew I used to drink when I lived in Maple, Ontario. Did I ever tell you about my third husband, the Canadian?"

***

Shortly after slurring stories of suburban Canada into the bottoms of four Rebag pitchers she had mostly downed by herself, Farah called it an early evening. Diya held her up by the waist, steering her back to the hotel room. The room was not very big—a bed, a table, a window overlooking the street—but it had that crisp smell of countryside bed-and-breakfasts. He dropped her on the bed with her boots on while Iris lumped a pillow under her head.

Farah threw her arm back over the pillow, revealing her tattoo, the inky fly impudently looking up at Iris from above the Latin words that stretched across her shiny skin like the Happy Birthday message on a balloon.

"What does it mean?" she whispered, hoping to get the truth out of the drunkard. Instead, Farah opened a beady eye and fixed her with Edgar Allen Poe intensity before she passed out.

They shut the door behind them and found themselves in a darkish hotel corridor. His breath smelled citrusy from the drink he had. He leaned in and held the back of her neck with his hand. His skin felt chapped and rough against her own. By the time their lips touched, she had already made up her mind that she was going to do it. They barely made it to her room and fell on top of each other, wolfing haphazard patches of skin rather than kissing. He felt like a fast car speeding through her excitement, swerving and drifting until her head was a fumbling blur led by a heated force that could not be controlled, stirring outward from the pit of her loins and spreading to the tips of her toes. She saw herself in a mirror, clinging onto his back so as not to fall, head thrown back, hair draping behind her like the mane of a horse. The scene made her sad somehow. Not because she felt ashamed, but because she had never felt so alive before, and it made her regular life seem like an endless sequence of dull and proper moments. There was nothing childish about him now—only an inexhaustible display of masculine energy, buzzing through her veins and charging her like a drug. For the first time since she had started on this trip, she didn't want to find Leborio because she forgot to think about him. And because she wanted Diya to last longer.

Later, against the clean roughness of her bed sheets, he told her stories about his mother's life, as if they were chapters in an epic. His voice was warm and subdued like that of a snake charmer. She could tell from it that his eyes were smiling again. She wanted him to shut up.

They barely slept, and yet she didn't feel tired. They agreed to part ways before Farah awoke from her drunken sleep, and he went back to their room quietly. Iris washed up and let her hair dry the way it was, knotted and curled from humidity. She picked up The Daily Telegraph from a shabby newsstand and read about sporadic hail and rain fall in Europe, dropping temperatures and terrible traffic, all announcing the impending arrival of a push-over autumn.

She looked up to the bright African sky, creamy blue and cloudless, and put the paper away. Staying here for another day seemed like a good idea now.

She made a collect call to Umberto, but he did not pick up. The line rang muffled and staticky as she rehearsed what she would say to him.

"I'm fine, yes. Sorry I haven't called. I'm in Gabon now. The weather is great. How is it over there? No, I haven't caught up with him yet."

Then that *him* would grow bigger and bigger, until nothing got through the imaginary phone line, not even words. Umberto's accusatory silence would make her choke with guilt, and she would hang up hating him. She wondered if there were women out there who could love a man like Umberto. If there were, they would have had to be much younger to find his type of anxiety romantic. There was nothing less attractive to her than a man who simmered in a pool of insecurities, all of his very own making. She imagined avoiding his phone calls, texting him noncommittal messages to postpone the inevitable meeting where she'd tell him that it was over, that for her it had never really begun. Umberto was not the kind of man you could break up with without feeling you've raped him deep inside.

Strong people were easy to break up with. And somehow, that made the decision harder, because it made them more beautiful. To hurt someone like Diya would have broken her heart. But saying good bye to Umberto was like shaking a bug off your shoe. There was no element of choice. You do it because it disgusts you, and there is no other reaction you could have.

Before hanging up the receiver, she thought about calling Snejana's mother, but telling her about Gabon would have only sent her over the edge. She would phone her once she had Snejana safely away from Leborio.

"And do you still want to find your evil man today?"

She turned to find Farah, who was wolfing down a rolled-up pita wrap, looking as fresh as a Basset hound, especially around the eyes.

"I know," she said. "I look exactly as I feel. One of the many side effects of my fondness for alcohol, right up there with headaches and pregnancy."

"Why drink, then?"

Farah finished chewing. "Because I like it."

"I like chocolate," said Iris pensively. "But I suppose that won't get me pregnant."

"No. Fat perhaps, but not pregnant."

They sat side-by-side on the edge of the sidewalk, not saying anything for a while, each with their own thoughts, both craving a fresh cup of coffee.

"Who were you calling just now?"

Iris looked back to the phone and shrugged. "No one important. It can wait until I get back home."

"Oh, I had one of those too. Did I ever tell you about my fourth husband?"

The younger woman shot her a look to state the obvious—it was too early in the day for a husband story, especially when it was becoming difficult to tell just how many stories and husbands there were.

"No, wait. It has a point, you'll see. Krystof was a Czech professor who lived half of his life in France teaching architecture at the Sorbonne. In his spare time, he wrote political novels denouncing communism in his motherland to show the local academia that he was a clever and sophisticated rogue and not a barbarian Slav, which was how he saw his people. You might think professors are a pompous lot, and you're probably right. I have only lived with one. But to hear him talk, you'd think the universe had expanded just from the sheer force of his intellect, stretching like an all-casting net between four pillars of himself as a combination of God, Le Corbusier, Solzhenitsyn, and the Peace Corps.

"I think he liked me because I added to his deviant image. He brought an entire faculty of very important people, mostly important to themselves, as it befits academicians, to have a look at his exotic bride, as if I were an artefact he'd dug out of an archaeological site or the last of an extinct indigenous tribe. They looked at me and asked me all sorts of questions in simple grammatical form, speaking slowly and loudly, so I'd understand."

"What did you do? You must have freaked out on them."

"I didn't. It was amusing in a way. But I knew then that I could not live in Krystof's world and that the only chance we stood was for him to come and live in mine. And so he did. For a few weeks. He came to Marrakech on a sabbatical and brought his typewriter with him so he could write the next great culture shock novel. He wasn't the only one looking to put the ultimate label on a place. All manner of men came to Morocco in those days, everything from Mediterranean playboys who bought raids to impress their girlfriends to political dissidents who wanted to lobby the playboys into spending money to wage civil wars in the name of liberation. Krystof found a new kind of entourage to replace the French academia and gawk at his unfinished writing. Only this time, he brought them in my house to eat my poorly cooked couscous and call my six-year-old boy precocious. I came home one day to find white wine chilling in the fridge in the place of my beer. That's when I knew that Krystof had to go. And so I told him that I'd decided we were better off living in France where there were four seasons, decent health care, and better opportunities for Diya. I sent him back and stayed behind to sell my house and pack."

Here, Farah stopped talking and began to roll a cigarette. Iris gave her a few moments, anticipating that the part of the story that was difficult to relate was stuck somewhere at the base of her throat, from whence only a puff of harsh tobacco could unhinge it.

"What happened after? If you feel like talking about it, that is."

Farah blinked with supreme serenity. "Nothing. I'm still packing."

"So you're still married to him?"

"Not in my opinion."

Iris gave her a look. "Marriage is not a matter of opinion."

"I argue the exact opposite. And I've done the damn thing enough times to know." She stood up to scout the street for a coffee shop. "To be honest, I like getting married. It holds such promise, such unknown potential. I don't enjoy divorce at all, and that's precisely why I've decided that I don't believe in it. I've only gotten divorced twice."

"But that makes you polygamous, Farah. Where I come from, that's a felony."

"Yet in some places it's a status symbol for a man to have multiple wives. Who sets the boundaries between these different worlds we live in? Who chooses where we should love and for how long? And by what laws do I have to deny having loved and deny it on paper? The rules of living keep changing as our needs as a society evolve. But sadly, the life of a single human being is too brief to ride out the slow tides of change. I'm not gonna live my life playing by arbitrary rules deemed fit by today's world in the hope that someday things will change."

They crossed to the sunny side of the street, where the outline of the hotel made jagged geometrical peaks into the asphalt.

"But what do you mean you don't believe in divorce? It's not like the horoscope or the Tooth Fairy. It's the law. Before you marry somebody new, you have to divorce the person you were married to in the first place."

"Says who? And for whose benefit? So that the bureaucrats at city hall can keep a record of all the papers that say two people belong together? I prefer to think of marriage as an act of collecting. As for divorce, the end of love is sad enough on its own that there's no need for informing civil authorities of it. What will a piece of paper show you that your heart doesn't already know? You must know couples who can barely tolerate one another. Is the marriage still valid just because a piece of paper says so or because it is the law?" Farah appeared encouraged by the younger woman's silence. "Come to think of it, I don't believe in the law either. It's all so relative. Four hundred years ago, it was the law to be killed because you spoke against the Church, and only a little more than a hundred years ago, the law allowed one human being to own another. Laws are the opinion of the privileged," she said, paying a street vendor for two sweaty bottles of Coke. Coffee would have been better, but in the absence of caffeine, Coke had to do for now. She handed one to Iris. "I prefer to live by my own moral compass. It's all that we have in the end."

They sat again and drank the cola, making satisfied noises after every gulp. Farah lit up one of her rollies and took content puffs, looking out at the hotel entrance.

"You're awfully open-minded this morning, letting me take the foundation of civilized society apart without even putting up a fight. If I didn't know better, I'd say you're considering my point. It's almost as if someone extracted that giant carrot you've been clamped to."

The image of herself as a clip-on toy riding a life-size carrot made her blush. It was strange that she felt closer to Farah now that she should have felt guilty. Obnoxious as she was, the woman guide had a point. Truth lasted longer than social conventions.

Iris caught a glimpse of the tattoo again but decided not to ask. For now, she was happy just to sit there next to Farah and take in the sour aroma of her cigarettes. The economy of her movement ended when Diya walked out of the hotel. Iris checked herself and crossed her legs into an X and then interlocked her fingers, only to shift back by the time he spotted them. Iris could feel Farah's inquisitive eyes follow her shuffles like lasers.

Small talk was made all through breakfast, mostly comparing the rich cuisine of Morocco with the austere food of central Africa. Diya touched Iris's foot under the table, and she twitched a little, excited by the prospect of being found. Even though she avoided his eyes, she could tell they were beaming with content and nowness.

By the time the three made it to town hall, the sun was shining at its highest point, and Monsieur Songoku was napping with his nose buried in a newspaper.

"He's always tired after police day," explained Diya. "It's a taxing job."

The old man awoke from hearing his voice and opened up the glass partition with a smile. He greeted the boy, shaking his hand with both of his, and they caught up in two different kinds of French. Once he was told who the women were, he took off his crème straw hat and made to kiss their hands, all the while standing behind the office counter. He didn't have to look through the archives, he said. He knew exactly where they could find this inherited land that belonged to a white man. The whole town knew it too. It had been an exciting month, what with having white people live with the local tribe, teaching the natives how to mine and speak English. The last time the tribe had had any guests, they had been mousy ministers who taught them boring stuff about Jesus, forbade them from participating in the iboga ritual, and insisted the natives would be dressed from head to toe, even in steamy jungle weather. The natives had soon lost interest in attending class, and the ministers went to look for other people they could dress up and preach to. But this new white man was a different sort of character, and everyone wanted to attend his mining class. To begin with, he did not look like a white man at all. He had cornrows, dressed like a witch doctor, and moved like a panther. The natives liked to watch him, even if they could not understand his words.

"Yeah, that sounds like him," said Iris. A small smirk of pride flickered over her rounded lips.

She checked herself, but it was too late. A quick glance was exchanged between Farah and her son. She hated these moments, when entire conversations between the three of them were had in the blink of an eye and without any words being exchanged. It made her feel clever, but it also made her feel confined to a suffocating and exhausting intimacy, the intimacy of communication without appeasement, without the closure that only words can bring. It was as if the three of them were the only ones attending a masquerade without a mask. They were naked together, but judged one another all the same because they saw through each other. It made her feel sad and lonely—just as she had felt in the presence of this man she was chasing, the man she had chased for the better part of her life. She told herself she was there to rescue her client's daughter. But it was just a different kind of chase.

"Ask him who the original owner was. Who did this white man get the land from?"

Monsieur Songoku licked his index finger and flipped some yellowed papers in a file. After a few moments of searching, he produced a name that required no translation.

"Gigi Borzelini."

Though vaguely, Iris remembered hearing stories of him when she was a child. There was a picture of him in Umberto's house, depicting a tiny and serious looking man with a large head, befitting of a scientist. The family thought he held such potential right up to the Cold War, when he disappeared completely along with the research facility he had designed for the USSR somewhere in Siberia. He stopped sending his favourite little sister Katyusha rocket launcher toys for her birthday, and for a while, Umberto's mother forgot about him. Umberto would sometimes look out a window and hum the chorus of the Katyusha song, and Iris knew then that he thought of his uncle. Iris thought it was strange that he should leave this land he apparently owned to Leborio when it was Umberto's mother he had favoured out of all his siblings.

"Iris." Diya's voice brought her out of her daydream. "What do you want to do?"

"What we came here to do. Let's go find him and bring the girl back."

His eyes were smiling again. It was so easy for him to light up, so easy to expect a reasonable denouement, and so easy to believe. She wanted to jump-start herself from his glow and generate her own. It was possible. That light had once been hers.

CHAPTER 17

BY THE RIVER

The stream was merely a tributary of the Ogooué River, but it was life-giving well to the people of the jungle and to the animals. Over many generations, men and animals had learned to dance around each other for the abundance of the river. The animals came to drink farther down from the settlement and only at midday, when the village fishermen went to rest. In turn, the people kept to their stretch of the watercourse and waited well until after noon to fill their pots and wash their clothes in the river. And if one should wish to wash or swim in the stream at a time when others might not be inclined to do so, one would have to do this when the sun was up at its highest, during the time when the river belonged to the animals.

Léonie had explained this to him through the laughter of their jesting, in the jungle, before Leborio raised his knife to Brother King. She had told him to meet her there, at the foot of the stream. But now things had changed for the two of them. She barely looked him in the eye and only answered when spoken to. He tried to wait it out at first, but it was plain to see she did not want him in the way she had before. Leborio understood enough about women to know that in order to get her to speak openly again, he had to catch her in a time of vulnerability. In his experience, human beings were at their most vulnerable when naked.

He followed her from a safe distance, careful not to step on dry leaves, careful not to make a sound. He hid behind the thicker trunks and only moved when she did to mask his presence behind hers. Close to the riverbanks, she looked back once more to make sure no one followed. Then, hopping along the stones on the shore, she pulled the white sarafan over her head and dropped it on the ground. Not too far from where she was, Leborio almost forgot himself and came out from behind the trees. Then she descended into the water, slowly, cautiously, her skin bristled from the cold waters of the river. She dipped her head in the water and remained under for a few moments. When she remerged, her black hair, usually coarse and shapeless, was hanging around her round face in dripping waves. From where he cowered, he could see her eyes were just as wet as the river, and for a moment he contemplated whether it was water or tears that he saw mirrored in them. She did not look happy. But she did not look sad either. This was how her people had always been when left in their element. Good or bad, their days would be peaceful for as long as they lived in the place where they belonged.

And Léonie belonged here. He saw it now without a doubt in the way she stretched her arms to caress the river and the jungle around it and in the way she treaded water as if it were family being embraced. This was her home in a way that it would never be his, land deed be damned. There was an openness in her carriage that existed only as a covenant between Léonie and the river in which she bathed and the forest in which she lived.

"Léonie."

She turned around, covering herself with both arms—the same

arms she opened for the river. Her eyes lost their soft wetness at the sight of him.

"Léonie, please listen to me. I'm sorry you had to see me fighting the gorilla."

"Fight? You did not fight. If you fight, you are dead."

"I understand that. I will not fight him, I promise."

Using the word *fight* did not make him feel more dignified. He could tell she was deciding whether to stay in the cover of the water or to make a run for her clothes. Somehow, being naked in front of him bothered her now. She had seen a side of him that was petty and deceitful. Stacked up against the gorilla that had saved his life, he was nothing but an ungrateful coward. He nodded. Yes, she was right. Yes, he was truly sorry. He would do whatever she wanted him to do. He would have her forgive him no matter the cost. He would tell her that he was a changed man and beg her to give him another chance. He would cry if he had to. He told himself it was because he did not want to lose the admiration of one so pure of heart. But he knew, deep down, that his inability to gain it back alarmed him. Once a girl like Léonie saw through him, there would be nothing he could do to go back to the way things were. She would have seen him for his true worth, and she would want nothing to do with the likes of him. Then she would still be out there, in the world, running around with this knowledge that he was nothing more than a crooked child, and every day, the truth would grow stronger and more difficult for him to suppress. A man should never have more than one nemesis, and Leborio already had one.

When young Tom figured he'd been seen by a girl¬—truly seen, as stark as the negative of pictures that had not yet been developed—he conjured the great Leborio Borzelini, colourful, in high definition, a callous monster with a charming smile and a clever turn of phrase, ready to see what people wanted and dangle it in front of their eyes for as long as it took to enchant them. That sort of thing worked well in the city. It was what he was good at. Here, in the middle of the African jungle, looking into the eyes of the chieftain's daughter, Leborio knew that he was very far from conquering the world, and that, in fact, the world had conquered him. If only he had a magic remote to rewind and undo the things he did not want Léonie to see. That ought to have been the future of television, anyway—stories and endings to be created by the viewer, after their own hearts and imagination.

Alas, intelligent viewing did not exist. Léonie had seen the unscripted version of Leborio and could not overlook it. She swam farther from the shore where he stood until she became a doll-sized spot in the water. He could not get to her now, and it would serve no purpose to try. His shoulders sank as he stood up, an upright ape trying to walk as a human, with his magnificent arms swinging by his side. He disappeared back into the steamy jungle, following his own tracks, his feet circling the estate like scissors cutting around a pattern.

He did not go back to his hut. He could not do it now. Instead, he followed the trail to Bongoville and walked right up to the woman cleaning the fish behind the counter of *L'Arbre de Bois Bistro*. The woman took one look at him and without a word, wiped her hands on the apron and handed him the phone. He dragged it to the first table and collapsed in one the seats, making the Coca-Cola umbrella shake and rattle above him. Slowly, he dialled the number. On the other end of the line, the voice of the secretary came through, cheerful like a songbird.

"I need to speak to Kodjo."

"He's not—"

"Put me through! Now."

The bistro keeper slithered from behind the counter with a cold bottle of Regab in her hand. She opened the beer with a small, reserved gesture and placed it in front of him. Moments later, Kodjo

C.R. Preston

Mba Nze's voice greeted him, a little irritated. He was busy and didn't have time to chat.

"I don't want to chat. I called to tell you that I have what you need. Send your men tomorrow night. Tell them to meet me halfway on the trail into town. I will take them to the spot."

CHAPTER 18

PRIDE AND PRE-JUSTICE

There are moments in life when time is measured by the space it occupies. Change the scene, and the speed of time passing changes to suit it, like a kaleidoscope rearranging its patterns with every switch of the wrist. Time spent in the nooks and folds of friendship went by too fast, giving way to duty and responsibilities. Afternoons of laughter came to an end in the blink of an eye, while days spent completing chores dragged on like slugs through the dirt.

She looked about the settlement anxiously and waited for Diya to speak with a few of the tribesmen. It was an unlikely place for Leborio to live. The sun glided unnoticeably above the matrons who folded hand woven rugs and straw mattresses over a tree branch and struck them with a wicker beater until a thin mist of dust floated and swarmed over their heads. Chores, she thought again, made time go by so slowly. She pushed her hair away from her face, turned to face the trees, then turned to inspect the dwellings again. They all looked the same, none taller or more ornate than the other.

Where was he?

Pacing away from Farah and her son, she checked her blouse was just the right amount of tucked in.

Then, suddenly, he appeared out of nowhere, zooming in on her from afar.

Time ceased to exist.

It stopped, the way it did whenever she first laid eyes on him in a room full of people or, as the case was now, in the middle of a tribal village in the Gabonese jungle. Bare-chested, tanned, and cornrowed, he was still the single most breathtaking creature she had ever seen. She'd know him anywhere, the way dogs know their home.

Before anything was said, they quietly agreed to move away from the others. Farah and Diya stayed behind to chat with the tribe's people. She wasn't sure if Diya had seen, but she didn't care. Not right now.

She barely noticed Leborio's surprise for her own racing heartbeat. He took her to the Coula tree and the two of them sat on thick roots bulging through the humid ground like rustic benches. He fiddled with the sash around his waist and touched his torso as if to button up an invisible shirt.

"I can't believe he sent you here to fight his fights," he said. "Actually, I *can* believe it. He's too cowardly to face me. But I have plans... plans to pay the ungrateful bastard back. Oh, the plans I have are going to shake his world and make him rue the day he was born. I'm going to destroy him."

"What are you talking about? Who are you going to destroy?"

"Umberto. Who else?"

"He didn't send me here, if that's what you mean. How would he know where to find you?"

"Oh, but I'm afraid my cousin knows exactly where I am."

Smiling superciliously, he pulled a crumpled piece of paper out of a pocket and passed it to her. *So long, your feudal highness.* Iris read it silently and gave it back to him.

"He left this in my pocket back in Portugal. Must've read my inheritance telegram."

She swallowed, unsure of what to say. For a moment, she felt relief. She didn't owe Umberto anything after all. His lie of omission would be her easy way out.

"Nice place you've got here," she said, avoiding eye contact.

Leborio cast an instinctive glance over the settlement.

"Yeah, it's authentic, isn't it? At first, I didn't expect this, but then it grew on me."

Like the coils on an old clock, time started slowly moving along again.

"What *did* you expect?"

"To be honest, diamonds. We're still mining for them now. It doesn't look very good, I'm afraid."

Iris took her shoes off and let her feet breathe. He used to laugh at the shape of her bunions, and she used to feel embarrassed. He looked at her for a moment, taking in the sight of her uncombed hair and cargo trousers.

"You've aged," he said, paying no mind to her feet. She checked her hair again with nervous fingers, discreetly touching her forehead to feel the depth of her frown lines. Time leaped forward, spinning out of control.

"It's only been a few weeks."

"Has it? It seems like a lifetime." His voice didn't rise or fall. It was the even voice of meteorological reports. "It didn't feel this way the times before—not when we fought and stopped seeing each other for a year at a time and not when you moved away. Somehow, you were always part of my routine, like an underlying thought that moved my day about safely and without fail. I would cross the street to the gym, brush my teeth in the morning, and pick up my mail, and you would always be there, just at the back of my mind. I'd think of you as if I had just seen you the day before, as if we might just bump into one another at any moment."

His scruffy face looked piratical and swarthy. It was hard to describe his expression, somewhere between bewilderment and disbelief, as if he couldn't imagine having ever felt that way about another person. She buried her feet in the dark, grainy dirt, peaking at him when he wasn't looking.

She made an effort to sound neutral. "Why do you say I've aged?"

He inspected her once again. "It's your eyes," he decided. "They had a light before, a sparkle of joy and purpose. I don't know how to describe it."

Instinctively, she looked for Diya. He and Farah seemed to have met Snejana and were now being given a tour of the settlement by a group of natives led by the chieftain himself. She was relieved to see the girl was in one piece, though even from afar, Snejana looked tired and worn out.

"Most women lose it in their late twenties, I've noticed," Leborio carried on. "In fact, I have a theory that ties it to the ticking of their biological clock and having to compromise what they really want for the sake of getting married to a decent provider. Would you like to hear it? No? Another time, perhaps."

A sort of half smile froze on her face, and she pretended not to care. She forced herself to watch Diya, but he was nothing but a blob of colour moving against the earth tones of the settlement, exchanging hand signs with the natives. He was no more than an imposed focal point to keep her from crumbling. Eventually, he turned and met her eyes for an instant, long enough to see the addict next to the poison of her choice, trembling and sweating, pupils dilated in begging anticipation. Here, next to Leborio, weakness spread through her veins like heroin. Time stood still, pressing against her chest, unable to break free. At last, she spoke:

"We all have to grow up sometime." Her voice was contained. "Most of us, at any rate. I probably look wiser."

"No. Just hopeless."

She wondered if he had prepared that answer or if disconcerting replies came to him extemporaneously and wavered on the tip of his tongue, ready to dive off like missiles.

"I probably look tired," he added. "It takes a lot out of me, civilizing these people. I've started a school you know."

"Oh yeah? What do you teach them?"

He cleared his throat, then lowered his voice so that she had to lean in to hear him.

"Kinetic interchange."

She laughed. "Meaning you mime stuff to each other? And how's that going for you?"

"That's not the only thing I teach them," he muttered. "It's a very special school. The things I teach are very...esoteric. Almost mystical. I teach them social entropy, that's what I teach them."

She raised both eyebrows.

"Did you just say that because most people don't know what it means?"

They both burst into laughter and for the first time he touched her hand over the bulbous bark of the tree and pulled it closer to where he sat. She didn't pull it back. Nothing was said for a while, and only the sounds of the natives' chatter interrupted the flow of their thoughts. Neither one of them wanted to move, certain that when they did, the warmth flowing through their joined hands would grow cold. Time ceased to exist once again, and from where they stood, all other moments outside of their covenant seemed chores, leading up to the minutes of peace they afforded. Did all of them, through the course of a lifetime, amount to a day, a week, a month?

Drops of water fell upon the back of her palm and she claimed it back looking up at the blue sky above.

"It's raining," she heard herself say.

"No it's not. *I'm* raining."

He was still smiling when he wiped the tears away with the back of his hand.

"Are you happy?" he asked, perhaps wanting to change the subject.

Iris took a deep breath and regained control over time once again.

"Right now?"

"No. In general."

She shrugged. "Happy enough, I guess." Her feet came together under layers of earthen brown granules and decaying leaves, two small creatures bundled as one to cover each other's nakedness. "My business is going very well, I am—or rather, was—in a good relationship, and I have many friends. Generally speaking, I have a good disposition. I make jokes all the time, and my friends love me for it. All in all, my life is pretty good."

"And yet there's something missing."

She nodded. Without noticing, he too had buried his feet in the moist dirt at the foot of the tree where they sat. He raked the sweet-smelling soil with fanned out toes, drawing patterns only he could follow, combing it all back over the top of his feet to cover himself.

"I know the feeling," he said. "Maybe it's because you betrayed me."

"Yes. There is that. How do you feel about it?"

"Like I'll never trust anyone," he said, simply. "Not that I ever had before. But now...now I walk around scanning those I meet and passing quick diagnoses: this one is weak like Snejana, that one is fickle like me, and this one is small-minded like Umberto. It takes the joy out of meeting people."

"I wish you wouldn't call him small-minded." Her voice was tiny now. "It forces me to be defensive, and I would like to be honest this time. What do you say to yourself when someone reminds you of me?"

"Stubborn and proud."

"That's not too bad, I guess," she said.

He didn't seem convinced. Moments went by too quickly, wasted, like empty storage boxes that could have been filled.

"Have you made many friends?" she tried again.

"Not many. Although I seem to be well known."

"So how do you pass the time?"

"I look at everything," he said, inspecting a small piece of wood he had dug out from under his toes. "There is time to see things over here. I mean really see them. And I've met a girl. She has a beautiful smile, dark skin, and a very good heart. She doesn't wear a puzzle ring. I think I love her."

She wanted time to move quicker. "Does she love you? Of course she does. All women do."

"Yes."

He seemed to have decided that the romance was doomed, so she didn't ask. It spared her having to hear it, and for a moment, she felt grateful. "Will you forgive me one day?"

"No, I think it's better that I don't." He shook the dirt off his feet and put his sandals back on. "I could forgive weakness because one cannot help it, fickleness because it's just another kind of attention deficit disorder, and stupidity because it's pathologic. But pride and stubbornness are sneaky. Or rather, those who suffer from it are. They lead you to believe that the ailment is curable, well worth the wait for a person who means a lot to you, and then they go and do something weak, fickle, and altogether stupid just to make a point. So you see, this is as bad as all the other flaws put together because it's so unpredictable."

Her thoughts strayed to the woman guide. Farah had also called pride the unpredictable sin, the most tragic of all human flaws. It sure didn't sound like much to her. Pride had a noble, romantic ring to it, an aristocratic quality to be had by knights and clever maidens. Was it really that bad to be proud? So many great novels had been written about proud people who denounced that which they desired most in the name of principle only to be rewarded tenfold for their virtue. Yet here she was, standing in front of a man who had adored her in his way and whom she still yearned for, a man who was now looking at her with the emptied eyes of disillusionment. Would it have been so bad to close a blind eye to his sins, if in the end it meant that he came back home to her? Would it have been so bad to live by rules of their own making? Deep down, the other women meant as little to her as they had meant to him. She knew full well that he had loved her, and that she had been the only one. And that was all her own love was contingent on.

That and the world around them, watching. For all her brave talk, she couldn't stand the world passing their judgements. She couldn't live a life of being secretly pitied for something other people decided was hurtful. He was right; her pride was weak, fickle, and altogether stupid.

"Oh, Iris, your foolishness has deprived me of my favourite person. You. Now, I'd rather be alone than with you."

It would have hurt less if there had been anger in his tone. Or hatred. She could have worked with hatred. His dispassionate reproach made her boil on the inside with a desperation that was only made greater by having to suppress it under the cover of fatigued honesty. Her heart pounded in her chest faster than a rabbit's.

"I'm sorry," she said. "Believe it or not, I can understand why you'd rather be alone because it's how I feel too. I would have loved you just the way you are, the hero of a novel that has only been written in your head, with your ridiculous wallpaper shirts and your roving eye. Because I know you, you see. I know you through and through.

But you do not know me. To you, I am the tragedy you need in order to be the hero of your own tale. The one who got away, the one who could've saved your soul but didn't. Blaming me is easier than loving me, and far more convenient to your lifestyle. And that's fine," she waved her hand dismissively. "Just so long as you know that's not love. It's not what I feel for you."

"You think I didn't love you," he said. It was a statement, not a question.

"I think you've cut your losses a long time ago."

"But I didn't. I never do...with you."

"You've made up your mind that you and your grand Destiny cannot afford a wife who may leave you some day, or get sick, or ...age badly."

"You probably will," he said, not without maliciousness.

"We'll see about that. In the meantime, good luck pretending that I don't exist. I almost feel bad for you, you see. By chance or divine design, you were given a match that is less than perfect. Live with it! We don't get to choose who we love, not if we're honest with ourselves."

She leaned closer, until the warmth of her bittersweet smile illuminated his skin. She touched his cheek with the back of her hand. It felt rough against her fingers.

"Not everything in your life has to be grandiose," she whispered. "I am who I am, and you love me just for that."

For a moment, their eyes locked and they breathed in each other's air. Leborio bit his lip. He pulled back and pushed her hand away from his face as if he hadn't heard a word she said.

"You're the one who betrayed me. Not the other way around."

She hid her hand in a pocket. "I'm sorry that's how you see it."

"How else could I see it?"

"You could look at it as being about me, not you. I must have had a reason to break the rules of our little...arrangement. Don't you think?"

"Arrangement? Did we have an arrangement that you will not be handing me to the cops on false accusations? I thought that was implied between old friends."

His eyes were averted in righteous indignation, his voice as clear as a bell chiming along the stillness of dishonesty. Behind the irony of his manner there was real hurt cleverly disguised as indifference. He never would have cared that she thought him a thief. He knew that no matter how grave a crime he committed, she was incapable of being disappointed in him enough to stop loving him. The betrayal lay in the aftermath of Portugal. Umberto. That was the taboo she had deliberately crossed. Not to say she had not cared for Umberto. But she could have cared for someone else just the same.

He didn't ask, so she did. "Do you know why I did it? Why I chose Umberto?"

Leborio's black eyes flashed with the darkness of hate, and time slowed down to allow for hope. Where there was hate there was intensity, an intensity that could only be matched by love. The fine line in between was something she could work with.

But then he spoke.

"Why are you here, Iris?"

It had been a long time since he called her by her name. It sounded just as he meant it, like an insult.

"Why have you come this far? I'm happy here. I'm in love with someone else. Deeply."

She knew he meant for the words to hurt, that the entire scene was contrived to show off his detachment and that it probably wasn't even true. Even if it were true, it wouldn't matter, not between them. But the words still cut right through her. Deeply.

She wanted to tell him that she was sorry for her part. She wanted to say if only they could start over again, she'd be good to him, and perhaps he could be good to her. They were old enough to know better now and young enough to forgive one another. She wanted to tell him…

"I haven't come to ask you to marry me, you know. I'm here for the girl. Snejana. Her mother wants me to bring her back home."

Those were not the words she had wanted to say.

"And why should I give her to you?"

"Because I am here to make amends. This is not a bad piece of land you know," she said, looking about her. "If Umberto knew what he was missing on, perhaps he'd want a piece of the action. But I won't put ideas in his head. Even though uncle Gigi would have wanted him to inherit it. You know how much he cared for Umberto's mother…"

His mouth parted to speak, but no words came out. She could tell he was computing his options.

"I'm not here to enforce his will," she added. "Or stir up trouble. I'm here for the girl. And I am willing to return with her as soon as she's ready to go."

"Oh good, then. You can have her. She's been cramping my style anyway. She'll need a few hours to get used to the idea. If you tell me where you're staying, I'll get her to you by tomorrow evening. I think after the time she's had, she's ready to get out of here as soon as possible."

She told him the name of the hotel and stood up. Their time was up.

"You can't keep living like this," she said.

"No. But it's fun trying."

And just like that, the moment had passed. There was nothing else left to say. She had come half a world away to be left with the same hole in her soul as before. She knew now why pride was the most harmful of sins and why it struck when you least expected it: because it reacted to words that could not do justice to thoughts, especially the kind that left you feeling like a naked beggar reaching out empty handed, and instead slipped out of our tongues into a frenzied dance of menacing demons. Pride clothed and comforted the bare, begging ego residing within. In turn, the ego grew stronger and more vicious, grasping at the soul and smothering it like a parasite feeding on its host until there was nothing left of it, nothing left to consume but bile and bitterness.

Yes, pride was the silent sin.

It was the sin of not speaking that which lies deep in the heart.

It was the sin of never finding the right time to do it.

CHAPTER 19

THE DREAMING TREE

Leborio didn't want to watch Iris leave. Instead, he walked off into the jungle, focusing his thoughts on Léonie, telling himself that he was heartbroken over her. He liked the feeling that settled in after he accepted that she would never take him back. It was little like pinching your fingers to relieve a splitting headache. It kept his mind off Iris.

The sun was beginning to set when he started back to the settlement. The closer he got to the clearing, the more he could make out the bowing silhouettes of a few natives, both men and women, fidgeting about the hearth of the tribe. At the center of the commotion was Monsieur Juste Bamba and Jean, the man in the beige suit. He had come to visit him. The sight of his Bongoville friend cheered him up, and he grabbed his hand, pulling him halfway into a hug. Smiling with his big, long teeth, Jean explained he had been there for a few hours, waiting for him to return from town. He had also brought his son, little Messi, who was playing a game of chasing and screaming with the tribe's children, huffing with excitement and anticipation. Leborio tried to recall if he had been as loud as a child and swiftly decided that he could not have. Good taste reined his childhood play, especially in retrospect.

"I had a feeling you were in town," said Jean. "A gentleman of the city can get restless in a place like this, handsome as it may be." He let Leborio guide him to the tree stumps outside his bark house. "I know—I have studied in Libreville and London. What a big city London is! A city of marvels and rain. Do you believe me when I tell you I would not want to live in such a city?"

"I do. Europe is a sinking ship," declared Leborio and sat down to face his guest.

"I do not know if it is. I should think it is a very beautiful one. But it is too cold for me."

"Yes, England has terrible weather. And food."

"I do not mean the weather. I mean the life of the people. Here, people know you and care for you. When you are lost, Mr. Songoku will bring you to my house. If you need sugar, somebody will lend it to you. They'll ask after your health and send good thoughts to your family. Here, everyone's your friend. I got lost in London—it is such a big city—and there was no one to help me. I bought a map that cost me a pound. One full pound. That is half a day's work in Bongoville. There were good things too, like free museums, squares as large as a village where people sit alone and read the paper, and great buildings—old ones with columns and new ones made of glass and steel. I would never dream of seeing them here in Africa. It is very good to see such things and to know they exist. One day I will send Messi to London to learn. But I do not think it is good to live there. One can lose oneself in such a big place. Better live here, where everyone knows who you are and will remind you of it in case you should forget."

"The people here don't know who I am," muttered Leborio ominously.

Jean seemed to ignore his words. "Yes, this is a good place to live.

People care for you here, no matter who you are. If you were a bad man, you can start anew here. You can look at the beautiful faces of the people and say to yourself, 'I will be like them. I will be good.' This is what I love about my land."

"You make it sound so black-and-white, my friend. You Gabonese have this habit of assigning people into two distinct categories: good or bad. There is nothing in between—no room for a margin of error, nothing connecting good and evil. I think you will find the world is not as Yin and Yang as you'd like it to be. There are many different shades of gray in between, as many as there are men and women."

"Yes, you are right. There is good and bad in all of us. But in every human heart, one side is bigger than the other. I think that is the one that matters."

To whom, wondered Leborio. Who stood to judge the hearts of humans, other than other humans who felt entitled to judge just by virtue of witnessing a tiny, random part of a whole? There was no one to judge us; no one who could truly make sense of it all. No one but ourselves. We are the only keepers of our true intentions, paving the road to nowhere else but here and now. Why should the good feel righteous and the evil feel remorse? How were they different in that that they took a stand true to their hearts? Both good and evil were born out of love, love that was given freely and love that was needed and perhaps not found.

"Well, it seems I have been deemed to be a bad man. And I wouldn't mind carrying out this role, if you will, as successfully as one possibly could, if only I could keep the things I like." He sighed, his eyes following Léonie's footsteps on the ground. She cut across from her father's hut to the cuisine, chatting with another young girl. The sight of her white sarafan made him feel inadequate somehow, and he wondered if Milton's Satan felt remorse after he set his plan in motion. Would he still be a fallen angel if he hadn't brought all Eden tumbling down? The trouble with revenge plots is that they are more difficult to call off than they are to come up with. They are mechanisms moved by hate and a collective will for destruction that, once released, do not cease to advance until they consume their victim and their maker alike.

Fallen angel sounded a whole lot more romantic than *bad man*. He regretted having called Kodjo now. It was too late to put the brakes on a plot that no longer belonged to him.

"A good woman can be a blessing and a curse," said Jean with a meaningful gaze. "I know. I was married to one. She was not perfect— no one ever is. But she was good. Sometimes she showed me things I did not want to see. I was an ambitious man back then, too ambitious for my own good. She nearly left me because of it. I was impossible to live with; I worked long hours at the office in Franceville and drove a fancy car, a Hyundai Sonata. Do you know it?"

Leborio did not reply, surprised to find there was a place on God's green earth where a Hyundai—any Hyundai—was considered to be a fancy car.

"Yes, it was a very good car. I sold it after my wife died. It is what she would have wanted, to work less and spend more time with my son, to take the time I need to be one with the people and the place of my birth. We are all connected, she used to say. When your heart beats, the gorillas feel it in their chest. This was also her saying. Be sure that when you do the right thing, they will know it in their hearts." He made a gyrating gesture with his hand, encompassing the settlement and all the people in it. "I only wish I saw this when my wife was still alive. She would have been very happy."

The two men sat in silence, each with their own thoughts. Leborio missed the tacit camaraderie between two men who know things, who have imparted their knowledge to the other the way women impart confidences. It used to be that way with Umberto, right up to the point when he was wrongfully accused of stealing the diamond necklace. How odd that he should lose his cousin's friendship for the one crime he did not commit. Yes, his true talent, if he actually had one, was combining the wrong time with the wrong place and darting right smack into the bull's-eye that was their intersection. He wondered how many more such moments he would be fated to be a part of.

Jean made for the well by the cuisine and pulled out a bucket filled with beer bottles. The bottles had been kept so cold that water droplets formed on the glass surface, just like in TV commercials. They clinked and cheered silently. Yes, it was good to be in the company of a man.

"It is a good day to have a cold Regab," nodded Jean, putting an end to his thoughts. "I used to have one to cool off after a row with my wife," he added with a wink. "No wonder you come to town so often."

"Oh, I didn't have time for that, my friend. My visit to town was more about business and less about pleasure."

Jean waited for a moment before shrugging. If Leborio wasn't going to tell him about his business, then he wasn't going to pry.

With a sharp thud, a light, worn football ricocheted off the rustic outer walls of the cuisine and into Leborio's shoulder. The two men looked over to find little Messi pursing his lips into an *oops*. Before his father could discipline him, Leborio held out the ball and waved the child over. He had extremely large eyes made even larger by a mix of curiosity and shame.

"Hello." The child spoke English for the first time. "What is your name?"

"That is one of two phrases he knows in English," explained his father. "He's excited to see you again and he wants to show you what he knows."

Leborio ran his palm over the top of the boy's head in a "there-there" gesture meant to pat the child's head or bounce a basketball—there really was no telling.

"Your father is teaching you English. That's excellent!" he enunciated. Then, to indulge the child, he told him his name was Leborio. Leborio Borzelini. A few steps away, the tribe's children were waiting for little Messi to retrieve the ball. The boy decided to show off a little, and imitating Leborio's tone and accent, he put out his hand too, like a grown up.

"My name is Messi. Messi Mba Nze."

"And that's the second phrase," said the father.

Leborio shook his hand. Somewhere between handing off the football to the child and reaching for his beer, a lightning bolt struck the soft of his head, and for a moment, he found he couldn't breathe. The name echoed ominously inside of his mind, making connections and altering plans. It all made sense, and none of it did. Messi was just about the right age to be the child in Kodjo's story. He wondered if Jean knew and if he had deliberately left out his surname when they first met. But then again, who wouldn't have, if their name were affiliated to the only known criminal in town?

One name, one woman, one gorilla, one death, one tragedy. Not two. One woman who had been somebody's sainted wife, but who had also been the sinner of her husband's brother. One woman who had been the mother of this little boy. One woman who had perhaps waited for her husband to come home every night, until she gave in to temptation and allowed his brother in her bed. One woman's death left two men wanting, one to make the changes he should have made while she was still alive and the other on an embittered crusade against all living apes. Jean could not have known, he decided. And Kodjo did not want him to know or he would have already told him. Compassion? Not likely from a man willing to steal his brother's wife and sell his people and the land they lived on piece by piece.

What did a man like that care for? The only thing he seemed to ever have loved was his brother's wife. Now that she was gone, what was left of that love? What was left of her?

Surrounded by the tribe's children, little Messi was yelling for the ball to be passed. When it finally reached him, he dribbled through a couple of other skinny legs and kicked it right through the trees that served as an impromptu net. He was all right as far as children go. Jean was bringing little Messi up to be a clever, well-behaved boy, and with a little luck, a future good man. Who wouldn't want that for their child?

Suddenly, Leborio knew there were brakes to the mechanism he had set in motion. But he was the only one to stand outside of it and see the whole picture for what it really was. Leborio Borzelini knew full well that he brought misery wherever he went. But he could change all that right now. He had what it took to stop Kodjo. He saw himself take Monsieur Juste Bamba into town at first light and have Monsieur Songoku notarize his boon of land onto the other rightful owner, making a better man the permanent protector of the land where the tribe was settled. What he did not see was all the time in between those two moments. He needed an ally, someone with a brain, someone remote enough to see the safest path.

He had only one ally in this town, one person who owed him beyond repair and cared for him enough to repay. She would do it out of principle, because she liked good people, and she would do it for him, because the alternative would be unthinkable to her. And he would give her what she came for in return.

"Would you do me a great kindness and take Snejana into town? I don't want her to cross the jungle alone at this hour."

Jean, who had not been planning to head back just yet, stood up obligingly and nodded. Of course he would take her wherever she needed to go.

"Finish your beer and get your son. I'll go get her!"

Moments later, Leborio emerged from his hut with a folded paper in one hand and Snejana in the other.

"Here. Please walk her right to the door of this address." He showed Jean the name of a Bongoville hotel, complete with the room number.

"Where am I going?" The girl began to panic, her big gray eyes moving quickly from Leborio to Jean.

"You'll see, Big Bird. It's a surprise. A pleasant one."

"What about the cat?"

"It must be somewhere around here. You'll see it when you come back."

"And when is that?"

"Soon."

Jean was watching them intently, without the trace of a smile on his face, like a child watching his parents tell the story of how the family pet is going for a really long drive.

"Put this letter in the hands of the white woman who's staying at this address." Leborio leaned in to give the other man a pat on the back. He slipped the folded paper in Jean's pocket. "Her name is Iris," he whispered before he turned away from them.

***

Later that night, Leborio waited until he was out of sight, hidden in the cover of darkness and the tropical forest, before he turned on the flashlight he'd taken from the shed where the men of the tribe kept tools and bits they used to make utensils. Once the flashlight was turned on, he knew there was no turning back. Mba Nze's men would have already seen him. He ran as fast as he could, holding the cat and the light with one hand and warding branches off with the other. The animal squeaked and squirmed to no avail. His arm was as strong as a vise, crushing the cat's tiny head until her eyes bulged out like fluorescent balloons.

The trail to town was difficult to see even during the day, but at night, it was nearly impossible to follow. After a while, he stopped to listen. The cat had nearly passed out from fright. It was hanging under his arm like a handbag, tamed and listless. He could only hear his own breath, panting from the run, rattled from the magnitude of what he was about to do. After this, there would be no turning back. Just as well. What was to become of him, out here, in the wilderness? Any illusions he might have harboured of having a peaceful life in the forest of Gabon had vanished with the loving look in Léonie's eyes. She had sent him away. If anyone were to blame, it would be her. No, he could not live out his life in the jungle of Western Africa. He was meant for—his thoughts trailed off into the abysmal darkness of the woods. What was he meant for? He had never really known. And now, waiting for the only group of bad men that could be found near the peaceful town of Bongoville, Gabon, Leborio Borzelini spat at the ground beneath his feet and cursed his fate.

He could return home to face justice, whatever forms it took for him. He would be beaten to a pulp by Placido's men until his beautiful face would become raw flesh, his chiselled jaw never to sit quite as handsomely without the teeth in his mouth. Then, after the beating, he would be locked up for stealing a diamond necklace another man had stolen. No one would care that he was not guilty of this crime. They would toss him in a cold, dark cell and call it karma. Let's not exaggerate, he thought. He could do all that if he were a braver man. But alas, he was quite fond of his teeth and his jaw. No, he could not go home—not if he wanted to ever make a name for himself. But he could stop by briefly to recharge on his way to a brighter future.

Provided his plan went like clockwork—something he could never really count on, especially when he involved the most unstable of variables—other people—he would make enough money to leave this godforsaken place and start anew. There were places in the world where, with a little money and brains, a man could start a business. Places like America or Canada. No, perhaps not Canada. Their taxes were too high.

He flashed his light three times, and soon he heard steps rummaging through the shrubbery. By a crooked bend in the path, more than a dozen men appeared from the dark, a few of them hauling bamboo sticks and ropes, perhaps to make a trellis that would carry the gorilla. They had left their trucks on the road about half a mile west of the settlement. He noticed they had tranquilizer guns hanging over their shoulders, and a few of them held rifles in their hands. He stood there, motionless, staring at the weapons. It seemed like an awful lot of artillery for one gorilla, even if it was a very large one. One man came forward and greeted him in broken English. He put out his hand to shake Leborio's. His grip was heavy and his back was wide. A string of fangs and ears—presumably belonging to gorillas he'd killed—hanged around his neck. He smelled like clotted blood and cinders, a pungent smell that made Leborio gag on the inside.

"Tell your men they're gonna have to be very quiet," he hissed. "*Silence!*"

The poachers exchanged glances. A few hands grasped the stock of their rifles. They were all big, strong mercenaries, some not as tall as Leborio, but there was strength in numbers. Leborio swallowed hard. There was silence now.

Behind the man who smelled of death, another poacher, with an eye-patch and a deep scar running across the bridge of his nose, nodded at the nearly passed out cat.

"*Pourquoi le chat?*"

Leborio took another look at their weapons and uttered in his best witch doctor voice, "The cat is magical, and it belongs to me."

The men gave him an ominous stare. Even if most of them didn't understand English, they understood *magical*, and it was enough for them. They fumbled through the darkness, following his footsteps until the dim light of the campfire began to play on the shapes of the trees. Farther along, where the bush met the great big Coula tree, he crouched down and used the pads of his feet to move stealthily, without crunching leaves and stumbling on rocks. He stopped behind the tree and listened. Nothing stirred. The natives were sleeping in their huts. It was now or never.

"There." He stretched out his index finger, pointing at the bush. "The gorillas are over there."

The man who smelled like blood made hand signals to the rest of his group. They followed him through the bush, holding their rifles at eye-level, moving quietly, like men who were trained to be shadows. Scratching his scar with the barrel of his weapon, the poacher with the eye-patch stayed behind, pointing his rifle at Leborio. He picked up a bag full of axes left behind by one of the other men, and started aiming at the Coula tree. Leborio flinched at the sound of the first axe hitting the tree. The one-eyed poacher still held the rifle in his other hand, a little lower than before. It would have taken him less than a second to point it back up. He threw another axe into the tree. And then another. Leborio pretended not to notice, and dropped the cat on the ground. With a feeble hiss, the animal disappeared into the bush.

Before he had time to brace himself, the man with the eye-patch came at Leborio, pushing him against the tree. The poacher shoved his rifle right against Leborio's chin, demanding to know something incomprehensible. He asked the same question a few times.

"I don't know what you mean," said Leborio, clenching his jaw bone to brace the cold steel. Beads of sweat formed around his face. The only thing he understood was that the poacher wasn't happy and that it had something to do with the cat.

Not as dumb as he looked, thought Leborio. The cat was the key to the entire plan. Although, the plan did not seem like such a good idea now that he was staring into the barrel of an angry man's gun. He looked the poacher into his one good eye, trying hard not to breathe.

Somewhere, not too far, a single devilish yelp broke the silence. It was the cat. The poacher with the eye-patch pressed the rifle to Leborio's forehead and clicked the bullet into place. Leborio's lips parted, but no sound came out. Perhaps he was destined to die in the jungle after all. He closed his eyes.

Then, suddenly a great stir of bodies and foliage coming together swooshed and slithered deep inside the bush. Something was happening. A struggle. The poacher lowered his rifle from in between Leborio's eyes and listened.

With one swift whip of the arm, Leborio elbowed the weapon away from his face. But he didn't succeed in knocking it out of his hands. The poacher shot his rifle. He missed. Leborio gripped the other man's wrists, pushing them away and squeezing as hard as he could. The poacher tripped him. They fell on top of each other, and rolled on the ground until Leborio's back stopped against something hard. The tree. They both strained to force the other to let go. The one-eyed man let out a fierce battle roar that sent chills up Leborio's spine, and surged forward. He tried to push from his feet, but the poacher was too heavy. Both of their hands were now locked onto the rifle. Every muscle in Leborio's body tensed. The poacher's breath was close. Close enough to smell. With a powerful jerk, he head butted Leborio, striking from below into an uppercut. Leborio's head hit the tree, and the bottom of his chin gashed open. It stung. Blood trickled down his neck. He didn't let go of the rifle. Neither did the poacher. He pushed with all his might against Leborio's fading strength.

They both groaned. Leborio's arms began to give in. If only he could get on top somehow. His whole frame trembled with effort. He could feel the other man gaining on him, inch by inch. His teeth, the back of his head, they all throbbed with pain. This wasn't a struggle for the rifle. It was a battle for his life. There was just enough strength left for one final kick. One blow. It was all that stood between this one-eyed killer and him. He used his knee to kick right between the other man's legs.

The poacher gasped in agony, and rolled off to one side. Leborio stood up quickly and picked up the rifle. He pointed it at the poacher. The man squirmed for a while before catching his breath again. A tirade of slurred French swear words followed, and then he fell on his back, exhausted. Leborio could see his one eye fixing him through the darkness.

"Don't even think about it," he hissed and armed the weapon again.

He wasn't sure he could shoot a man, but held the rifle like he meant it. The poacher watched him still. Leborio listened for steps. It was quiet. Too quiet. Everyone must have heard the gun shot. Where were they? The struggle in the bush appeared to have ended, but the other poachers weren't back yet. That, at least, was a good sign.

A few of the natives had come out ready to defend their homes. He could see their shadows crouching along the huts, looking to spot the unseen enemy. Go back inside, he thought. For this to work, the natives needed to be left out of it. He didn't even want to think of the white sarafan. Or of what would happen if she came out. A feeling of doom took a hold of his heart. Help should have been there by now. It should have never got to this, he thought, clutching the poacher's weapon with both hands. For all he knew, he was fighting alone.

He heard the cocking of another rifle right behind him, and the smell of dried blood made him freeze in his tracks. How did he get back unnoticed? He turned to see the head poacher pointing his own gun at him, grinning. Here was a man who had no trouble shooting another. Leborio dropped his weapon.

He counted the ears on the poacher's chain. Same as before. He hadn't killed any of the gorillas. He dared to hope the cat had succeeded in leading the apes away from danger. Brother King looked after the bloody cat as if it were his baby. And the troop followed the alpha male. He felt resigned to his fate now. He'd done something good and it felt oddly gratifying. So that's how being selfless feels like, he thought. He closed his eyes again, waiting for the bullet.

Seeing somebody had his back, the one eyed poacher made to get up. He picked up an axe left on the ground and lifted it up in the air. Leborio took one last breath. He would have preferred the bullet. Then suddenly, he heard a loud thump and opened his eyes to see the poacher boss passed out on the ground. A neon yellow arrow came out of his left shoulder. Tranquilizer guns. The special forces were here. He spun into an elbow kick, sending the axe and the one-eyed poacher back to the ground. This time he'd hit his head hard. Leborio left him unconscious in the dirt.

He rubbed his elbow and made for the nearest hiding spot, behind the cuisine. There were battle roars, the swishing of tranquilizer guns, and then silence. Men dressed in dark uniforms came to pull out the immobilized poachers before the tribesmen could get to them. The natives ran around in complete chaos. There were screams, panic, and a whirlwind of leaves and dust covered the clearing. Crouched by the dying fire, the women held their children to their breasts and began to wail. They had all come out to seek the shelter and safety of numbers and of warm bodies. There was no one left sleeping.

Leborio took off his caftan and pressed it against his chin to stop the bleeding. He stood and watched with trembling knees how the villagers moved in a frenzied dervish from the hearth to the edge of the clearing, to their homes, to their children. No one noticed the cat, with its wrinkly pale skin, slithering swiftly through the shadows cast by the hearth flames. She hid in the cuisine, disappearing through the door-like gaping. And then there was a shadow, many times bigger than the cat, and then another one, and another one, until Leborio had counted fourteen. He let out a sound of somewhere between relief and frustration. The first good deed he had ever done, and there would be no one to praise him.

"We are even now, beast," he muttered, staring into the obscurity of the cuisine.

***

The next day was a blur for most people of the tribe. The men had mobilized into a small army, and stood holding on to tools and knives, ready to defend their own. These were not warriors fighting for riches and glory; they were peaceful people fighting for their homes and families. They were the same men he wanted to fashion into miners, the pupils who giggled in his class and made farting sounds when he drew pictures in the dirt. Yet the determination in their eyes left little doubt that they meant to put their lives on the line if it came to that. He felt the unbearable urge to defend them both, villagers and apes, to use his strength to send away the misfortune he had brought on them, even if it was the more temporary and lesser of two evils.

The elders urged appeasement. Monsieur Juste Bamba kneeled by the fire and began to chant, smearing ashes over his face and waving his arms in the air. Was that the best a chieftain could do, wail like a widow? Leborio undid his gypsy knife from its sash and wielded it over his head to let the other men know he was prepared to fight by their sides. The men looked at him as if he were a character from a silent movie and then turned to Léonie for an explanation. The chieftain's daughter spoke, for the first time in days, looking Leborio in the eyes.

"The bad men came for the gorillas," she said. Her eyes had gone rigid. They were the shiny black found on a beetle wing. "They came for Brother King," she added, as if to summon a debt he owed.

His knife still hanged in limbo in his hand, ready to part through the moist air of the jungle. But the next time she opened her mouth, Léonie spoke to her people without translating. They looked at her with the unequivocal approval of a mob led by a leader who is both strong and fair. He noticed the young woman's long-fingered hand resting on her deliciously curved belly, and thoughts of her body took hold of his mind once again. Undoubtedly, she would one day be Mother Earth to her people. The Léonie of the future was strong and just, a goddess of fecundity, brimming with children that would listen to her stories of ancestors and love for the land, stories told by the hearth where the tribe's women were lamenting now, the anima to some shaman of the jungle. The Léonie of the future would not be very different from Léonie now. But would they ever be lovers again? Doubtful, he thought.

They waited until the sun came up to go searching for clues. He walked behind Léonie, alongside the few men she had named to come with her. She hadn't named him, but he came anyway. The smell of blood trailing through the jungle filled the air and mixed with the smoke from the burnt out torches. The poachers had put up a fight before they were taken with the same courtesy they practiced in their trade. Iris had come through. First, Kodjo's men were rounded up by the antipoaching unit, a faction of the state army of Gabon. Then, Kodjo himself was brought in. Before the men gave him up, he confessed to running the entire operation. It seemed he didn't want his son to be dragged into his underworld. He loved his child enough to know it was better that a good man raised him. Leborio understood that now. He understood love.

Behind them, the bush had been stripped naked of its shrubbery, and everywhere there were lianas curling on the ground like shrivelled umbilical cords. Markings of wheels and footprints told the story of what happened. In the middle of all this, the Coula tree stood tall, a ring of axes piercing through every side of its formidable trunk like the cufflink on a chain.

"The tree—look at it!" spoke Léonie. "They marked it for death. The bad men will come again."

He allowed himself a smug shake of the head. "I wouldn't worry about them, Léonie. The poachers are not going to bother anyone for a while—animals or trees. Besides, this land belongs to me."

Léonie barely glanced at him, but when she did, her look was bitter.

"Do you love it, this land?" he heard her ask as she turned to face the men. He felt her deadened stare burn a hole though him. There would be no lovemaking. Now or ever. An awkward, ignominious grimace flickered over his lips. His mind was telling him that he should not feel guilty, yet every fibre of his being was under the duress of self-justification. He could feel himself wanting to make his case, passionately and defensively, like a husband caught out on a date with another woman, arguing that it was all for the sake of spicing up the marriage. And like an adulterous husband, he felt the pang of guilt struggling to break through the absurd theatrics of self-righteousness.

He inhaled sharply. "The bad men did not get a chance to harm your gorillas because they were rounded up and taken by the special antipoaching unit. They will be kept behind bars for a very long time. In jail. Do you understand jail, Léonie?"

Léonie shook her head. She said something that was not French or English. The words must have been "I don't care!"

"This is...*très dangereux*. Do you understand? We want peace. We do not want problems." And then more quietly, she repeated her question. "Do you love this land?"

Her eyes inadvertently lingered over the Coula tree. There was sap dripping from the wound in the bark where the axes were wedged. Leborio didn't bother denying he was responsible for bringing the bad men into the jungle, and he didn't try to explain he had in fact set a trap for the poachers to save the gorillas. Her meaning was not that the conflict had been won. It was that it had been started in the first place. Tactical gambits be damned. He wasn't going to wield his words to convince her. They would have been but jesters dancing lewdly around her simple, decent, and compelling words.

Such was the power of decency, it seemed. He knew now that loss was the true measure of love. Umberto would take good care of this land. He would be hugging trees in no time. And like this land that had once belonged to him, Léonie would one day belong to someone more worthy—a lover of nature, a shepherd of men, a man who could not be tempted. He breathed in the humid air that smelled of sweating vegetation.

The best thing Satan had done for the Garden of Eden was leave it.

CHAPTER 20

AWAY FROM THE FALLS

She could see Diya's sullen face from the corner of her eye. On the pretext that he wanted to stretch his legs, he took the seat next to Snejana, by the emergency exit, closer to the front of the plane. Farah had given Snejana an herbal tonic to calm her nerves, and she was knocked out for the flight, her head resting against the folded out food tray like a giant egg. Mission accomplished, thought Iris grimly. The girl was hours away from being delivered back to her mother, where she would remain perfectly safe until Leborio would seek her out again, looking for money or a way to use her. But, at least for now, Snejana was on her way home. After all, that was what Iris had come here to do, even though she may have done a few other things along the way. Her gaze fell back to Diya, who looked upset in the way of a child who had been deprived of a beloved toy, an important toy, a toy that held the meaning of life as he knew it thus far, like a bike or an imaginary friend. And like a child's, his eyes still held the light of hope in the face of injustice. He would be fine. As soon as tomorrow.

She, on the other hand, would not. The vast and wretched scenery of the Moroccan desert stretched before her, like the rest of her life. The plane swerved ever so slightly, and for a moment, the sky became a small strip of milky blue running through a great big sea of arid nothing that stretched as far as the eye could take in. No oasis in sight—not a single shadow of movement between the rust hued dunes.

Hell was slow, dried-out living. And nothing she could ever do would change that. Yes, Diya would be fine. And she would trade all that she had to switch places with him, to hurt and hope and hurt again.

"Handsome villain we had back there," remarked Farah with a quizzical smile.

"Yeah, he's not bad looking. Though I couldn't help notice a receding hairline behind the cornrows. Pity! He had such nice hair."

"Why haven't you brought him back with you?"

There was no point denying any of it. She knew Farah had been watching her silently for a while.

"He didn't want to come."

"How do you know? Have you asked him?"

"I didn't have to. He was pretty clear on where he stood. I've done something he will never forgive."

The woman guide put her leathery hand on top of hers, in an awkward gesture of sympathy that resembled fly swatting. This was why personal robots would never take, thought Iris. Too much to learn about human expression.

"People make mistakes," said Farah. "Have I ever told you about my fifth husband?"

"No, you haven't. And you're not going to. For once, I'm going to tell you about my—I don't know what I should call him. Friend… perhaps."

What do people call someone who is an extension of their own bodies and minds? Family? They were not family. Besides, blood seldom guarantees kinship. She gave up trying to find the right word.

"I've wronged him on purpose, you see. That is why he's there now. That is why he won't come back with me. Men do not guess at the reasons behind a woman's betrayal. They take it as it is and walk with it. I mean, yes, I was disloyal! There was nothing else I could do to preserve myself from becoming who he wanted me to be. I had to break the chains he tied around my ankles; I had to fight for the survival of the self. My disloyalty was deliberate and painful. Even as I wielded the knife, I knew it would pierce not one but two hearts, inextricably linked to each other, and that in betraying him I would really be betraying myself. And yet I had to do it and would do it again if I were to go back to that very same crossroads. In time—much of it perhaps—he would have changed. His demons would have subsided, and we could have aged together as parents to children born out of true love. But in that time, I would have grown accustomed to my cage. I would have purged my spirit of all desires—to expand my mind, to create, to know myself—until I became one and the same with what he saw in me, the me who lived only to love him. That is not love. That is possession. To truly love another, you must allow their mind a space of its own and you must wish for them to seek this freedom. Otherwise, what is it that you love? A shadow? Your own image reflected in the mirror? Or an enchanted slave?"

Farah retracted her hand and wiped the clamminess along the back of her thighs.

"You could have told him this now. He's lived through some strange times. Perhaps he could have understood."

"I asked him. Once. Sincerely. He declined in words that rang false and stank of his wounded ego. He told me it was too late and that he loved another."

"The chieftain's daughter," nodded Farah. "I saw the way she looked at him. She's carrying his child, but he does not yet know this."

"She's what?"

"She's pregnant with his child."

"How can you tell?"

"I can." Farah shrugged as if to say, *Must you still doubt me after all we've been through?* "I am a mother."

She knew Farah was probably right and yet her world did not spin madly. After all, what difference did it make that he had fathered an unborn child somewhere, in central Africa? He would find a way to mess it up, just as he had every other thing in his life.

"I did not only see the way she looked at him," Farah carried on. "I also saw the way he looked at her, and he does not love this girl. He loves the idea of a girl in a white sarafan."

"It doesn't matter if he loves her. That was not the point. The point was telling me that he did. He savoured every word like a petty child, inviting me to partake in the same old show of feathers that had us doomed from the first day. There is no other way that he can be with me."

"And what did you answer?"

"What could I answer? I saw him as he had always been: proud, insecure, and unchanged, so much like me and yet knowing so little about himself."

"That's all very poetic," remarked Farah. "So you said nothing."

"Nothing. What could I have said? No words exist for such occasions."

"What will become of him?"

"I don't know. Not much. Not as much as it should. Potential without truth is nothing but a string of celebrated failures."

"Ah, but at least they will be celebrated." The web of lines around Farah's eyes closed in into a singular smile. "If you ask me, I think you and your man friend suffer from the same problem."

"Yeah, I know. Pride?"

"No. You both need to drink more."

And with that, she threw her head back and downed a tiny bottle of whiskey. Without looking at Iris, she flicked her wrist like a magician and dropped another tiny bottle in her lap. The younger woman obeyed at once. It wasn't as bad as she expected. Her belly warmed up, and the knot in her throat let loose. Just outside their window, little patches of clouds formed out of thin air, keeping track of their descent. Farah noted they would be there soon. With her aquiline outline, she looked like a prophetess reflecting back from the obscure center of a crystal ball.

"I'm sorry about your son," added Iris, casting a glance in Diya's direction.

The woman guide waved her hand magnanimously.

"Don't mention it! He'll be fine. Such are the double standards of our age. A boy is not a man until he loves a woman, and a woman does not know that she's a woman until she loves a boy. Funny how that works out. The important thing is that we found the lost girl, and you can bring her back to her mother. What will you do now about your...friend?"

"What *can* I do?" she shrugged. "Can I tell him there is no fundamental difference between the child I once knew and the man he claims to be now? If he does not know that I can see that in him, that every time I look into his eyes I still see my face, then he is not my soul's equal. Death by banality—that is how it shall be. I'll keep on living my life, aware that we are two of a kind in this world and that even though we can coexist, we cannot live together. I'm fine with that, as long as my life is my own, as long as I am not enslaved to another."

"That sounds lonelier than being alone."

"Does it? I wouldn't know the difference." It sounded sad when she thought about it, but she could avoid thinking about it. After all, we each have to carry our crosses, and we manage it as best we can, some days better than others, every day less clumsy than before. There are better things one could invest energy into than the pain and suffering of love. Iris knew now that she was an excellent investigator woman. She could find anything that needed to be found: stolen treasures, missing people, and delicate secrets. After all, she had found the most difficult of all elusive truths: she had found herself.

Farah reached for the overhead compartment, showing her the thin skin on the inner part of her triceps. The blue fly elongated under the pull of gravity, seemingly grasping to stay put. Iris read the Latin script again. *Aquila non capit muscas.*

"What does it mean?" she caught herself ask for the third time since she had known Farah. The question had become more of a mantra of self-assurance. She didn't really expect an answer, seeing as Farah hadn't given her one yet.

"You know what it means. But you want to know what it means to me." And then, just like that, the woman guide answered the question. "It means nothing. I woke up with it after a drunken night in Bangkok."

"What were you doing in Bangkok?"

"Oh, I lived there for a little while. Did I ever tell you about my sixth husband?"

Listening to Farah's voice, Iris's eyes closed, and she slowly drifted back into a dream of the muddy brown river. Alone in her boat carved from the empty shell of a hollowed-out tree trunk that glided through the heart of an unnamed jungle toward the faint throbs of a waterfall, she reached deep into the belly of the wooden dugout and pulled out a paddle. There was still time. She steered to the shore and away from the waterfalls.

CHAPTER 21

TIME TO MOVE ON

The next evening, life had returned to its tedious paces. During the day, the villagers had set up traps around the settlement to prevent intruders from breaching it again, and now they rested by the hearth, unsmiling and silent. Monsieur Juste Bamba had been watching the fire, frowning with concern. Around him, the older men had gathered to say a prayer to the ancestor spirits. Their humming voices filled the clearing and echoed back to them as if from under the dome of any one of those large marble cathedrals of Europe. The women stared with pious eyes and mouthed the words silently. Removed from their tropical setting, the tribe could have been any other group of people in any other part of the world, brought together under the ancestral rites of faith and kinship.

Leborio had never felt part of such a group. He had never belonged to the church of his forbearers, to the humble rituals of the poor people of Eastern Europe. But if there ever had been a place that resonated with his nature, that place would have had to be the city where he was born, the capital city of an inconsequential country, a place ruled by complexes and resentments, where modesty was renounced for arrogance and pride and common sense was exchanged for a sense of self-importance. He belonged to the city that wanted to be the hub of something important. He belonged to its crooked streets and dark folds. He belonged to the rituals of wealth and display carried out by others, who, like him, wanted to believe they were almost legendary. For the first time since he left home, Leborio felt a longing to return. He knew it would pass and that for him there was nothing to go back to, but right then and there, he wanted to indulge in the sweet pain of missing and imagine himself as the brave, ancient hero pining for his homeland, a little flawed by hubris and beautifully doomed.

He was aware of the chieftain's piercing gaze and thought it wouldn't hurt to look as vulnerable and broken as he felt, to ingratiate him with the elder. He wondered if the chieftain knew about him and Léonie, but somehow he could not imagine her saying anything.

He kept to himself, feeding pieces of chopped fish to the hairless cat under the great big Coula tree that marked the spot between his school and the jungle. The tree was still maimed by the ring of axes, and no one dared take them out just yet because the natives believed the tree would bleed too much. It was better to wait for the tree to heal before removing them.

There was no wind to sweep through the darkness, and the stars were covered by a thick layer of clouds. A few of the children tiptoed around the camp fire, making dancing shadows with their arms, exchanging complicit glances, and giggling quietly so that the elders would not hear them and get cross. The chieftain gave an order to one of the other elders, propped himself up on his wooden staff, and stared Leborio from afar. He hit the ground twice with the blunt edge of his stick, like a judge using his gavel to bring silence to the court, punctuating the ruling verdict against the ground beneath their feet— the ground that still belonged to Leborio, by law. But out here, on his land, two laws coexisted like two unlike brothers: the law of the people and that of the jungle. And by the law of the jungle, he knew he had committed the harshest of crimes. He had brought intruders into the heart of the woods. It was of little importance that in doing this he'd rid the land of its foremost menace, Kodjo Mba Nze's poachers. Truly bad men were now locked away for a very long time. The jungle would be safe, at least until the void left by Kodjo's influence would be filled by someone else, another bad man.

"Hello," mouthed the younger man, uncomfortably. He returned the older man's piercing look with a daft smile, searching to find a shred of the candour and hospitality with which Monsieur Juste Bamba had first received him. But there was nothing there besides disillusionment and suspicion, as unflinching as his wooden sceptre, looking the young man in the eye and showing him he was no longer wanted on his own land. Half expecting lightning bolts to come out of the chieftain's walking stick, Leborio feigned a wave of sorts, as if to say 'so long'. A strange feeling of sorrow took over him while he thought this was probably the last time he'd see the crazy warlock. If we spend enough time in the company of those who judge us, we come to miss their disapproving glares. How else would we ever miss our families?

He was gone by the next morning. He took with him the gypsy knife and the clothes off his back. He left behind the hairless cat, now shepherd to a troop of gorillas. Léonie came out of her father's hut, hands folded over the lap of her white sarafan, a glimmering pale stain in the middle of her lower lip. That was how he would always remember her. She was the last thing Leborio saw before he disappeared into the foliage of the jungle.

CHAPTER 22

THE OSTRICH FARMER

"The castle was first built around 1212 AD by Teutonic knights meaning to protect trade in the mountain valley. But because it was only built in wood, it was easily destroyed by the Mongols during one of their invasions. More than a hundred years later, the Saxons had the castle rebuilt in stone, and this is the structure we see today."

The group followed the tour guide's hand flourish to the large window overlooking the valley, crowding to take pictures of the pristine vista: green valleys as far as one could see and colourful flowers dressing the silky grass in a vivid paisley.

After an awkwardly timed dramatic pause, the guide continued:

"The red-tiled rooftops were inspired by the Germanic roots of the first builders, and they served as a sort of lighthouse to travellers crossing the mountains. Over the years, it was used as a fortress against the Ottomans and as a custom post between the two provinces it borders."

"Yes, yes. But how about the vampires?"

The tour guide cast a snubbed but dignified look to a young blonde who continued to stare him in the eye with consumer impudence, blinking impatiently as if to signal she didn't have all day.

"There are no vampires, madam," spoke the guide with the heavy enunciation of Eastern languages. His English sounded a lot like any other tongue of the Balkans. "These vampire stories were invented by a mad Irishman who had never set foot in our lands. His Dracula was one of our best princes who rid the land of invaders and impaled rapists and murderers. He was a great ruler, but I assure you he was not a vampire."

"Oh, don't be ridiculous. Of course there are vampires." The girl raised a dismissive hand. A red scarf framed the stem of her pale neck. "I've read books, I've watched the movies, and I came here to see the real thing. Maybe your prince took his name after the real Dracula. Everyone knows he was the king of vampires. It even says so in the latest vampire saga—and I've watched all five instalments. That's what we all came here to see." The rest of the group stood behind her in acquiescent silence. "Why else do you think we'd come here? This ain't the Versailles, you know."

Heads shook disapprovingly, and hands dipped in trouser pockets, clenching fat leather wallets. Two-by-two, disgruntled eyeballs measured the austere furniture up and down. It was unanimously found lacking. They had all paid to hear vampire stories, to see crumbling crypts held ajar by bloody stakes, and to behold preserved vampire fangs. Some of them might have even harboured the hope that a hellish immortal had somehow managed to penetrate the group, looking for a victim, cleverly disguised as a handsome security guard. The sound of foreign disappointment filled the room all the way up to its bare high ceilings.

The tour guide surveyed the room with the ashen look of a diabetic low on blood sugar, and as his shoulders folded in, he shook his head slowly, from one side to the other, uttering a few words in his own language. Desperately, he lifted his hands in the air, supplicating

C.R. Preston

an unnamed divinity—perhaps the god of the tour guides and high school teachers—a divinity not well known for answering prayers.

At this juncture, an unusually handsome young man with a shaved head and magnificent arms emerged from behind the group and cut in.

"What my colleague means is that vampires do not like to be talked about, especially during daylight. Something about those who speak about them growing impotent," he added with a mischievous wink.

A few of the men in the group looked down for reassurance. Leborio flashed an impudent smirk to the women who were slowly gliding to the front of the crowd, nearing in for a better view. He flexed his arms ever so slightly, bearing in mind that muscles bursting with manly good health were not a favourite with the vampire crowd. He lowered his jaw just enough for his glimmering eyes to stare out affect-edly from under his monobrow. His lips seemed darker and thinner now, giving him the air of mystery and febrile torment becoming of a night creature. Suddenly, the impatient blonde seemed interested.

"But what I can tell you," he continued, lowering his voice just above the sound of a whisper, "is that although he inexplicably only came out at night, Vlad was a very charismatic prince, and that no one, but no one, was able to resist his charms. Man or vampire, it is said that he was an outstanding lover. He took thousands of women to his bed."

The guide's eyes opened up like saucers. Vlad the Impaler was known for many things, but his skill as a lover was not one of them.

"Yes, Vlad bedded all kinds of women. Younger, older, married, widowed—he pleased them all. And then he drank the blood of their husbands to keep up his stamina."

A few tourists gasped in horror. He could tell the women enjoyed his story a whole lot more than the men did.

"Dracula was fast—the fastest man who ever lived or died. He could cross the mountain valley faster than the fastest horse, and this is why it is said he was in more than two places at a time. Many say it was the magic of vampires and that he flew over the valley at night. But I assure you, dear guests, that there was no magic at play. There is a perfectly good explanation to account for Vlad's speed and mobility, one supported by history and…physics, all at once."

This was followed by a deliberate pause. And sure enough, one of the women asked, "Well, what is it?"

He waited to be coerced into spilling the story. With false reluctance, he continued, "Of course, most of you know that Vlad was raised as an Ottoman captive, in the lads of the East, where curious creatures roamed the grounds. He studied all these creatures with great care until he found just the right one to carry him. A creature of stealth and strength." He paused again for effect. "Vlad brought this animal back with him when he returned from captivity, and it still lives here, now, amongst us."

"Is it a horse?" gasped the blond girl, who looked incredibly familiar to him.

"No, it isn't. I've already said this other animal is faster than a horse." The blonde was getting ready to guess again, and so he spoke quickly, hissing and moving his hands like a warlock to describe the mysterious being. "There is only one type of animal in these parts that could carry the Prince of Darkness. One kick from this creature can send a grown man to his grave. It moves as swiftly as a shadow and as lethally as a…ninja. Can you guess what this creature that I speak of is? No? I don't blame you. Most people lack imagination."

He waited for everyone to get closer.

"Alas, it is the mighty ostrich!"

"The ostrich?"

"Yes. The ostrich." His eyes narrowed in on the blonde, as if to pull her into this wondrous world forged together by the sacred brother-hood between vampires and ostriches. She smelled of baby powder and crushed candy. Her scent reminded him of wet wipes, and he contracted his buttocks ever so slightly.

"The ostrich is one of the strongest animals to ever have lived," he continued in a conspiratorial voice. "It moves as fast as a hundred kilometres per hour, fast enough to take Prince Dracula from his castle to any one point you can see though this window here, quicker than you could say the evening prayer."

The tourists flocked around the window once again under the perplexed eye of the guide, who fell into a chair, dumbfounded.

"I'm afraid you can't sit there." Leborio leaned in with a wink. "You told the last group that the chair is a precious artefact, at least a few hundred years old."

The guide jumped out of his seat.

"No worries. Your secret's safe with me."

"Who are you?"

"I am the man who singlehandedly saved your career today. The name's Leborio. Leborio Borzelini. You see, I own a small ostrich farm, just a few kilometres north of the palace."

"Ostriches? Here, in the mountains?"

"Yes, they're adaptable creatures, you know."

"How did you get them here?"

"I bought them in Africa for the price of a family heirloom. A gypsy knife encrusted with precious stones...but that's a story for another time."

The guide listened in complete astonishment.

"Honestly, how do you expect to sell tickets to this monastery of a castle if you insist on being historically accurate?" he went on, encouraged by the other man's silence. "Who wants to hear there are no vampires at a castle that is only known for being mentioned in vampire novels? You might as well put a sign up saying there is no Santa Clause during a Christmas sale."

The tour guide fiddled with the pockets of his cheap suit jacket. It appeared he was at a crossroads between integrity and success, as so many men of minor importance often are. Sensing his conundrum, Leborio shrouded the man under the persuasive weight of one of his magnificent arms and held him as close as a brother.

"Perhaps we can help one another, my friend. Business has been a little slow for me, what with the recession and all. And so I'm branching out into ecotourism."

"With vampires?"

"No. With ostriches. Haven't you been listening to a word I said? We've found them a purpose, you see—as vampire carriers. You, my friend, need vampires just as badly as I do. Without them, there is no story to be told here. But if you were to send me a few busloads of Americans every day, I would be more than happy to think up ways to revive your…presentations. I have men on my farm who would make great drop-in vampires. Just imagine how it would be if in the middle of that history bit you were doing earlier, a couple of vampires were to be sighted lurking in a far off corner of the room. We could even get a couple of coffins in here to hike up your ratings."

"Ratings?"

"Well, who's to say you won't get to be in a series or a documentary on the History Channel? We can really help each other, you see. With a little bit of cross-advertising, the sky's the limit, my friend. What do you say?"

The guide blotted his forehead with a folded handkerchief. Leborio did not wait for the man to reply. Instead, he gave out brochures, working the room like a lobbyist before a campaign.

"You really shouldn't wear that perfume." He winked at the blond girl, whose cotton candy scent now filled the air. "Mosquitoes and vampires are attracted to the smell of sugar."

The girl barely smiled, and when she did, she held her phone up above her.

"You won't get signal up here, I'm afraid. I'm Leborio, by the way." He put out his hand. "Have we met before? I get the distinct feeling that we have."

"No, I don't think so."

"You look familiar somehow."

"I get that all the time. Do you watch *Gossip Girl*?"

It all came back to him then. She wasn't really looking for phone signal. He took the phone out of her hand, held it up above eye level, and snapped a picture of the girl, just as her mouth formed a perfectly shaped, indignant O.

"Here you go, Blake! Add that to your Facebook."

Leborio walked out into the darkness of the cloistered exit and looked back in from the window at the mindless crowd that swerved through the room like billiard balls on the table, colliding with purpose and stopping to examine perfectly uninteresting surfaces, brochure in hand, cameras and smiles ready.

What made a good billiards player was his ability to lay out trajectories in his mind and predict what balls to sink and when. Leborio wasn't very good at predicting what balls on a felt table would do, but he had always been able to predict what people would do and trigger reactions they might've never wanted to have. The game was already in motion—a beautiful piece of precision machinery and impressive kinetic art. He had tapped his aim lightly against the intended trigger and was now watching the balls skitter and roll in an elaborately choreographed dance. The guide was answering questions the Americans were asking, a few families had decided to visit his ostrich farm, and one newly separated corpulent man fiddled with the brochure, torn between viewing tonight's porn feature at the hotel or visiting the ostrich farm on an impulse. He was going to visit the farm. At the farm, he was going to see Leborio's curvy female assistant feeding the ostrich babies and fall in love with her. She was going to smile the freshest smile he'd ever seen, and, within a week's time, he was going to buy the farm from Leborio, who would sell it all for a passport, a plane ticket to Chicago, and thirty thousand hard-earned American dollars to get him through the first couple of months of projecting a successful, independent image.

Then, he would move into Blake's posh studio—paid for by her father—and encourage her to take an internship that would help the blonde become a wildlife photographer someday never, but that would keep her travelling to faraway places. Her father would grow embarrassed about their dalliance and invest in his future son-in-law's custom furniture factory so he could tell his golf buddies that his daughter was marrying rich. Leborio wouldn't marry her, of course, but he would take the business and have disabled people run it from top to bottom, because it hadn't been done before and because it would get him the cover of a couple of rich people magazines, the kinds that even ambassadors read while they're at the dentist.

He was going to be successful.

He was going to be American.

He was going to be pursued by a narcissistic heiress in three… two…one:

"How did you know my name?" He heard the voice of the blond girl as she stood cautiously a few feet away and knew she had picked up the brochure he left behind.

Also available from CR Preston:

THE SPANISH GURU

The Spanish Guru is the first installment of the *Leborio Borzelini* series. Meet the antihero in his natural habitat, the hot spots of post-communist Eastern Europe. Guru by day and gigolo by night, Leborio's adventures take him and his entourage all the way to sunny Portugal. Love triangles, stolen diamonds, and secret investigations are just a few of the ingredients making up this wonderfully kooky story.

Follow Leborio:

Twitter: http://www.twitter.com/Leborio
Facebook: http://www.facebook.com/Leborio

www.ingramcontent.com/pod-product-compliance
Lightning Source LLC
Chambersburg PA
CBHW030923120626
46554CB00001B/257